WINTER'S MAGE

MIRIAM GREYSTONE

CITY OWL
PRESS

WINTER'S MAGE
Outcast Mage: Book Two

CITY OWL PRESS
www.cityowlpress.com

Cover Design by Mibl Art and Tina Moss. All stock photos licensed appropriately.

Edited by Heather McCorkle.

Author Photo by Fox and Owl Photography.

For information on subsidiary rights, please contact the publisher at info@cityowlpress.com.

Print Edition ISBN: 978-1-944728-73-1

Digital Edition ISBN: 978-1-944728-72-4

Printed in the United States of America

For Josh
"This is my beloved, and this is my friend."
-Shir HaShirim, 5:16

"Truthsight offers unusual details that keep the reading experience fresh; an infant earth spirit running amok in Rowan's house is a moment not soon forgotten."
- *Publisher's Weekly*

"A fun, fast-paced read with a compelling main character, excellent world-building, and refreshingly unique mythological creatures. Greystone delivers an impressive start to an intriguing new series."
- *Leah Cypess, Author of MISTWOOD*

"From the first page, Truthsight reaches out insistently, drawing us into hidden corners of our world, into shadowy places populated by pixies and centaurs, by harpies and elves—all with plenty of magical qualities to fascinate us, all with enough humanity to seem utterly real. It is fast-paced, and suspenseful. It is also heart-breaking, funny, terrifying, and passionate. It is, in the end, deeply satisfying. It is not to be missed."
- *B.K. Stevens, Agatha-, Anthony-, and Macavity-nominated author*

"Truthsight is a compelling debut novel with a smart, forthright heroine, a good-hearted but rough around the edges hero, and a unique approach to supernatural creatures. Not the sweet little fairy type either. Like humans, they run the spectrum from kind to vile. But vile is good when it makes you squirm. Not to mention appreciate the heroine's toughness that much more."
- *Michelle Markey Butler, Author of HOMEGOING*

"An epic, beautiful, heartbreaking struggle against enemies both seen and unseen. A beautiful tapestry of magic, myth, and the power of choice. Highly recommended!"
- Red Hot Books

PROLOGUE

IT TURNS OUT THAT, IN THE AFTERMATH OF BEING ATTACKED BY A clan of bloodthirsty mages out for carnage and revenge, centaurs can get a little bit twitchy.

"You are being ridiculous and you have to stop," I told Crinea, who pawed at the ground with apparent frustration as she glared at me.

Smaller than the average centaur, what she lacked in stature she made up for with the ferocity of her expression. She stood with her long brown braids flung over her shoulder and the creamy tan, horse-like portion of her body practically dancing with frustration.

I set down the heavy armful of books I had been collecting, and crossed my arms over my own chest, mirroring her stance. Trying to make it clear that I had no intention of backing down. "I opened this clinic years before we ever had centaur guards here. We can certainly make it through one night on our own." My eyes flicked over to Jason, who sat on a nearby tabletop, swinging his legs back and forth and watching our exchange with wide eyes. He seemed determined to do the smart thing and stay out of this conversation.

"I'm just saying that you might enjoy spending the night in the safety of the centaur camp," Crinea said, her tone a bit too sharp to sound cajoling, her eyes flashing. "I don't understand why you won't consider coming."

"I wouldn't be allowed to attend your super-secret centaur ritual, right? The one that even the clinic guards have to be at?"

Crinea hesitated before giving a grudging nod.

"So, I would be coming to the camp in order to spend the night sitting all by myself, doing nothing, sleeping on the ground instead of in my own bed, and generally wondering what in the world I had been thinking when I accepted your invitation?"

"Not on the ground," Crinea responded coolly. "We have straw."

I huffed out a sigh of exasperation and threw my hands up in the air.

Jason seemed to realize things were getting out of hand. He hopped down from the table and came to stand beside me. "I know you were pretty shaken up by what happened, Crinea," he said, his tone placating. "We all were."

Crinea's brow wrinkled. "Shaken?" She peered at Jason with an expression that betrayed no small degree of concern for his mental well-being. "No one has shaken me. Should anyone *try* to 'shake me up,' I assure you his head would roll at my feet as soon as he laid a hand upon me."

Jason's response caught in his throat, and he coughed, his face flushing pink. I couldn't be sure if he was choking down a chuckle, or if Crinea's words had simply surprised him. Having seen her behead an enemy before, I didn't feel particularly inclined to laughter.

"What I mean to say," he continued after regaining control of himself, "is that Amy's foster mother, Meri, is back in charge of the mage clan. She's incredibly powerful—the most powerful mage in the world, according to Amy. And Meri is making sure that none of the mages come after Amy anymore. All of that is over now."

Crinea cocked a disbelieving eyebrow at Jason, and then swiveled her head around to frown at me. "Your actions have angered an exceptionally powerful group of people, have they not?"

"Yes, but..."

"And these people have already tried to kill you on multiple occasions."

"Well, yes, but that was all while Meri was imprisoned. She's free now."

"Being free is not the same thing as being firmly back in power." Crinea's hooves clicked against the wooden floorboards. "Your foster mother was weakened by being held captive for many long years. And after you rescued her, she completely used up the Pearl, her great reservoir of power, to save herself from death and at least partially repair your own injuries." Crinea's eyes flicked to the wound that still lingered on my chest. "Who is to say she can fully control the actions of all the mages who wish to do you harm?"

I didn't have a good answer. Jason's eyes darkened, and I knew before he spoke that he had started to waver.

He turned around to face me, his hands held out, palms up. "Maybe it wouldn't be such a bad thing to take tonight off, Amy."

I shot him a dirty look. "Traitor."

He lifted his hand up, as though in surrender. "Since you started taking shifts at the ER again, you've been working long days, and then nights at the clinic, too. You're still recovering from your injuries. You could use a little extra rest."

"I am only back at the ER two days a week," I told him, though he was perfectly aware of this already. The hospital had been very understanding about my sudden disappearance several weeks ago. The fact that I had a significant injury that I couldn't very well conceal from them helped. I made up a story involving an accident while rock-climbing, and they believed me and welcomed me back, even insisting on reducing my work load until I had made a full recovery. "I don't want less work—I want more. And if I *did* take a night off I would spend it at home, in my own space."

"You are vulnerable here," Crinea insisted. "You will have no guard and, since Lord Rowan must be present for the ceremony, he cannot take the centaur's place. He's concerned for your safety."

"Rowan hasn't shown his face here in the last five weeks," I snapped, my words sharper than I meant them to be. Crinea was only trying to help, and didn't really deserve my anger. But she should have known better than to bring Rowan up. "If he cares so much for my well-being, then he can damn well come here and talk to me about it himself, face to face, instead of sending you as his messenger." The pain of his absence pulsed inside me, and I ran my hands roughly over my face. I wasn't going to talk about Rowan. I saw twin expressions of poorly disguised sympathy on Crinea's and Jason's faces, and that irritated me even more. "I shouldn't have to remind you I am not some help-less, run-of-the-mill human. I am a powerful mage. I can take care of myself."

Jason grimaced. "No offense, Amy. Really. But you're a healer. If some pissed-off mages barge in here, what would you do to them, exactly? Heal them of any injuries or broken bones, cure them of their sore throats or sinus infections, and hope that will distract them long enough for you to run out the back?"

I scowled at him. He was supposed to be on my side. The fact that he had a good point only made this more frustrating.

"Dr. Jason is right." Crinea made her words a pronouncement. "Have you ever used your magic to defend yourself? Have you ever used it for violence?"

"Of course not!" I exclaimed, horrified. "That isn't what my gift is for. I would never use my abilities to cause harm." Then I real-ized I had just lost the argument.

"Jason isn't human, either!" I protested, in a weak, final attempt to save myself from a night of useless boredom. "He has abilities."

Crinea arched a single eyebrow. "Dr. Jason's origin is unknown. Thus far, his supernatural abilities have expressed themselves through powerful nausea, insomnia, weakness of the limbs, and occasional fits of dizziness. He hardly qualifies as a fit preternatural guard."

Leave it to a centaur to be brutally blunt. Out of the corner of my eye, I saw Jason wince at her unfortunate, if accurate, description of his condition.

"And besides," Crinea added, "mages are not the only things that may emerge from the forest, wishing to do you harm." She glanced over her shoulder toward the open door of the clinic, at the sunset and the growing darkness, her face drawn and serious.

I forced a long, slow breath through my teeth, and closed my eyes for a second. This bickering was getting us nowhere. These were my friends. They were worried for my safety and, given all the revealed secrets and sudden violence that had damn near turned our world upside down less than two months ago, I couldn't really blame them. Besides, the person who I was really furious with wasn't here.

Again.

"Okay," I said, nodding and snapping my eyes open. "Let's compromise. I get that you guys are worried about me, and I appreciate it."

Jason raised his eyebrows skeptically, and I half-laughed at his expression.

"Really," I told him. "How about this? Jason and I will stay here, but we'll close the clinic for the night. We've been talking about doing some remodeling for weeks. This will give us a chance to get started on the work."

"No patients?" Crinea asked, her expression suspicious, as though she thought I would smuggle some ailing pixies in the back door.

"No patients," I assured her. "The centaur chief and I agreed that he would provide guards only while the clinic is open. With the clinic closed, he won't have to feel he is breaking his word."

Not that long ago I had saved the life of both Crinea and her son, and in return the chief had promised to provide the clinic with guards every night.

"Jason and I will use the night to do some stuff around here." I took a step closer to her, smiling a little. "You don't have to worry so much, Crinea," I said, my voice softening. "I'll be fine."

After a moment of intense consideration, Crinea's scowl melted away. She nodded. "Very well."

Jason heaved a sigh of relief. "All right, then. That's settled. Amy and I'll stay here and lie low. We won't pollute your centaur-only ritual with our presence, and you won't have to worry about us being in harm's way."

My eyebrows climbed. The bitterness that had seeped into Jason's voice surprised me.

Crinea's gaze flicked to him. She had heard it too. Her tail swished back and forth nervously. "We mean no insult by excluding you," she said, her voice anxious.

Jason ducked his head with apparent embarrassment. "I know, Crinea. I'm not offended. Sorry." Jason rubbed the back of his neck, looking anywhere but her face. "I'm just a little bit touchy recently."

"We know that some things are only for your tribe," I hurried to add, forcing a smile. But Crinea did not seem convinced.

"Even Lord Rowan cannot participate. He may only observe, and pay his respects," she explained, her voice urgent. I knew she did not want to offend Jason or me. Offense is something centaurs take very seriously. "Tonight is the final rite of passage for Mattis. Six weeks have passed since he was murdered by the mages, and it is time for his spirit to move on. Tonight we bid him a final farewell. It is fitting for us, who were his family, to send him on his journey to the next world."

I tried to ignore the throb of pain that Crinea's mention of family had set off inside me. The mages had been my family once, but that was over now. And Rowan, who I had thought might be a part of the next chapter of my life, had moved on. But I still had Jason, and Meri. They would have to be family enough.

"Of course," I told her. "I understand." I also understood what Crinea wasn't saying: that Natia, Mattis's pregnant widow, was still in deep mourning, and the sight of humans, let alone a mage like me, would be too painful for her on the night of this final ceremony.

"Well," Jason said, giving a halfhearted grin. "I'm glad we've worked that out. I didn't want to have to pull you two apart if this thing came to blows. Just kidding!" He hurried to add, when Crinea's eyes widened, "I know you two wouldn't really fight. Probably." His hand fell to his stomach. "Anyway," he said, "I'm starving. Why don't I run out and grab us a pizza or something, Amy, if that sounds good to you? After we eat, we can get to work cleaning the library."

"Yeah, sure. That sounds great," I answered, trying to sound enthusiastic.

"Great." Jason pulled his jacket from the back of a nearby chair. "It'll be just like old times. I'll be back in about a half-hour. I'll see you later, Crinea!" He beat a hasty retreat.

"Goodbye, Jason," Crinea called out after him. Unspoken understanding passed between us, and we waited in silence until we were alone.

"What aren't you telling me?" I demanded, as soon the door banged shut.

She shook her head, a movement more of refusal than denial.

"Why are you so worried about the guards being away? We haven't even had them for that long. You never used to worry about the safety of the clinic before."

Crinea hesitated. Again, she glanced over her shoulder, towards the darkness and the woods. Her eyebrows drew together and, for a second, I thought she would really tell me what was on her mind. But then she shrugged, her shoulders lifting and falling delicately. "There are some things it is better not to speak of."

"Why? Because I'm not part of your tribe?"

Her eyes flashed a little as she responded. "*No*. Because to speak of them only increases their power."

I wanted to argue, but instead I swallowed hard and forced myself to silence. I knew Crinea well enough to know that, if she thought it better not to tell me, no amount of prodding would get her to change her mind.

"How is Natia doing?" I asked instead, and Crinea's tail swished anxiously.

"About the same," she admitted. "Time does not seem to be enough to ease her grief. We will have to hope that, once the baby is born, it will be a comfort for her. But how are you, Amy?" she asked, stepping closer. She hesitated, and then laid a hand on my shoulder. "Really?"

If Crinea had been only human, I would have smiled and said I felt fine. But centaurs can tell when you're lying, and they generally take it as an insult. So instead I just shrugged. "I'm being an idiot. Two months ago, I thought I was going to be killed by people who I used to think of as friends—almost as family. Now I don't have to live in hiding anymore. I can use my abilities; I can keep the clinic open. I don't have to hide who I am. I can even use my real name. And Meri, who is like a mother to me, is safe. I should be happy." I scowled at myself. "I ought to be satisfied with this."

"But Rowan—"

"Never promised me anything," I broke in, not wanting her to finish that sentence. No matter how confused my own feelings toward him might be, the idea of someone else criticizing Rowan hurt. "We were thrown together at a time when we both thought we had no future. We were able to help each other through it. It doesn't have to be anything more than that."

Despite the things that Rowan had said, despite everything we had shared and my feeling that we fit together so perfectly…part of me wasn't really surprised by his desertion. I had learned about loss at a young age, with the sudden death of my parents, and had experienced it over and over again, in a variety of forms and permutations, throughout my adult life. On the deepest, most instinctual level, I had never expected to get to keep the happiness that I felt with him. When Rowan had first made it clear he no longer had any desire to see or speak to me, I had felt more a dull, numb grief than shock or outrage. I had pushed my feelings grimly aside, determined to get on with my life and not show anyone, least of all myself, how deep the pain went under the surface. But it still lurked there, waiting for a moment of weakness, when it could well up in my throat and send its shooting pain coursing through my heart.

I told myself, firmly, over and over, that I didn't blame Rowan for moving on. Not just because leshies mate for life, which made romance so high-stakes for them. But, now that he had successfully bonded with this land, Rowan had become its incredibly powerful guardian. He didn't need me anymore. I couldn't really be surprised he didn't want to continue to see me. I just wished he would come and tell me to my face.

Crinea shook her head, her face twisted with an uncertainty that was unusual for her. "I wish I knew how to advise you," she said. "But I know little of human affairs, and even less of how leshies handle these matters. It is so much simpler for us centaurs."

"How did you find Finar?" I asked, genuinely curious. A few weeks ago, I would have been afraid to ask such an intimate question, as centaurs are so secretive. But now I knew Crinea better, and I didn't think she would take offense.

"It was written in the stars, soon after I was born," Crinea answered, a small smile curling the edges of her lips. "My mother read my future there, and she announced it to our herd. Finar and I were always together after that."

"That does sound nice," I admitted. "To have the certainty of your happiness written in the sky."

Crinea pursed her lips. "Nothing is certain," she said, her voice suddenly quiet. "The stars cannot truly tell us our fate. They can only say what is most likely. Our actions determine what will really come to be."

"Have you seen my stars?" I asked before I could stop myself, already sure I would regret asking the question. But Crinea only laughed.

"I have never had the gift of reading the skies." She chuckled. "My brother says I am too much of a warrior for stargazing. He says that the greatest warriors do not read their future. They write it."

"The chief is a wise man," I said, smiling back at her. "You don't really seem the type for accepting your fate quietly."

Crinea's hand tightened on my shoulder. "I would say the same of you, my friend."

I huffed out a breath of surprise. "I don't know what you mean by that. I'm no warrior."

"There is more than one kind of warrior." Crinea's hand dropped from my shoulder, and she turned toward the door. "And if the stars do not smile on us all, then soon there will be more than one kind of battle that must be fought. I should go. There are preparations that must be made before the ceremony can begin." She cantered off into the night, disappearing into the darkness before I could ask her what the hell she meant by that.

ONE

"Lift with your legs, Amy! I mean, Asa," Jason cried later that night, lunging forward with his hands held out, ready to catch the box if it slid out of my hands. "Be careful! You'll hurt yourself."

I grunted as I hefted the cardboard box and then let it slam down onto the cart.

"I'm fine, Jason." I straightened back up and pushed sweat-drenched hair out of my eyes. "I'm being careful."

"You are not fine. Not until those stitches in your chest come out. You already busted them open once a few weeks ago. If you do it a second time, they'll have to stay in even longer."

Actually, I had already broken them open a second time. But I had quietly sewn them back up by myself. There was no reason Jason had to know it had happened. He was enjoying his new status as mother hen entirely too much already.

My fingers moved of their own volition up to my collarbone, tracing the still-tender wound that trailed diagonally all the way down my chest, between my breasts, and almost to my rib cage.

It was an injury that should have killed me.

For years, I had carried a pearl of power hidden in my body for my almost-mother, Meri. Removing it ripped a hole right in the middle of my chest. Meri had repaired much of the damage, and later I had done more healing of myself. But there are limits to how fast a human body can mend, even with magical inducement. So, what should have been a life-ending trauma had become instead an ongoing nuisance. Though the healing was slow and would leave me with one hell of a scar, I still felt pretty damn lucky. Things could have been much, much worse.

The gemstone bracelet I wore wrapped around my wrist had slipped out of place, and I adjusted it. My preternatural patients paid me with those stones. Usually, I wore them as a necklace. But, since being injured, it was too painful to wear a necklace that lay against my chest, so—knowing how important it was that I show my patients how much I valued the payments that they gave me—I had taken to wrapping the necklace around my wrist.

"Maybe getting started on remodeling tonight wasn't such a hot idea after all," Jason commented. He was breathing harder than I would have liked, standing with his hands on his hips as he surveyed the progress we had made on the barn. His sandy blond hair was sweaty and sticking to his forehead. I resisted the urge to ask him how he was feeling or tell him to sit down and rest. Instead, I wiped the dust and sawdust that were clinging to my palms off onto my jeans and looked around the clinic with an appraising eye.

"We've gotten most of the books out of the library and into the house," I observed, trying to sound upbeat. I had to admit, converting the clinic's small, one-room library into another patient room would be a bigger project than I had imagined. We'd been working for hours, and so far, we'd only managed to clear the room out. "Only two boxes left to carry over to the house, and the library will be totally empty. That's real progress."

"We also nearly polished off a whole pizza," he commented, grimacing and placing a hand over his stomach.

"Well, I did more than my fair share there," I admitted, trying to sound remorseful, but failing. The pizza had been delicious. Now that the Pearl had been removed from my body, the constant aching pain deep inside my chest was gone, and I could finally eat normally again. I wasn't the slightest bit sorry my jeans felt a bit tight. "Wanna take a break for a minute?"

"Yeah," he answered, and the moroseness of his tone told me just how sick he felt. I cursed inwardly. We had worked so hard for so long to get him feeling better, and I knew he had been meeting regularly with Rowan. I had hoped that would help, too. But clearly something wasn't right.

The long tables that stretched down the center of the barn were strewn with plywood, hammers, and duct tape, and Jason had to shove things aside to make room for the cooler he set down between us. He opened it and tossed me a bottle of water before twisting his own open and taking a long drink.

"So," I said, after a moment. "How are you feeling?" Then in a lower voice that didn't pretend any cheerfulness, I added, "How bad is it right now?"

Jason didn't meet my eyes, which by itself told me the answer wouldn't be good. The silence stretched on, twisting into something heavy and painful between us. "I thought Rowan was helping you!" I exclaimed when I couldn't stand it anymore. "I thought you were meeting with him."

Jason shook his head slowly, his jaw clenched, muscles in his neck standing out. "I have been meeting with him. With *Lord* Rowan." He managed to make the title sound like an insult. "He's been giving me lots of instructions about how to take care of myself. Edicts, really. And I'm not following them. Not a damn one." He looked up at me, his eyes flashing, daring me to argue. "I won't do anything he tells me to do until he gives me some answers. It isn't right, Amy. He's so secretive. With you, it was different. Neither of us knew what was wrong with me, and we were a team, working together. Trying to figure out something that would make me better. But this is completely different. He knows. He knows what I am, where I came from. Everything I've been waiting my whole life to find out. But he won't tell me! Do you have any idea how infuriating that is?"

"No," I answered softly. "I can't imagine."

"Every time I press him, he tells me I'm not ready. That I have to be patient. As though I haven't been being patient for my whole damn life already. I can't stand it." Jason's voice dropped to a low, tortured whisper. "It gets so bad that I just want to haul off and punch him in the face. But I *can't*." His voice broke, and I knew that, in some ways, this was the real crux of the problem. Since Jason did not have a tribe or group that he was part of, he now fell under Rowan's direct authority. From what I had seen, that power was at times an overpowering, terrifying force. "When he's standing there, in front of me, it's all I can do not to fall on my face at his feet. Because he's my king." Jason finally looked up at me, and his eyes were wide and frightened. "*My* king. I don't even know how that happened. I don't want it. I didn't sign up for any of this, Amy. And to be totally honest, right now, when it isn't making me furious, it's scaring the hell out of me."

I was about to respond, when something caught my attention. Despite the cold of late fall in South Dakota, we had thrown the barn doors open to the night air, welcoming the breeze on our faces as we hauled heavy boxes across the barn. Now I saw something stir, out in the dark, just past the barn doors. Something I couldn't quite see, but, still, I knew it was there.

A piece of darkness, a small mass of black, only distinguishable from the gloom of the night because it moved. Something lurking just outside the faint glow of the lights strung up by the clinic's front door.

"Amy?" Jason asked, "What's the matter? Are you all right?"

"Shh!" I motioned with my right hand, stepping in front of him as I moved towards the door. "Something's out there."

"When you say 'something,'" he breathed, taking in the urgency of my voice and following my gaze until he, too, was staring out into the darkness, "I take it you mean something other than one of our normal clientele?"

"Something dangerous," I confirmed, moving towards whatever it was with slow, measured steps. "Don't make a sound or move until I tell you."

Instantly, Jason was as still as a tree when no wind passes by. It was one of the reasons I liked working with him so much. He knew how to take direction.

There was another movement outside, but I did not increase my pace. Whatever it was, and whatever it wanted, there seemed to be no reason to rush towards it.

I'm safe here, I reminded myself, even as my heart rate sped up. *Meri is back, in charge of the clan. No one is hunting me anymore. That is all over and done. I am safe.*

But there was no denying what I felt: a deep sense of dread, and a twisting, sinuous sensation of fear that wound around my spine and inched slowly up my back.

I reached the barn door and stepped out into the night, to stand in the warm circle of light that spilled out from the lights inside. The night clung eerie and silent around me, the cold air stinging against my cheeks. On the nights the clinic was open, we turned on the Christmas lights that lined the walkway up to the barn. Tonight they hung, dark and lifeless, swaying limply back and forth, pushed by the cold breeze that swept up against me, their cheerful glow absent, somehow making the darkness around them seem thicker. Something rustled again just a few feet to my left, coming closer.

For a second, I didn't understand what I saw.

In the movies, a swell of dramatic music comes before tragedy strikes. The camera pulls back. Everything switches to slow motion. In the real world, an earth-shattering event can happen in a bare and silent second. The world doesn't do you the favor of slowing down, so you can process what's happening. The moments that take our lives and rend them end to end happen while no one is paying much attention, in the dark, still night, in no more time than it takes a dream to die.

I felt a sudden, savage stinging in my eyes, like someone had thrown a cup of acid against my face. A scream rose in my throat, but almost as soon as the pain started, it vanished. The scream distorted, and became a strangled whimper. I bent over, clutching my stomach as a feeling, like a tidal wave inside my body, swept through me. My eyes burned. I felt wetness on my cheeks. The ground tilted beneath my feet, and for a second I thought I would fall over. Then the ground righted itself. The pain receded. I lifted my hand to my face, and wiped my cheek. When I looked at my fingertips, my tears were tinged with red.

The curse took hold.

I knew enough to know what had just happened to me. Grief and loss roared in my ears as my heart rate peaked, and my breath caught in my throat. It was already too late. The damage had been done.

I thought of Meri, who didn't have any family except for me, and of what this would do to her. My heart ached. Behind me, the thin light from the open barn door still stretched out, like a thin, weak hand beckoning me home.

I blinked and shook my head, trying to push everything aside: my confusion, my fear for myself and for Meri. I couldn't feel them now. I would only allow myself to think about the most important thing—the one thing that had not changed in that devastating moment: a creature crouched on the ground in front of me, bleeding and in desperate need of help.

"It's all right," I said, not sure it would understand but knowing that the words were important to say. "Really. I understand. You can come out."

The hellhound inched closer, one of its back paws dragging,

useless, on the ground. It stood, still just outside the light, and we stared at each other. Was I imagining the look of sympathy in its eyes? Slowly I squatted down, making myself as small as possible.

What must it be like, I wondered with an ache, to be a creature who brought a curse of death to all who saw it? What must it be like to carry that kind of power, that kind of venom, in your gaze?

"It's all right," I said again, slowly. "I'll care for you."

I had promised Crinea I wouldn't see any patients, but that hardly seemed to matter now. I reached out my hand, and the creature took another painful step closer and then, suddenly, crumpled to the ground.

I scooted closer to it, unwilling to stand up, not wanting it to feel threatened if it was still conscious but simply unable to stand. If the wounded creature lashed out at me, the curse would strike in the most painful, horrible way.

Fear made my throat constrict. My hands trembled as I forced myself to move closer.

The hound wasn't much bigger than a German Shepherd, its body slender, built more for speed than for girth. Thick, bristle-sharp black hair covered it and stood out from its hide like the prickles of a porcupine. It stank. The quick puffs of its breath that made tiny clouds in the cool night air smelled like rotted flesh. Its eyes were closed, but I could see a faint glow of red from under-neath its lids. Its mouth lolled open, and its black tongue hung out to the side. Double rows of teeth—like a shark— stood out, unnervingly white in the black night.

I would have to carry it, and I couldn't tie its jaws closed. It would almost certainly see that as an attack, and wake up fighting. I would have to risk a bite, which I tried not to think about as I hefted it in my arms. I walked back to the barn, calling loudly ahead of me.

"Jason! Get the hell out of here. Quick. Get in your truck and take off. I'll call you first thing in the morning."

Carefully I lowered the hound onto the table in the middle of the barn, pushing plywood and hammers out of my way and letting them clatter to the ground before flipping on the light next to the exam table to get a better look at the hound's wounds. They were extensive. Outside I had only noticed his paw, which seemed to have been gnawed on. But his right flank had been torn into, leaving a large strip of flesh dangling. There was a lot of blood, and I saw a white flash of bone. I was so engrossed that I didn't notice Jason walking up behind me until he spoke.

"What is that thing?"

I cursed and dove for a blanket, and hastily pulling it over the unconscious hound's face. According to what I had read, the hell-hound's curse could only be spread with eye-to-eye contact. I hoped desperately that the book had been right, and that it wouldn't harm Jason to just look at it, so long as the beast was sleeping.

"You've got to get out of here." I rounded on Jason, who had come to stand behind me. "Seriously. You don't want to have any part of this."

"Let me help you, okay? It's unconscious. It isn't a threat to anyone right now." Jason leaned in, looking closer, his eyes narrowing. "What is that thing, anyway?"

Suddenly comprehension kicked in and he jerked his head back.

"Holy shit. Is that what I think it is?"

"Like I said: go." I pointed at the door.

"You can't have that thing be in here! Jesus, Amy. What have you done? You've got to get rid of it!"

I shook my head.

"It's hurt. It stays."

"You don't understand. That thing is a *hellhound*." Jason took half a step backward, raising his hands up and away from the creature. "It isn't just that it's cursed—it is a curse. A living, breathing curse that spreads to whoever it looks at, and you went out there and had a freaking conversation with it and then carried it around like a goddamn baby!"

I turned away from Jason and focused back on the wound in the hound's side. The blood that oozed from it was almost as dark as his fur. I would have to check to make sure none of its bones were fractured.

"Amy? Are you listening to me?"

I didn't turn my head.

"No, I'm not. This is my clinic, and I make the rules. I say who stays and who goes. He stays, and you go; it's as simple as that."

"There is no way in hell I'm leaving you alone with that thing."

"Listen." I spun to face him, heat rising in my cheeks. "I already made eye contact with it. That damage is done. But I can handle this myself, and there is no reason for you to be exposed. I won't let you put yourself in danger."

"You won't *let* me?" Jason's cheeks flushed with emotion, and he took a step closer to me. "I think having Rowan order me around all day is already more than enough. I'll make my own decisions about putting myself in danger."

"Not here you won't." I let my voice climb, staring him down, determined to win this fight. In that moment, I didn't care if he hated me afterwards. I just wanted him *safe*. "My clinic. My rules. Get the hell out. Now."

A low growl thundered from behind me, deep and savage, a rumbling warning of imminent harm.

"Crap." I turned away from Jason to lean over the hellhound, trying to calm it back down while simultaneously adding *having a screaming fight while standing inches away from an injured, frightened, and immeasurably dangerous supernatural beast* to my mental list of the stupidest things I'd ever done. The list, I noted distractedly, was getting rather long.

"Don't worry," I whispered, gently touching its flank, where I hoped my touch would cause no pain. "You're safe here. Nothing is going to hurt you. I'm going to fix you up, and then you'll be on your way. You're going to be fine."

A second growl answered my words and I froze. For a split second the simple shock of it made me feel dizzy. Because the hellhound in front of me was still deeply unconscious, his eyes firmly closed. Slowly, very slowly, I pivoted, until I could see the second hellhound that, half-crouched, stalked in from the night.

TWO

"Jason," I breathed, my voice little more than a whisper, "don't run. Turn your back, *very* slowly, and don't look at it."

He rotated slowly on his heel until his back was turned, and then froze as though he had turned to stone. My eyes focused on the dark shape that stalked closer, its red eyes glinting and focused on the still form that lay on the exam table beside me. It moved with predatory grace, and I felt sure that the blood that was smeared thickly on its snout was not its own.

Stupid, I thought. *So stupid not to wonder how the first had gotten his injury, not to think that whatever he escaped from might be coming after him.*

"Don't get between them," Jason urged with his back turned. "Just step away."

"I can't," I murmured. "I told him he was safe."

I took a deep breath before speaking to the second hellhound. I had never done an in-depth study on the legends surrounding hellhounds, a decision I suddenly regretted with bitter intensity. I knew they were extremely intelligent, but I couldn't be sure whether or not they understood human speech. Still, whether he could understand me or not, it was my tone that mattered most. I knew enough about predators to understand that if there was fear in my voice, he would attack.

"This is a clinic," I said, my voice firm and even. "If you are hurt, I'm happy to treat you. But I will not allow you to harm my patient. This is neutral ground."

The hound made no noise, but his eyes turned to me, and he straightened out of his crouch, displaying his full height. Much bigger than the injured hound, he came up well past my thigh, with a much thicker body. I would never have been able to carry this one in my arms. His nose wrinkled, and he pulled his lips back from his teeth in a crazed grin, displaying hundreds of razor-sharp teeth. They were dyed red with blood.

I took another step, so that I stood blocking his path to the unconscious hound. "You are not welcome here," I told it. *"Leave."*

The sound that it made in response was somewhere between a roar and the bay of a hunting dog that has scented its prey. The sound reverberated off the walls, making my ears ring.

Wow, I thought to myself, *that curse worked quickly. Less than fifteen minutes from seeing the first hound to dying. I wonder if that's some kind of record?* But if this creature thought I was going to turn and run, it was in for a surprise.

It took a step closer, and, without looking away, I reached out. My fingers closed on one of the pieces of plywood that Jason had left lying on the table.

The hellhound snarled. Its body tensed, like a spring pulled tight. When it leaped, I could see no more than a blur of motion, a black smear of fury arching toward me through the night. I jumped forward, moving toward it, swinging the plywood in front of me like a club, bringing it smashing up into the hound's face. The hound barked once in surprise, and crashed hard onto the floor. It lay on its side for a dazed half-second. Then it scrabbled furiously back onto its feet, its long, curved claws leaving deep scratches on the wooden floor.

It lunged at me again.

I swung the board in an arc, again making contact with the hound's face, feeling a rush of satisfaction as I saw a few of his teeth fly away.

The hound stumbled backwards.

"Out!" I shrieked, moving closer as I swung the wood again. But my aim was off this time, and I hit nothing but air. My heart rate soared, sending adrenaline pounding through my veins. It washed everything away, and suddenly there was no fear, no curse, no pain where the stitches pulled tight and angry on my chest. No ache of loneliness or burn of betrayal as I waited, day after day, for someone who did not come.

It felt so good.

I took a long stride toward the hound, bending my knees as I swung again.

"I said get out, you prickly bastard. He is *my* patient! Mine!"

The hound snarled and snapped, but it fell back a pace. The weight of its gaze made my skin prickle and crawl. But no pain followed; the damage from curse was already over and done. I saw a trace of confusion in the hound's eyes. It wasn't used to its victims fighting back.

I kept going until I had driven him out of the barn and into the night. Again and again, he darted forward, but every time he moved I swung, and I hit more often than I missed. His growls got deeper and more furious, but I could tell he was getting tired, too. He was used to hunting by stealth, tracking prey that fled from him and never stood its ground. By the time we reached the edge of the forest, sweat was dripping down my face despite the cool night air. Finally, he lunged, and when I brought the plywood down it connected with a distinctive crack. The hound yowled in pain and frustration, then turned and sprinted away into the trees.

I stood in the darkness and watched it go, gasping for breath, suddenly feeling the cold night air that pressed against me.

"Are you hurt?" Jason hurried up behind me. His voice was

calm, but I knew him well enough to hear the panic that hid beneath his words.

"I'm not sure where I hit it, exactly," I said, ignoring Jason's question. "But I broke something." I rounded on him. "You didn't make eye-contact with it, did you?"

Jason's eyes searched mine as he shook his head. "No. I saw a dark form running off into the woods. Nothing more."

"Good." I started back to the barn, Jason hurrying behind me. "You should be all right. The curse won't spread to you." I dropped the plywood to the ground with numb fingers. I didn't want to bring it back inside the clinic—it was splattered with blood. My body vibrated with nerves and adrenaline, but I forced myself to turn and look straight at Jason, tried to make my voice calm and even. "You've got to head on home. I'll be fine—I'm just going to tend to the other one."

"Amy?" Jason said, his voice oddly vulnerable. "The curse. Can you fix it?"

"No." I said it with no inflection in my voice. I didn't even feel that upset about it, at the moment. The shock was still too strong. Nothing felt completely real.

"Don't say that. Of course you can." Jason's pale face stared at me from the shadows. "You just need time to figure out how to cure it."

"You can't cure a curse." I raised my hand and touched the skin just below my right eye. Was I imagining it, or was there a faint, oily residue there? As though, when it had struck, the curse had left behind some sort of thin, noxious coating on my skin?

"You can't be sure of that," Jason protested. "Not really."

"Yes, I can be, actually. I've seen this before." I closed my eyes, trying to control the flood of memories, trying not to see the images that surged like an unruly mob to the surface of my consciousness. "I was young. No more than twelve. They brought her to Meri first, of course." I opened my eyes, schooling my features so the pain wouldn't show. "It was only after Meri had done everything she could think of that they brought the girl to me."

Jason was staring at me dumbly. I didn't want to talk about this, didn't want to remember anything from that time. The swirl of confusion as my gifts began to pulse inside me, pulling my insides this way and that. The raw, open wound in my heart as the grief over my parents' death festered and took root, growing into a dark shadow that hung over my every moment and word. A little girl with tight black curls, convulsing under my fingers.

"I tried everything I could think of for her. The whole clan did. Helen was only six years old. We all wanted so badly to save her. But a hellhound curse isn't a sickness that can be cured. It isn't even a spell that can be undone. It changes you. Changes your future. It corrupts your fate."

I shrugged, looking up at the stars in the night sky. The cold air felt so good on my cheeks. We were far enough away from any major cities that the sky here was free of light pollution. The stars shone so brightly, as though they were pressing themselves as hard as they could against the firm, cold face of the night. Determined to shine a little longer, desperate to shed whatever small portion of light they could. The moon was pale and distant, a thin sliver of muted white, hanging uncertainly in a distant corner of the sky.

"What happened to the girl?" Jason asked. I wished he hadn't asked, that he hadn't forced me to say it out loud. I smiled around the hard lump in my throat.

"I watched her die in her mother's arms," I told him. "She was the first patient to die under my care."

For a second Jason stayed rooted to where he stood. "How long do we have?" he called out from behind me. "How long to figure out a cure?"

There would be no cure. But I didn't feel like arguing.

"I'm not sure," I said. "It seemed to lie dormant for a while. I don't know what activates it. For all I know, it could be days, even months, before it strikes. But once the curse is active, it hits pretty hard." I flinched away from the next memory that came, pushing the image of the little girl's face away, to the place deep inside me where my worst fears and deepest regrets were stored. Jason came and stood so close beside me that the warm flannel of his shirt brushed against my arm.

"What are we going to do?" he asked, his voice hushed and frightened.

Our hands brushed against each other. His fingers were cold, almost as cold as mine. I reached over, wrapping his hands in mine, trying to warm us both up a little. "*We* aren't going to do anything," I insisted. "Please, listen to me. Go. Right now. There is absolutely no reason why both of us should be endangered by this."

I didn't want to lie to him. But false hope wasn't exactly the same thing as a lie, and I would have said almost anything to keep him safe. "If you keep yourself out of danger, then you'll be better able to help me figure out how to beat the curse. I'll need you—strong and healthy—to figure out how to get through this. Go home for now." I squeezed his fingers. "In the morning, you can come over. I've got all those books that we just carried into the house. Maybe there's something in one of them that can give us an idea of what to do. We can tear the library apart, search for answers. We can figure something out together." I clung to his hands now. As much as I wanted him to leave, I wasn't sure I could bear to let go. "Please, listen to me. Go home. Be safe. Just for tonight."

Jason wasn't looking at me. His eyes were trained resolutely over my shoulder, and he swallowed hard before he looked back at my face.

"You know I have trouble saying no to you," he whispered, his voice raw with emotion, and I smiled. A real, true smile this time.

"Yes, I know. It's one of your best qualities."

"You're sure you want me to go?"

I nodded.

"All right." Jason nodded jerkily. "I'll go now, and be back at first light. We can fix this. You and I together. We'll figure something out. You'll be all right. I promise."

And then he bent down, and kissed me.

I wasn't expecting it, and I didn't have time to think. The night air whipped around us, and Jason clutched my cold fingers with his own. Only our lips and our hands touched, and for a moment it felt to me as though Jason and I were the only two people in the world. He leaned into me, the press of his lips warm and insistent. There was something urgent, almost sorrowful, in the way he touched me, his fingers twisting around mine so tightly it hurt.

Then he pulled away. I tried to think of something to say, tried to even understand how I felt. His hands slipped from mine. He turned and ran off, into the dark.

My feet felt heavy and clumsy as I turned and walked back into the barn. I had wanted Jason to go, would have given almost anything to make him leave. But now the night felt huge and hostile, and I felt very, very alone. I walked over to the exam table, where the injured hound lay, still unconscious, and breathing shallow, painful-looking breaths. I spread my arms wide and leaned against the table, bowing my head and closing my eyes, trying to fight off the exhaustion that suddenly surged inside me. I was almost glad the hellhound's wounds were so severe. It left me no choice but to force all other thoughts away. I had been a doctor long enough to learn how to turn on the intense concentration I needed in the moments when a patient's life hung in the balance. I reached for that focus now, and almost instantly my fingertips began tingling as my gift rose inside me, aching to be used.

I had gone without using my Truthsight for all the long years that I had lived in hiding. Now that Meri was free, I could access my abilities again. Still, I hesitated. Even with Meri's promise that she would keep me safe from the mages who continued to hate me, I couldn't shake the feeling of vulnerability that came with tapping into the Source. I knew that once I used my abilities, the other mages would be able to see me, would know what I was doing.

They would know where I was.

But I wasn't living in hiding anymore. I shook myself, forcing the irrational fear aside. Every second I wasted was a second the hound grew weaker. I looked down at his face, at the rapid rise and fall of his chest, and I let the magic out.

The instant I called on it, Truthsight bubbled up inside me. Silver swept over my vision in a blinding flash, falling like a thick rain that first coated and then transformed the world around me. Suddenly I could see the Source, a silver river of power rushing along just inches from my feet. I looked around me. Seen through my Truthsight, the barn glinted in bright colors of silver and gold, and the very air seemed to whisper, "home." The air smelled like cinnamon and vanilla, and the paper lanterns that hung from the ceiling cast a brilliant, glittering light on everything.

But despite the beauty of my ability and the joy of being able to use it freely, I still felt a shiver of unease. I glanced around me, looking for any sign that I had caught the attention of the other mages. There was nothing. I shook myself, trying to rid my mind of the discomfort, and I looked down at the hellhound.

His true-self looked more reptilian than mammal. The black fur had given way to pitch-black scales, many of which were torn and bleeding. His whole form vibrated, and he made a constant, high-pitched whine of distress that was pathetic and painful to hear. He stirred, and looked up at me. The ominous red glow of his eyes was gone. The eyes that gazed up at me now were chocolate brown, and wide with fear. His whole body stilled, and I could feel how helpless he felt, how vulnerable. I reached out, touching him just under the chin, the way I would calm my own dog when he was frightened.

"I'm going to patch you up now," I said, keeping my voice even and calm. "You just hold on. You're going to feel better soon." And then I set to work.

I had spent so many years treating creatures in my clinic without using magic that now using my Truthsight felt a little like cheating. A few months ago, treating the hound's wounds would have taken hours of careful stitching. I would have been plagued by fear of infection, always concerned there was something I was missing, some deeper injury that was escaping my notice.

Now my power thrummed inside me like a constant, steady drumbeat, and my fingers tingled as his skin knit itself back together under my touch. My eyes saw everything. There was a fracture in one of his rear legs. I reached down and the bones felt like wax, warm and pliable in my hand. I smoothed the pieces back together, watching with satisfaction as it mended and then solidified. When I was done, he wouldn't even limp. I turned my focus to the deeper wound in his chest. After a few moments, he stopped making the high-pitched keening sound, and his body relaxed under my hands as his pain eased. When I looked up from my work, he was watching me, his eyes clear, alert, and full of intelligence.

"Your friend came looking for you while you were sleeping," I warned him. With his wounds fully mended, I got a cool, damp cloth to wipe the remaining blood away from his fur.

"I made it clear he wasn't welcome, and he ran off. Still, you should be careful. He's looking for you. You need to rest and get your strength back. You're a nice hellhound." The words sounded funny, but as I reached over to scratch behind his ear, I believed them. "I want you to be safe."

Gently, I ran my fingers from his forehead, between his eyes, and down the length of his snout. He sighed deeply, lifting his nose up to nuzzle my palm in seeming appreciation.

"You're all fixed up now," I told him. "You should try to sleep."

But the hound was already pulling his feet beneath him, and struggling to rise.

"Are you sure?" I protested, fighting the instinct to reach out and pull him back down. No matter what camaraderie had passed between us, I was pretty sure that doing so would cost me an arm. "You can stay for the night, or for however long you need. I'll sit up with you and keep watch while you're resting."

But with a lightness that surprised me, given both his size and his recent wounds, the hellhound leaped down to the floor. He shook himself tentatively, testing how his body felt. He stood with his feet spread wide beneath him, looking slightly dazed.

"Let me get you something to drink." I hurried to the sink in the back and filled up a bowl. I brought it back to him, ignoring the water that sloshed over the sides and onto my shoes. I wished I could offer him something to eat, but I didn't know what his diet was, and I had a sneaking suspicion I really, really didn't want to know. He drank deeply, nearly emptying the bowl. When he finished, he stood a little steadier. Moving with a slow, steady gait, he started for the door.

"You're sure you want to go?" I called after him, and he turned to look at me. There was no mistaking the apology in his eyes.

"It's okay," I murmured. "I don't blame you. I'm glad I could help." I stood and watched him shuffle away into the darkness.

When he was gone, I turned back to the table. I wiped my hands with a towel, pushed some stray hair back behind my ears. I knew I was stalling, but it was a moment before I could force myself to do what I knew I had to next. I took a deep breath and, using my Truthsight, looked down at my own body.

At first, I couldn't see anything at all. My body was healthy, strong. My Truthsight showed me my vitality, coursing under my skin like sap through a young, strong tree. For a brief, heady second, I thought that I must have been wrong. The curse hadn't touched me, after all. All that drama and worry for nothing.

Then I saw a shadow dancing deep under my skin.

It was a flicker of black, a quick glimpse of something foreign and deadly that waved like the fins of a deadly fish deep in the water, only visible for a second before it disappeared. I froze, holding perfectly still, looking down at myself with my Truthsight flowing inside me. An instant later I saw it again, but it had moved from my abdomen, and now flashed dark and deadly in my right arm. Then it was gone, again. I touched the skin where it had been just a second ago, searching for some evidence of taint: an infection, a wound. A fever I could fix. A traumatic wound I could at least understand. But this...I swallowed, trying to force the panic down.

I'd known that the curse was not a sickness. But it felt harder now, to see for certain that there was nothing I could do.

Feeling suddenly shaky, I let go of my Truthsight. The barn shimmered brightly for a second, and then I was firmly back in the real world.

The bright, warm light was gone. The beat of power inside me stilled. The night outside was dark, ominous. The adrenaline that had carried me through the moment of crisis dissolved like dew in the morning sun, and when I looked down at my hands, they were shaking. I rubbed my fingertips together slowly. What was I going to do?

A sudden bang sounded.

I spun around, in time to see the back door of the barn fly open and Rowan storm in.

THREE

THE NIGHT AIR SWIRLED IN HIS SHOULDER-LENGTH GRAY HAIR, AND the thick half-crescent horns that curled around his ears glinted a little in the moonlight. His wide, high cheekbones framed blazing eyes the color of a blue topaz stone.

There had been a change in him since the last time I had seen him. Then, he had still been regaining his strength, recovering from the exile that had nearly cost him his life. Now, his bond with this land was solid and strong, and he bristled with power that went beyond the thick build of his arms, or the stark outline of muscles that I could see through the thin layer of fur that covered his chest. He moved with grace and purpose, and when he drew to a halt and stared at me, I could feel the weight of his regard like an invisible hand, warm and heavy against my face.

It would have been easier to hate him, so much simpler if the warm knot of anger that churned in my belly had burned all my desire for him away. But as soon as I saw him, a different kind of heat ran through me. I remembered the feel of resting my head on his shoulder. My body had fit so perfectly against his. The night we had spent holding each other felt a lifetime away, but I could still feel the warmth of his fur on my fingers as I'd run my hand across his chest. More than anything, I remembered the feeling of being chosen and treasured, and of choosing him in return.

Longing shot through me, and I reached back and hung onto the cool metal of the table behind me, in an attempt to anchor myself in place. I wanted to run to him, to wrap my arms around his waist, to lean against his chest and have him bend down and press his lips to mine. But his absence had made it very clear he had no interest in my affection. Tears pricked in the corners of my eyes, but I blinked them back and lifted my chin, forcing the expression on my face to remain cold and distant.

Whatever irrational longings might linger in my heart, he had demonstrated he did not deserve to be trusted with my tears.

"What do you want, Rowan?" I demanded, proud that my voice was so measured and calm. "What are you doing here?"

In two long strides, he covered the distance between us. Then his hands, warm and rough with calluses, slid up my neck, cradling my head as he lifted my chin up and stared down into my eyes with a burning intensity.

"When did this happen?" he growled through clenched teeth, the gentleness of his touch at complete odds with the seething ferocity in his tone.

"What?" I asked, somewhat breathlessly.

It was hard to think of anything but how warm his skin was against mine. His bare chest pressed up against me, and he smelled of pine needles and the smoke of a good cooking fire. His new strength had erased the aching red lines that had inched up his arms, signaling his desperate need to find a home, and now only his tattoo was left: black ivy weaving up and around his right arm. He wore a knife strapped to his left arm. The thunderbird talon, a symbol of his kingship, hung like a curved sword across his back.

"The curse this creature has laid on you. When did it take hold?"

"Oh. Right." The softness of his touch was not affection; it was his wariness of harming a fragile human. I lifted my hands and pushed him away from my face. He let go immediately, and I took a step to the side, further away from him. I folded my arms across my chest. "Just now—two, maybe three hours ago. How did you know?"

Rowan did not answer, and his stony face gave nothing away but still, after just a moment of wondering, I knew.

"Jason." Of course, it had been Jason. Only now did I realize I had never heard his truck pull away, that when he had turned and pelted away into the darkness, he had not been returning home, but hurrying into the forest to get Rowan's help. "He came and told you what happened, didn't he?"

Rowan gave a minuscule nod. "He came running into the centaur camp at full speed, practically incoherent, desperate to find me." Rowan didn't really make eye contact with me. His gaze ran up and down my body, probing, using his own magic to try to sense where the curse had struck.

"Can you feel it, Asa?" he whispered.

I nodded, running a finger under my right eye, where I could feel the curse like a light residue on my skin, sinking slowly, deeper and deeper.

"Does it hurt you?"

"No." I shook my head, my eyes narrowing as he watched me. I couldn't understand the emotions on his face. He was flushed, his eyebrows drawn, his teeth clenched. He wouldn't look right at me, but when I could see his eyes, they burned.

He had left me. He had refused to even come see me, to tell me face-to-face why he had changed his mind. He had ignored all the messages I sent to him.

So why did he look like he was in pain?

"Why do you care, Rowan?" I couldn't keep the anger out of my voice, and I didn't want to. The anger was a shield I could throw up between us, a way I could at least keep him from seeing the anguish his absence had caused me. "It hasn't been worth your time for the last five weeks to come by and see me. Why are you here now?"

He still wouldn't meet my gaze. His eyes fixated on my chest, but it wasn't my figure he was admiring. I was suddenly uncomfortably aware of the way the top I was wearing left my still-forming scar visible. I wished I had worn something with a higher neckline, one that covered up the stitches, something that would keep him from gazing with such a tortured expression at the long, red gash still healing on my chest.

When he spoke, his voice was a rough, choked hiss. "You have suffered enough." There was a small hiss as he slid his knife out of the sheath on his arm. "It will be all right. Stay here. I will take care of this." He looked around the barn, his eyes lit with new fire: the excitement of the hunt. "Where is the beast now?"

For a second I stared at him, not understanding.

"What do you mean?"

"When the beast dies, its curse dies with it," Rowan said, as though the information was obvious. Seeming satisfied that the hound was no longer in the barn, he stepped past me, toward the doors. "Rest yourself. It will not take me long to put an end to this."

"What? No!" I said, but shock made my voice small and hollow, and he kept moving as though he had not heard me.

"I said no, Rowan!" I cried, running forward and putting myself between him and the door. "You can't do this!"

"Asa," Rowan said. The muscles in his neck stood out as he struggled to stand still and speak to me. "This creature has harmed you. *Fatally* wounded you." His voice broke a little at the words. "It is a crime that cannot be forgiven. I will not rest until you are safe, and it is dead."

"The hound didn't mean any harm, Rowan. You can't hurt it." I stretched my arms out to the sides, blocking his path. "It isn't his fault that he infected me."

Rowan shook his head, his eyes widening with confusion. "It

makes no difference how or why it brought this harm upon you. It has been done, and the creature's life is forfeit. I will make its death a clean and quick one, if that is your wish. But it dies tonight."

"You can't do that! The hound is an innocent. And you didn't seem so concerned for my well-being these last weeks, when you wouldn't even come and tell me to my face that you didn't want me. What is it, Rowan? The only one who's allowed to hurt me is you?"

Rowan's head jerked back as though I had slapped him. But he took another step closer to the door. "There is no time to waste arguing. You are under my protection, and this creature has wounded you. The trail grows colder by the moment. There is nothing more to say."

"There sure as hell is more to say! The hound is my patient. He came to me, to this clinic—to this place where he could be *safe!*"

"It makes no difference. I am the ruler here," Rowan growled, gesturing with the knife in his hand, "and that creature is under my authority."

"This clinic is neutral ground. It is a safe haven for anyone who needs it. I built it with my own hands, long before you ever came here!"

Seeming to accept that I was not going to move out of his path, Rowan stepped around me.

"You have no right to go after my patient!" I screamed. "This isn't right, Rowan. You've got to listen to me! Deep down, you must know that you can't do this."

"That's where you're wrong, Asa. I can do this, and I must." He didn't even look back at me as he said it. He was already most of the way to the door.

I wasn't going to be able to stop him.

I was a mage, but even if I had been able and willing to use my magic to impede him, Rowan was immune to my sort of magic. I had seen him bat another mage's spells away with no effort at all, shattering them like glass on the pavement. He moved further away from me. Once he disappeared into the night, there would be nothing I could do to stop him, and I had no doubt he could track down the hound and execute it before morning's first light.

There was only one thing left that I could do.

"You owe me," I called after him, my voice cold and clear.

Rowan froze. For a second, silence, pure and piercing, rang between us. Then, slowly, he turned to face me. Finally, he looked me in the eyes.

"I treated your father," I said, knowing the words would hurt him, but not allowing myself to care. "I eased his pain. Then I put myself in danger to save the life of your friend." The words tumbled out, fast and hard, and I hated each and every one that fell from my lips. "When we first came here, I was the one who stopped the centaurs from attacking us. You were weak. You had just lost your home. If I hadn't stopped them, they would have killed us both."

"I know," he breathed.

I could see the toll my words were taking. He stared at me with wide eyes and a wild, trapped expression, as though he wanted desperately to look away, but couldn't. His breath came fast and ragged. He deflated as strength drained out of him. His shoulders hunched as the weight of his debt bore down on him. Debt was a burden most preternatural creatures cannot bear to carry. I was playing dirty, using his own nature against him. But I didn't know what else to do.

"If I hadn't brought you here, you wouldn't have met the chief, and he would never have suggested that you try to bond with this land. And when the land tried you, I stood by you and strengthened you, so that you could pass its tests. When the mages attacked you, I was the one who healed you from that wound."

"Yes," Rowan gasped. His face white as a sheet, he looked like he might fall down.

I walked up close to him, holding his gaze, staring him down.

"If I hadn't helped you, you never would have become the ruler here. Without me, you wouldn't have survived."

His knife fell from his hand, clattering onto the floor at my feet. He made a sound deep in his chest that was half groan, half snarl of frustration. He struggled against his nature. His feet shook with the effort to keep moving toward the door. He took a stumbling step forward and lost his balance, catching the corner of the exam table as he fell to one knee. His head bent forward as he grunted with effort and tried to pull himself back up. I backed away, hating myself for doing this to him, frightened by the effect my words had. His muscles strained with terrible effort as he managed to haul himself up to his feet. He stood, leaning heavily against the table, pulling in fast, uneven breaths.

For a moment neither of us spoke. The sight of him so weakened shocked me into silence, and he stood with his head bowed, his hair forming a curtain around his face, hiding his expression from me.

"What do you want?" he rasped.

"I want you to let the hound go."

He swung his head back and forth, his hair still obscuring his face. "Pick something else. A different payment."

I trembled, but when I answered him my voice was steady and sharp.

"I will not buy my own life at the cost of another's. I can't sacrifice a patient's well-being for my own. It would betray everything I am, everything I have built here. No."

Rowan brought his fist down on the exam table with a terrible crash. "Pick something *else*, Asa! Anything. You know I will pay my debt." He looked up at me, his eyes burning through the shadows on his face. In an instant, his voice changed from a howl to a whisper. "Don't do this," he pleaded. "Let me keep you safe."

I fought down the emotion that surged in my breast. I had no desire to weaken Rowan, no desire to cause him pain. But this was something I had to do.

"That creature was my patient. I took it under my care. I *promised* him that he was safe. *No.*"

I could hear Rowan grinding his teeth, trying to find a way to refuse me. But the debt was too much.

"So be it," he cried at last. "I will grant you the life of this creature in exchange for the aid you have rendered to me." He looked up at me, raw fury in his eyes. "We are agreed?"

"Yes," I breathed, and now I was the one who couldn't look away.

"And my debt is paid?" he prompted me.

"Yes." I swallowed hard. "Paid in full."

His head snapped up. In an instant his strength was restored, and he straightened back up to his full height. His hand snaked out and picked his knife up from where it had fallen to the floor, and he slid it silently back into its sheath. Then he stalked to me, until he stood towering over me, his gaze pinning me where I stood.

"What will you do now, Asa?" he hissed. "If you will not permit me to kill the beast? Can your Meri undo this curse?"

"No," I told him, my mouth dry. "She is powerful, but her magic won't help her undo a curse like this. She's tried to fix this kind of damage before. So have I." I shook my head at the memory. "This isn't something mages can fix."

"Then how will you save yourself from its poison?"

I looked away. I didn't want him to see the desire that still surged within me, or the pain that followed closely in its wake.

"That's my concern, Rowan. You've made it very clear that you want no part of my life." I meant to stop there, but the words kept coming. "You didn't owe me your love," I said. "That night, when you said all those things—even then I told you that you didn't really mean them. The fact that I reciprocated those feelings— that's on me, not you. But you should have talked to me. You should have done that much." I looked up at him, but his eyes were fixed on the door, a hard, distant expression on his face. "We could have at least been friends."

"You don't know what you are saying," he snarled. "And you couldn't possibly understand." Then he stormed past me, back out into the night.

FOUR

WHEN HE WAS GONE, I DIDN'T SHAKE OR TREMBLE. I DIDN'T EVEN cry. I felt nothing, really, just a deep, aching exhaustion that sapped the strength from my bones, and made me want to curl up right there on the floor and sleep for a week.

But I didn't.

No matter how much the news would pain her, Meri needed to know what had happened. And, if I was honest with myself, I needed to see her, to hear her voice. To take whatever comfort could be found in sharing the burden of this fear and uncertainty with someone who loved me.

Out of habit, my hand fell to my belt loop, searching for the clamshell that Meri had given me a few weeks ago, but my fingers met with empty air. I looked down, and cursed quietly. I had forgotten to wear it again. Meri was probably half-mad with worry already.

Not long after leaving with the rest of the mages, Meri had sent me the shell. Although we had already set up a communication portal in my house, it wasn't enough for her. She worried about me, she was lonely, and she wanted a way to hear my voice more often. She had made the magical device herself, taking the two halves of a clamshell and imbuing them with power. Since they were two halves of a whole, they maintained a natural connection with each other, even over great distances. By magically enhancing that connection, Meri created a way for us to speak to each other. When I was a girl, I would sometimes run my finger around and around the edge of a wine glass, until the vibrating glass hummed. The clamshell worked much the same way. If I ran my finger around the edge of the shell a few times, it would hum. And then it would link to its other half, and Meri and I heard each other's voices.

I had teased Meri about it, pointing out that buying a cell phone and signing up for a data plan would have been less trouble.

I smiled as I remembered the way her eyebrows arched and her voice grew slightly icy as she told me, "Darling, I am over two hundred years old. I do not *text*." She said the word as though it was both unfamiliar and, somehow, a little indecent.

It was for the best, anyway, as many of my preternatural clients were uncomfortable around modern technology. And the truth was that I loved the clamshell and its gentle curves of delicate shades of pink and cream. Meri had hung it on a chain for me to wear around my neck, as she wore her half. But the shell had bumped against my stitches, and I had taken to clipping it to my belt loop instead.

But I loved it so much that I was a little wary of wearing it all the time, as it seemed so fragile. I didn't want it to shatter if I banged against a table accidentally. I often left it on my dresser instead of wearing it, and, invariably, when I left it would be the exact time Meri tried to contact me. Unable to reach me, she would quickly progress from mild concern to full-fledged panic.

Meri had always been overprotective, and all the horrible things that had happened to her over the last few years had only made it worse. After being betrayed by a member of the clan, she had been subjected to years of torturous captivity. Now that she was free, I couldn't blame her for her constant anxiety and hawk-eyed protectiveness. And there was a part of me that didn't really mind having someone care about me so intensely. But I still hoped that, with time, she would come to be less fearful.

But even her worry and occasional prying couldn't dampen the simple joy of having back the woman who had been like a mother to me for most of my childhood. I loved having her to talk to again. Loved knowing that, at almost any time or day or night, I could reach her if I needed to ask a question, or just to tell her about my day. Having her back in my life was a warm touchstone, an anchor. Meri lived hours and hours away, but she always felt close. Sometimes I almost thought I caught a whiff of her perfume in the hall. Or felt her hand, pushing my hair back from my forehead while I drifted off to sleep. The rocking chair in the spare room would creak as though, just a moment earlier, she had been sitting in it. I always had the feeling she was watching over me.

It comforted me.

I left the lights in the clinic on and let myself out the back door. It only took a few minutes to cross the grass that separated the barn from the old farm house that was my home, but the air was sharp and the cold pressed against me in the gray light of early morning. I walked faster, tucking my fingers under my arms and wishing I had put on a coat.

I went inside and climbed the wooden steps to my bedroom, not sure if it was the strain of the day that made my legs feel so heavy, or the weight of the conversation I was about to have.

I got to my room, switched on the bedside light, and settled down on the floor in front of the mirror. It had been Meri's idea, and had taken her a few days to set up. Not knowing anything about portals of any kind, I'd been more than happy to let her handle setting it up. The floor-to-ceiling mirror was so large that, when I sat on one side and she on the other, it felt like being in the same room.

I tapped on the glass twice, paused, then tapped twice more.

Then I waited. Less than a minute later the same sound echoed back to me. Tap-tap. Pause. Tap-tap. The mirror shivered, then rippled like a silver pond disturbed by a single, well-thrown stone. With a small, muted flash of light, my reflection disappeared, and Meri sat cross-legged on her own floor, looking back at me.

"Meri," I breathed. "It's good to see you."

It was true.

Just the sight of her, in her black jeans and old sweatshirt, did my heart good. She sat in her own bedroom, a fire crackling warmly in the hearth behind her, the warm light of the flames reflecting off the polished wooden floor she sat on. Her hair had changed color while she was imprisoned, shifting from the pale-yellow I remembered as a girl to a dull, brittle white. Now it shone again, falling smooth and golden across her shoulders. Looking at her, it was hard to remember that she was the most powerful mage in living memory. Her silver eyes sparkled as she smiled at me.

"Hello sweetheart," she exclaimed. "I was so worried! I tried to contact you and then..." Her smile faded. She leaned closer to the mirror, studying my face. "What's wrong, Asa?" she asked, the lighthearted tone gone from her voice. "What's happened?"

A lump formed in my throat, and I found myself utterly tongue-tied.

"Are you all right?" Meri demanded. "Did something happen to one of your patients? To one of your friends?"

"My friends" was the closest she ever came to mentioning Rowan. Her lips thinned and she quickly changed the subject whenever I mentioned his name. Luckily for her, his name hadn't come up in conversation for several weeks.

I cleared my throat. Drawing this out would only make it harder for both of us.

"Something did happen," I admitted, trying to think of a way to say this that wouldn't send her straight into a panic attack.

Nothing came to mind. "Not to one of my friends. Something has happened...to me."

Meri's body went rigid, and her eyes widened.

"What...what are you talking about, Asa?" she demanded, her voice rising an octave.

I grimaced. "A patient came to the clinic. It didn't mean to hurt me, but...well, it couldn't really help itself."

"What patient?" Meri crossed her arms tight against her chest. I could see her fingernails digging into her arms.

I sighed deeply and closed my eyes. I couldn't bear to look at Meri's face while I told her. "It was a hellhound, Meri." I said. "I made eye contact with it."

I didn't need to say any more. Meri knew what it meant. She gasped, and then a long silence stretched between us. When I finally opened my eyes, her head was bowed, her hands covering her face. Her lips were moving, but at first I couldn't make out what she was saying.

"...no, no, no," she whispered, over and over. "...not possible. This can't be true."

"I'm so sorry," I murmured, rubbing my hands together, wishing there was something I could do to ease her pain. "I'll try to figure something out. I know we've seen this before, but maybe I can learn something we didn't know then. Something that will help us."

Meri looked up. All the color had drained from her face. Her eyes looked hollow and haunted. My heart ached. She looked so much like she had when I rescued her, more dead than alive, from the imprisonment that had nearly ended her life.

"Come home to me, Asa," she moaned, her voice cracking. "Come home right now."

My heart sank. I should have anticipated this request, should have thought of what to say. I spread my hand out in front of me, helpless.

"I'm sorry," I said. "You know that I can't."

"Why?" Meri brought a slamming fist down on the wooden floor. "You know that I cannot possibly leave the clan now—not when I have just returned to power, and my hold is not as strong as it ought to be. Why do you refuse to come to me, even now?"

I ran a hand over my eyes, suddenly bone-achingly tired. "We have been over this, and over this," I said, keeping my voice as even as I could, but knowing I couldn't completely hide my frustration. "The mages hate me. It's not like they've kept that a secret, not even now, with you back in control. Other than you and Greg, there isn't a single mage who won't be happy to hear about the hellhound curse. If it weren't for me, the clan would still be the only ones who can access magic. I tore down the barriers, gave mages who aren't part of the clan, and even other preternatural creatures, access to the Source. The mages in the clan won't ever forget that."

"You don't have to fear them," Meri said, her jaw clenched. "Not anymore. I don't know how many times I have to explain that to you."

"I'm not staying away because I'm frightened," I exclaimed, running my fingers through my hair. "I'm staying here because I don't enjoy being surrounded by people who wish I were dead. My life is here. I've got my clinic, my friends..."

"That's what it really comes down to, isn't it?" Meri's voice was cold. "Even now, with all that has happened. Even when we do not know how much time you even have left." Angry tears gathered in the corners of her eyes. "You still choose that creature over me."

I closed my eyes, willing myself to stay calm.

"This isn't about Rowan, Meri," I said at last. "I am going to do everything I can to find out more about the curse and how to get rid of it. I promise." I pressed my hand up against the glass. "We can fight this," I told her, and her eyes softened. All her anger melted away.

"I just got you back, child." Her voice quivered. "I cannot bear to lose you again."

"I know." I nodded. "I won't let that happen."

"I will do what I can here," Meri said, rousing herself, forcing her voice to an unnatural, businesslike tone. "I have books and scrolls I can search. Perhaps one of them will have some information we can use."

I nodded.

"Please, at least do this much for me," Meri pleaded. "Keep the clamshell with you all the time. If you feel unwell, or if anything happens..."

"I will," I promised, and smiled, trying to reassure her as much as I could. "We can talk every five minutes, if that will make you feel better."

"I'm not sure that would be enough." Meri's eyes filled with tears again. "I will talk to you soon, child." Then the silver shimmered, and she was gone.

For a minute I sat, just staring at my own reflection. I wasn't sure how well I knew the person who looked back at me. Some things I recognized. My dirty-blond hair still fell in tight, chaotic curls to my shoulders. The gemstone necklace wrapped around my wrist glittered softly, a touchstone of connection to every patient I had healed in the night clinic. With the pearl gone from my body, my stomach no longer roiled and rebelled every time I tried to eat, and over the last few weeks my face had lost its angry, harsh angles. It had softened, rounding out a bit. Looking more like the girl I remembered from before the world turned upside down.

The angry red gash in my chest still lingered, a reminder of choices I had made, and the consequences that continued to find me. I could no longer regret what I had done. When I had pulled down the barriers to the Source, I had only been trying to heal Meri. But my actions had allowed magic to flow freely to mages who were not part of my clan. It turned out, though I hadn't known it at the time, that my actions also allowed magic to flow freely to other preternatural creatures. The mages in the clan still hated me for taking away their monopoly on magical power. But now that I knew my actions were helping preternatural creatures grow stronger and survive, I could no longer feel the guilt that had once plagued me.

But I could feel lonely. And sitting alone in my room, staring at my own pale reflection, I felt very much alone.

I shook myself, stood up, and rubbed my legs. My foot had fallen asleep while I sat cross-legged on the floor. Sitting around feeling sorry for myself was not going to do anyone any good. I glanced over at my bed. I often slept in the mornings, after being up all night in the clinic. But right now I couldn't imagine lying down.

I had too much to do.

I grabbed the clamshell necklace and hooked it to my belt loop. Then I hurried down the stairs, and back out into the cold.

FIVE

No matter what I had said to placate Jason and Meri, I didn't really believe that either Meri's books, or the ones piled high in cardboard boxes in the middle of my living room floor, held the secret to curing a hellhound curse.

Which meant I had to turn somewhere else for help.

I slipped through the back door of the clinic and began to gather up all the things I would need. It took some time. I retrieved my favorite jacket and pulled it on. I'd found it some time ago at an army surplus store. It was green on the outside and orange and brown plaid on the inside which made it ugly, sort of, but I loved it. Roomy, warm, and softer than it looked, it had a million pockets, all waterproof. I could load that coat up with tubs of ointment, vials of medicine, anything I needed, and it never seemed to run out of space. Now I stuffed a box of matches deep in one pocket, and a mini-flashlight in the other. I grabbed an old, scratchy blanket for good measure.

I slung my messenger bag over my shoulder and walked to the back of the barn, where our two refrigerators hummed. I pawed through the fridge's contents and shoved item after item into the bag, until it was nearly overflowing. I slipped a few more things into my pockets. I tucked a large stainless steel oval bowl under my arm and carried a jug of water in my hand. I hesitated at the door, then walked back and grabbed two pieces of cold pizza. When my arms and pockets were too full to hold anything else, I turned from the barn and trudged out into the trees.

Winter in South Dakota starts early and stays late. Technically, it was still fall, but the cold was here already, sinking its claws deep into the land, preparing to hang on for as long as it could. Even with my jacket, after just a minute of walking, gooseflesh covered my arms and my nose ran.

I trudged out into the trees that stood behind the barn, and walked into the forest. Instantly the trees closed around me, the light of the nascent sunrise swallowed up by the dangling tree limbs, naked and skeletal in the frigid breeze. It was quiet. No birds sang in the trees, and the noise of my own feet on the dead leaves and decomposing pine needles seemed thunderous and out of place. Frigid air filled my lungs, and the first hint of sunlight changed the sky from black to a smudged, dull blue-gray. I could barely see where I was going in the dim light among the trees. Stray branches scraped against my coat and caught in my hair. The recent rain had left the ground soft and muddy, and I lost my footing on the slick leaves, stumbling and nearly falling.

When I caught my balance, I stood still in the gloom, looking down at my shoes, now encased in a thick layer of mud that crept up the ankles of my jeans.

The silence seemed to coalesce and harden all around me, and a strange prickling sensation tickled the back of my neck.

I stiffened.

The feeling intensified and I stood stock-still, frozen in place, my breath making small, ghostly clouds in the air. Apprehension uncurled in my belly, and I fought down the sudden urge to bolt. I forced myself to turn, slowly, slowly, and looked into the trees behind me.

Nothing.

Nothing moved, nothing stirred. No mages jumped from the darkness, blades drawn, crying out for revenge. No bogeymen stomped out of the shade of the trees, fangs bared and claws reaching out.

For another moment, I stood stock-still, breathing hard, torn between berating myself for my childishness and still not quite believing I was safe. But I couldn't turn back. If there were answers in this forest, I would find them. I refused to be scared away by a formless, faceless fear.

I adjusted the strap of my bag on my shoulder, spun on my heel, and continued on my way. Five minutes later, when no danger had materialized and no threat had appeared, the cold that stung my nose and numbed my fingers, combined with the damp-ness creeping through the soles of my shoes, took center stage in my mind.

Ten minutes later, I had put the non-incident completely out of my mind.

I knew the general area I was trying to find, and when I ran out of trail I just kept going, pushing through tangling branches and hanging ivy, ignoring the pine boughs that brushed against my face. I didn't need to go to any one specific spot. This was more of a fishing expedition. All I could do was pick a place that seemed likely, settle in, and throw out the bait.

When I felt more or less certain that I had come far enough, I settled down in a spot where the trees were thin and the ground was liberally coated with leaves in various stages of decay. Though the sun was fully up, the day was cloudy, and the tree branches held out most of the light. I dropped my bag to the ground before settling down with my back against a large, black oak tree. I folded my legs beneath me and, shivering, wrapped the old blanket around my shoulders.

Then I set to work.

I had guessed that the ground would be too wet to easily get a good fire started, but the bowl I had brought was wide and deep enough to hold the kindling I had brought. I poured the kindling in and fished the matches from my pocket. I tossed a firestarter lighter cube into the bowl, and then the match. I blew on the embers until I had coaxed them into a steady, glowing flame. Then I set the small grate I had brought with me over the top of the bowl, creating a small, instant grill.

As a rule, I try to keep the clinic fridge stocked for any eventuality, but with me still recovering and the larger than usual volume of patients we'd had over the last several weeks, we had been eating into our stores. The only package of sausages that I could find in the clinic fridge had already been opened. Still, there were four left, and I laid them out to cook above the fire, along with several sardines that I pulled out of a can. The smoke that went up from my little impromptu cooking fire was thick and fragrant, billowing up like a gray welcoming beacon and wafting through the leaves of nearby trees, filling the air around me with the meat's rich aroma. I pulled two bottles of beer out from the bottom of the bag, popped one open, and set it out on the ground across from me. Then I leaned back against the tree to wait.

A little time passed. I turned the sausages twice, so that they browned evenly and didn't burn. I ate one of the cold pieces of pizza.

There came a faint rustling of leaves.

"You know, it's rude to stare at people," I said without looking up.

"Humph. It's rude to go tramping over the tops of people's homes!"

"I didn't tramp over your home," I replied, then paused and looked up, suddenly nervous. "Did I?"

"Like a great earthquake, you are," Baxin shrilled as he pushed his way out of the bushes. The bald, red-faced gnome glowered at me, his chest puffed out and his head gleaming as he planted himself in front of me.

Still, I couldn't be in too much trouble, if he was showing himself.

"Thundering right over our roof. My wife is still picking up all the pots you knocked off the shelves."

"You're married, Baxin? I had no idea."

"Near to a hundred years now, more's the pity." He shook his head, making his long, black beard sweep back and forth over his chest. His eyes fixed on the sausages. "Quite the feast you have here, healer. More than a little thing like you can hope to eat all by her lonesome."

I choked down a laugh at having Baxin call me little. If I had been standing, the top of his head would have almost come up to my knees. Seated on the ground as I was, we were more or less eye to eye. His head was the largest part of him, with his big green eyes set round and round with wrinkles. If it hadn't been for those eyes, wrinkles would have been his dominant feature. They curled around the corner of his eyes and ran like rivulets of water down his face. But his eyes shone so brightly, full of mischief and humor in equal measure, that when you looked at him you just wanted to smile in return. And check your pockets, to be sure nothing edible had disappeared.

"I don't know." I tsked and rubbed my stomach. "I'm pretty hungry. I haven't had much to eat so far today. But I suppose there's enough for two."

Baxin had been inching closer, and now he picked up the open beer bottle and took a deep sniff, closing his eyes with pleasure as he breathed the smell of it in.

"And what would the price of this here feast be, missy?" he asked, his eyes narrowing even as he plopped down on the ground and made himself at home.

I shrugged. "Same as always, Baxin. Just stories."

"Ahhh." He took a deep, long swig from the bottle, which I took as implicit acceptance of my terms. When he was done he burped delicately and wiped his mouth with the corner of his sleeve. "Well, stories I have, and plenty. Now." He sat up straight, his eyes alight. "How's about you pass me some of that meat?"

We didn't talk much while we were eating. Baxin was too busy feasting, and I didn't want to rush him. The quality of his stories would be directly proportional to how much he enjoyed his meal. Gnomes are generally shy and grumpy, and in those regards Baxin, if anything, outdid his peers. I had heard that he was by far the oldest gnome in the area, which I suppose gave him a right to be a bit cranky. It also made him an excellent source of information, if I could manage to coax him out into the open and get him into a talkative mood. He was a hard creature to get a hold of. Though many gnomes had come, however reluctantly, to the clinic for treatment over the years, Baxin never had. I wasn't sure if he just couldn't bring himself to trust a human enough to put himself into my care or if, like some preternatural creatures, his advanced age made him stronger and healthier, rather than the reverse. I watched him eating out of the corner of my eye, careful not to show too much open attention.

He was very focused on the food, eating in quick, precise bites, pausing every once in a while to close his eyes with appreciation before digging back in. He wore pale blue trousers and a tunic that were finely spun and thickly embroidered with tiny images of flowers and leaves. Though he was bald, his beard was a thick, deep black, without even a hint of gray or white.

"How old are you, Baxin?" I asked, before I could stop myself. It was the wrong thing to ask—he might feel insulted and, besides, I had more urgent questions. But it spilled out of my lips before I could stop myself. Baxin paused mid-bite, and looked at me. I could see him deciding whether or not to take offense. Then he smiled, and shook his head a little.

"I stopped counting when I hit five hundred, dearie. Seemed rather pointless, after that."

The breath froze in my lungs. He couldn't mean that...except I was almost certain that he did. He had said he had been married for a hundred years, but I had assumed he was joking. Now it dawned on me that he may have been telling the literal truth.

"You aren't lying to me, are you?" I whispered.

Baxin wrinkled his nose, as though he smelled something unpleasant. "My kind can lie; don't let anybody tell you different. But it costs us." He looked up at me, and there was nothing sparkling in his eye now. His green eyes glimmered, and I saw him for what he was: an incredibly ancient creature with powers I had not yet even begun to understand. "I'm telling ya the truth, healer." His voice was deeper than it had been a moment ago, and the timbre had changed, as though he had decided to let some degree of illusion fall away.

I stiffened, suddenly aware of how deep into the woods I had come to seek him, of how far I was from any source of help. I had not even told anyone where I was going. And if Baxin really was that ancient, then he was a creature to be both respected and feared. No creature that is purely innocent and jovial can survive for five hundred years.

He sighed, as though he sensed my sudden reassessment of him, and was saddened by it. He leaned forward a little, and the dying fire lit up his face. "You need not be frightened, child. There's a black cloud followin' you around, and you seem in need of a friend. That's fine by me. But friends ought to know each other truly."

I nodded, and swallowed hard. He was right, about everything. "I'd like to be your friend, Baxin," I admitted.

"Well, then!" He leaned back and licked the last of the sausage juice from his fingers. "Why don't you take out the pipe that you've got hidden away in your jacket pocket, pass it on over to me, and tell old Baxin what has made yer heart so heavy."

I told him everything.

It had been my plan to obscure things, to speak in hypotheticals, to get as much information about hellhounds as I could without actually telling him what had happened. Then, to get him to spin me some yarns about hellhounds, and then use whatever information I could. But once I started speaking, I found it almost impossible to stop. He didn't interrupt me, didn't even look right at me. He folded his arms over his chest and puffed thoughtfully on his pipe, staring at the ground with narrowed eyes and nodding whenever I paused, prompting me to go on. Other things came out, too. I told him about Meri, and the blow I knew this news had been to her. I told him about Jason and Rowan. I talked until my throat was raw and my words ran out. When I had finished, I felt empty. But better.

We sat in silence for a few minutes, while he thought. Finally, he took the pipe from between his lips, and knocked it against the ground to empty it out.

"I don't know any way to remove the creature's curse, child. I'm sorry."

I let out a long, shaky breath. I hadn't known if he would or not. But it had been a hope.

"I've heard tales of those creatures, but nothing much that would be of help to you. They don't come through these parts too often, so I haven't had much cause to hear about them. From what I've heard, cold hurts 'em. They don't stay for long in any place that gets as cold as it does in these parts. What brought two of them here, of all places, and at the same time, is a question well worth asking."

I closed my eyes. Hoping Baxin would know some secret cure for hellhound curses had been unrealistic.

"Do you know how long I have?" I asked, forcing myself to open my eyes. Hiding from the truth wouldn't make things any better. "It takes some time, doesn't it, before the curse becomes active?"

"Aye. The hell-beast's curse takes time to build. Death is a part of life; every living thing has some measure of darkness living inside it. But death is usually patient. There is no need for it to chase you down—it knows well enough that it'll win in the end.

But the hellhound's gaze—it wakes the darkness. Makes it hungry. Eager. In the space of one moon's rising, it gathers itself together. Then it comes after you. Once the new moon has risen, and it has gathered itself for the pounce, the curse just waits for an opportunity. Maybe it's a common cold. Or you take a tumble. Whatever small misfortune befalls you, once the hound has cursed you, death is just waiting for its chance to strike."

I nodded, feeling numb.

"'Bout three weeks' time, then," he said, peering up through the tree branches, as though checking the moon's fullness, though it was daylight now. "You've got that much time, at least."

I shook my head. "It isn't enough."

"Enough for what, dearie?"

"Not enough time to find a cure! Or to find someone who knows what to do, or...or," I threw my hands up, Rowan's face flashing in my mind. "...or anything!"

Baxin sat silent for a moment, his chin tucked in against his chest, his face drawn. Then he took the pipe out of his mouth, and leaned in closer to me.

"I've more than five hundred years under my belt," he said, "Would you like me to tell you a secret?"

I stared for a second, and then nodded.

"We none of us get to choose, child. More time, less time." He snorted. "I've seen creatures burdened by a hundred years, groaning from the weight of the time they carried. I've seen pixies who were born and lived and died in just five summers' passing, who loved and lived and laughed more in those years than any other creature I've ever seen. The number of days doesn't matter as much as we think it does."

"That's very easy for you to say," I cried. I didn't want to offend Baxin. I knew that he was trying to help. But really, this was too much. "You've lived five hundred years! It isn't like that for me."

Baxin looked down at the ground, and for a second the light in his eyes was gone. In its place was something deep and dark and aching. "I've buried three wives," he said, his voice suddenly rough and deeper than I'd ever heard it. "I have buried five of my children with my own hands." He looked down at his hands, moving his fingers a little, as though he could still feel damp soil beneath his nails.

When he looked up at me, there were tiny tears glinting in the corners of his eyes. "Everything in this life comes at a price, healer. Everything. If I could have chosen to live less, and lose less, I would have done it." He closed his eyes, shaking his head a little as if to force old memories away. When he looked back up at me, the tears were gone. "I've had to make my peace with it. Nothing else for me to do, really."

"Baxin," I said, stunned. "I'm so, so sorry."

"As I am for you, child." He reached out and patted my hand. "But don't despair. You've got a light, burning inside you. As long as you're alive, as long as that light is still burning, you've got a chance to make things right. Both in getting rid of this curse, and in working things out with that young man of yours."

I stared at him blankly, for a moment. "Which do you mean?" I asked. "Rowan or Jason?"

At that Baxin laughed outright, and the familiar twinkle in his eyes was glimmering again. "Ah, girlie," he chortled, rubbing his beard, "I'll let you figure out the answer to that one on yer own." And he stood up and handed the pipe back to me.

"But what do I do now?" I asked, as he brushed a bit of ash from the front of his shirt.

"Live," he said, as if it was the most obvious thing in the world. "Live as much and as fully as you can. Fight the curse with everything you have in you, but if you can't beat it by getting rid of it, then beat it by fitting a lifetime's worth of living into the next few weeks. You can do it, too," he said. "I can see that much about you." Then he smiled a little, and gave a small wave, before turning away and disappearing back into the brush with a rustle of leaves.

"I don't think I know how to do that!" I called out after him. But Baxin was already gone.

Smoke stung my eyes as I extinguished the smoldering embers. I cleaned up the debris from our little feast, tucked the now-empty metal bowl under my arm, and turned toward home. My whole body felt heavy, and the way back seemed much longer than I remembered it. I knew this patch of the forest fairly well, and before it had always seemed a green and light-filled place. Now it felt shadow-filled and menacing, and I walked quickly despite my weariness.

Eventually the trees thinned, and I stepped out of the forest and onto the small meadow that lead up to my home. Even now, when I could finally escape of the gloom of the trees, I felt none of the safety and contentment that usually filled me when my home came into view. The sun was up, but the heavily clouded sky only let a dim, heavily filtered light shine down on the converted barn and little farm house. The air was frigid and the wind picking up. I hunched my shoulders and trudged toward the clinic, wanting nothing more than to drop my things on the clinic floor and then hurry to the house. Soon, I told myself, I would be home. I would be able to think things through, make some sense of all the disjointed thoughts and emotions swirling inside me. I would kick off my shoes, which were still wet from tramping through the mud and morning dew, sit down at my own kitchen table, and make myself a cup of hot raspberry tea.

And then the world exploded.

SIX

INCHES FROM MY FEET, THE GROUND ERUPTED. SUDDENLY THE AIR was full of flying dirt and bits of stone. A form hurtled toward me. The world seemed to stutter and freeze. I registered a flash of black, bulging eyes. A mouth, open in a silent scream. Teeth as long and sharp as needles. Thick claws the color of bone.

My feet flew out from under me. My hands clutched at open air, finding nothing to hold onto. The creature lunged for my throat.

I fell.

It, whatever *it* was, had been lying in wait, burrowed just below the surface of the ground, at the entrance to the clinic. When it burst out of its hiding place it knocked me over, and as I fell backward, its teeth snapped shut in exactly the space where my neck had been a split second before. I rolled when I hit the ground, avoiding the razor-sharp claws that swiped out at me by bare inches.

There was no time to think, no chance to plan. Everything narrowed down to the tingle of shock in my fingertips, and the suddenly-staccato beating of my heart. I gasped for breath, my chest tight with fear, my shoulder throbbing from the impact on the frozen ground.

I heard a whistling sound and, functioning on raw instinct, I held the large metal bowl up like a shield over my head and shoulders. There was a sound like screaming as the creature's claws shirred through the bowl in a single blow, leaving me lying on the ground, holding a few shards of frayed metal in my hands.

I stared up at a creature made more of nightmare than of flesh.

In the years since I had opened the night clinic, an almost countless number of creatures had come through my door. I had seen creatures with limbs of mismatched sizes, with long, haggard faces, with serrated teeth and eyes that had no pupils. I had once treated a creature whose species I could not name, who had long, tentacle-like fingers and proboscis instead of a mouth. None of those could have been called traditionally beautiful, but I had been fascinated by each one, filled with awe by their complexity, their uniqueness. Never, until this moment, had I looked at a living thing and felt nothing but horror.

The creature was taller than an average man, its frame tortured and skeletal. Rotting skin pulled so tightly against its body that I could see each rib. Its head was bald, save for a small tuft of frazzled, white hair at the base of its neck. It screamed, a howl both high-pitched and hacking, out of a mouth of needle-like teeth, and raised its claws to strike again.

When the creature came close, I pulled an empty beer bottle from my pocket and brought it up, smashing it into the creature's face. The glass cut deep into rancid flesh that did not bleed, and it reared back, more surprised than wounded.

For a moment, I lay on my back, stunned, staring up at the creature as it shook itself, like a dog shaking wet fur. Its wound leaked thick, gray pus. As far as I could see, it felt no pain—it was more enraged than anything else, and moved as though it were not wounded at all.

My hands fumbled on the ground as I searched wildly for something…anything that I could use to defend myself. My fingers closed around cool, rough wood: the piece of plywood I had dropped on the ground after driving away the second hellhound. I seized it and scooted backward, scrambling to my feet and clutching the wood with numb fingers, knowing it would not be enough to force this attacker away. But it was better than nothing.

The creature looked at me, its black eyes wide, and staring.

"Who are you?" I demanded, trying not to sound frightened and failing miserably. My breath came in hard, wheezing gasps. "What do you want?"

For a second the creature tilted its head, as though trying to understand what I had said. Then it hissed, and threw itself at me.

I swung the plywood in a wide, clumsy arc in front, hitting the creature in the side with every ounce of my strength. But my shoulder was still throbbing from my fall, and my arm felt numb. The weak blow only deflected the creature's attack. I didn't hurt it at all; it simply spun and lunged at me again. This time I managed to hit with more force, and I yelled wordlessly as I brought the wooden stick crashing into its side. The creature stumbled, and for a split-second I felt a thrill of hope. Then I realized the force of the blow had broken the wood. I stood, holding a few sorry inches of splintered wood in my hand, utterly defenseless as the creature shook itself. Moving with a slow, predatory caution, it pivoted to attack me again.

I gritted my teeth and braced my feet against the soil, ready to fight for as long as I was able. I tried not to think about the fact that this was a fight I could not win, or to imagine the damage those teeth would do sinking into human flesh. I was so focused on the creature, I did not even notice my hand tingling. It wasn't until later, looking back and trying to parse everything out second by second, that I managed to recall the cool sensation against my skin, the chill of unfamiliar power itching against my palm. I brought the splintered plywood up in front of me.

It wasn't a piece of splintered plywood anymore.

The wood was a living thing. It had stretched, sprouted leaves. It was a branch, still growing, but already longer than my arm; thin, strong, and spear-like. As I watched a wicked, long thorn pushed out of the end, transforming the wood into a wicked weapon, its thorn-blade razor-sharp and jagged.

Out of the corner of my eye, I saw a flash of red and a flutter of movement in the bushes. Long, black hair swirled.

For a second my mind reeled with shock, and I stared down at the weapon that had grown in my hands.

Then the creature pounced on me, and there was no more time for wonder.

I brought the spear up in front of me, and struck. The thorn tore into the gray matter that made up the creature's arm, and it howled, if not with pain, then at least with fury. Again and again it struck, and again and again I swung out, not hurting it badly, but managing to keep it from getting its teeth into my flesh.

It was not very cunning. It made the same moves over and over, and each time I succeeded in knocking its assault aside. But even as I fought back as fiercely as I could, deep down I knew it wouldn't be enough. The creature didn't need to be clever to defeat me. It just had to outlast me. None of my blows seemed to hurt it, and it showed no signs of fatigue. I was streaming with sweat and already gasping for breath. There was no question the stitches in my chest had broken open. I could feel a thin, warm trickle of blood between my breasts.

I narrowed my eyes, and drew in a deep breath, summoning up the same numb, emotionless detachment that I forced on myself when I was treating a patient and things were at their worst. There was no point in thinking of what would happen five minutes from now – that might as well be a century away. No point in thinking of what I might have done differently if I had different resources, or if I had known ten minutes ago what I knew now. All I had was this moment, these tools. I had a weapon in my hand. I was standing on my own two feet. My breath came short and ragged, but I still breathed. I was alive. And there was plenty of fight still in me. I might not be able to defeat this creature, but I could damn well make him work for every inch of ground he gained.

I raised the spear, and struck again.

I was so focused that I didn't falter at all when a savage roar sounded in the distance. I only saw a streak of gray fur and white horns out of the corner of my eye. Rowan hurtled out of the trees and planted himself by my side. He already held the thunderbird talon naked in his hand, brandishing it in front of him like a scythe, and his teeth were barred in a furious snarl.

"Monster," he growled in a dangerous, low voice. "You will find no easy prey here."

He slashed out with his weapon, but the creature paid no more attention to the gash Rowan made in its side than it had to any of the wounds I had managed to give it. The three of us became locked in a furious exchange of blows. The creature spun, lashing out toward Rowan, bending low to slip below his blade and closer to his body. Its claws tore into Rowan's shoulder, raking through flesh and fur, leaving four deep red gashes in their wake.

I screamed.

Rowan ignored his wounds and moved swiftly to take advantage of the creature's closeness, delivering a savage blow to its middle. The thunderbird talon ran the creature through, piercing its stomach and coming out the other side of its body. But even this was not enough to stop it. The creature snarled and pulled itself free from Rowan's blade.

Desperate to do anything to slow the creature down, not knowing how bad Rowan's injuries were, I ran forward. I ducked low to the ground and used my spear, sweeping the creature's legs out from underneath it. It gave a rasping scream as it plummeted to the ground, crashing to the earth with a dull thud. Immediately, it hissed and tried to scramble to its feet.

Except that it could not rise.

Thick curls of ivy slithered out of the ground, wrapping themselves like thin, green snakes around the creature's ankles and arms, binding it to the soil. The creature struggled, and the ivy thickened, moving like a living thing, encircling the creature's limbs and holding it down. Rowan darted forward and struck a final blow, bringing his black talon sword down, slicing diagonally across the creature's body, cleaving its chest and torso in two, leaving masses of black, putrid organs open to the air. The creature's heart was a glutinous gray mass that still pulsated faintly. Immediately the air was filled with the smell of soured milk and spoiled meat.

Only then did I realize I was shaking. The day suddenly seemed unnaturally quiet, now that the creature's hissing had died away. Rowan stood over it and lifted his face to the sky. His face contorted, something raw and savage in his expression that I had never seen before, and the sound that poured out of him was a deep, bass cry of fury and victory combined. The sound pressed against my eardrums, making the air ring and clouds of birds startle from the trees.

When Rowan's roar faded, he turned to me.

"Are you wounded?" he asked, his voice urgent.

But I couldn't answer. My eyes were still locked on the creature. I saw one of its claws twitch.

"What is it?" I whispered, knowing as I spoke that it was still alive, still breathing. I had never seen a creature that could survive a wound like that. My stomach turned.

A growl rumbled deep in Rowan's chest. He motioned with his hand for me to move further away.

"A trespasser," he snarled.

He dropped the talon, letting it fall to the grass beside him. He spread his feet wide. I could feel something happening in the air around him. Gasping, I backed a few feet away. A faint smell of smoke swirled around him and pressure built in the air. Rowan's jaw clenched. He brought his hands up and, in a sudden, swift motion, clapped them together over his head.

The reaction was instantaneous. The second his palms touched, the earth convulsed. The ground under the creature opened, dirt streaming up into the air on either side of it, like the yawning jaws of some angry beast. The soil under the creature fell away, and the still-living carcass plummeted down into darkness. The earth closed up over it, the dirt seething like brown water boiling in a pot. A moment later, the ground where the creature had lain was smooth, quiet dirt.

Rowan turned his face to the side, and I saw a flash of pain in his eyes. He hunched his shoulders, grimacing, and spat out forcefully onto the ground.

We both stood for a second, staring at the earth, at the large, brown circle of lifeless dirt.

"It will take some time," he said, his voice still a little breathless, "for this patch of land to fully repair itself. That creature is an abomination. Absorbing it will be a strain. Let the land rest through the winter. Come spring, you can plant something new here. Something beautiful, to counteract the horror that lies beneath it. The land will be ready then, to heal itself and grow again."

I nodded. I still held the spear in my hand. New leaves were sprouting, and a tiny flower bud dangled from one of the new-sprung branches. A few leaves were unfurling, as though it were a small tree, with a sharp, deadly point instead of roots. I walked over to the center of the circle of dirt and, without quite knowing why I did so, I lifted the spear high above my head and then drove the thorny point of it deep into the soil.

"This branch belongs here," I said, with a bone-deep certainty. I looked toward the trees, and saw a flash of red, an eye that looked out from between the branches and then blinked away. Then there was nothing, and I turned to Rowan.

"How badly are you hurt?" I asked, hurrying over to him,

concerned by the amount of blood that had spilled down his chest, and the pallid color of his cheek. "Do you want me to…?"

He shied away from me, shaking his head in a stiff, quick motion of denial, his eyes on the ground. He leaned down, wiping the talon clean on the grass before slinging it once again across his back. He walked several feet away from me to an overgrown spot where the native grasses grew tall and thick. Moving like it hurt him, he sank down onto his knees. He ran his fingers through the grass, winding it around his fingers, then bent down to press his palms against the earth. He closed his eyes and took a deep, shuddering breath.

Suddenly, his face relaxed. There was no wind, but the grass all around him moved as though in a gentle breeze. As I watched, the red gashes in his shoulder closed up. New skin rippled like water as it grew over the wounds. Fur sprouted like wheat, pushing out of the bare, freshly healed skin, and quickly growing dark and thick, replacing what he had lost. After only a moment, Rowan's chest looked as though no harm had been done.

Rowan opened his eyes. They were dull. Tired. His shoulders bowed as though under a heavy burden. He didn't move, but stayed on the ground, looking up at me.

We stared at each other.

The danger was over, but somehow my heart beat faster than ever. I didn't feel the hurt and anger that had been ricocheting inside me for so long. I looked back at Rowan, and I didn't see the person who had disappeared from my life with no explanation, who had hurt me and left me without a word.

I saw a friend. Someone who had run to my aid when my life was in danger. An ally.

I looked into his eyes, and I saw his own longing and need staring back.

The moment stretched on, and something changed. Our eyes stayed locked together. A force, like a magnetic pull, filled the air between us

Rowan jerked his head back, tearing his eyes from mine with visible effort. "I must go," he muttered. But he didn't move.

"No," I said, and moved toward him.

"No?"

I crouched down on the ground across from him. I looked him right in the eye.

"No," I repeated softly. "I'm through letting you run away from me."

Then I leaned in, and pressed my lips to his. For a second he froze. Then his body seemed to warm and melt around me. He moaned softly, his lips rough and hungry as they pressed against mine. His arms circled around my waist, his hands warm on my back, and he pulled me tight, tight, against his body.

I might not get to ever do this again, I thought sadly, as I ran my fingers up the length of his arm, relishing his warmth, the hard steel of his muscle beneath the soft satin of skin.

He shuddered. He leaned his head back, pulling away from me, his eyes still half-closed, his whole body vibrating. Goosebumps rose on his arm, showing the trail my touch had made.

"Please, Asa," he choked out. "Don't. You don't understand."

"I know," I murmured. I lifted my hand to stroke the rough bristle of his check. Rowan leaned his head, heavy, into my palm. "You haven't tried to tell me, and I have been too hurt to know how to ask. But we need to talk now. Okay? I don't want there to be this horrible tension between us. We've been through too much together." Rowan opened his eyes, his expression searching and uncertain.

After a long minute, he nodded.

I rose, taking his hands in mine.

"Will you come?" I asked.

"Where?"

"To my house." I wasn't sure why I suddenly felt so shy. "I could make us some tea, and we could sit and talk awhile." I smiled. "Have you ever had raspberry tea?"

His fingers tightened around mine. "I don't believe so."

"Well, you're about to experience it for the first time." I began to pull him after me. "I can almost guarantee you'll like it. It is one of my favorite things in the world."

"Asa."

Something about his voice made my feet freeze in place. His eyes were wide and troubled.

"You just saw me brutally kill that creature. Are you sure you still wish to invite me into your home?"

My eyebrows knotted together. "Well...yes," I answered, not quite understanding. The confusion must have sounded like hesitation, because Rowan began to pull his hand from mine.

"It is all right, Asa," he said, not looking at me. "You are not under any obligation. You do not owe me anything."

"Rowan, wait!" I cried, confused. "I am not inviting you because I feel I owe you some kind of debt! I'm inviting you because I want to sit and talk with you. Because you are my friend."

Rowan stilled, his fingers still tangled in mine. "Friend?" he asked, his voice uncertain, and I couldn't tell if he thought my description of our relationship said too little or too much.

"Friend. Ally." I stepped closer to him, and again the magnetic pull resonated in the air between us. "For starters."

At that, the corner of Rowan's mouth quirked up.

"Come on," I urged him, and in answer he took a long stride toward the house.

SEVEN

THE WOODEN PORCH STEPS CREAKED UNEASILY UNDER ROWAN'S
unfamiliar weight. I pulled the screen door open, holding it for
him. He crouched a little as he walked through the doorway, as if
afraid he wouldn't fit through, though there were a few inches of
space between the tops of his horns and the door's awning.

Sunlight poured into the kitchen, glinting off the linoleum
floor, filtering through the red and white checkered curtains. The
old furnace rattled away with grim determination as it fought to
hold the cold at bay. The rush of warm air was a welcome relief
and I kicked my shoes off, unwilling to track mud onto my
shining floor. I left them tipped over on the welcome mat, and
took a deep breath. The house smelled of lemonade and fresh
linen. Something hard and painful in my chest un-knotted a little.

It felt so good to be home.

"Please," I told Rowan, motioning broadly to my somewhat
battered wooden kitchen table. "Sit down before you fall down.
You still look pretty pale. You should rest while I make the tea.
This will only take a minute."

I turned toward the stove, grateful for the distraction. It was
easier to catch my breath and slow my heart with my back to him

and my hands busy. Slipping into the familiar routine of making tea was as welcome as slipping into a warm bath. I relished the clang of the teakettle as I set it onto the stovetop, and the hesitant click of the pilot light as it sputtered and then caught hold of the flame. I pulled open the cupboard above the sink, fumbling around until my fingers found the things I would need. Then I stood, leaned against the counter, closed my eyes, and just let myself breathe. Really breathe, so that my chest expanded and my lungs filled with air. It felt like hours since I had really been able to just stand still and take a breath.

It felt like just a moment later when the kettle sang. I took two blue ceramic mugs off the shelf and dropped a bag of raspberry tea into each before filling them with steaming water and a spoonful of wildflower honey. Taking a final deep breath to steady myself, I turned back to Rowan.

He sat on the floor, his hands perched on his knees, his elbows held carefully close to his sides, leaning gingerly against the far wall of the kitchen. I froze in momentary confusion.

"Don't you want to sit in a chair?" I motioned toward it as best I could with a mug in each hand. "We can sit at the table."

"I'm afraid I would break them," he admitted after a pause. I started to argue, but then stopped, remembering that I had inherited the chairs from the home's previous owners. Though I doubted they would technically qualify as antiques, they were definitely old, and probably not all that sturdy. And Rowan was... Rowan. He was at least a foot taller than me, and the thick slate-gray hair that covered his chest did little to obscure how inhumanly muscular he was. Next to him, my dining room table seemed like something intended for a child.

"Okay." I shrugged. "Don't worry about it. The floor works fine. Here."

I handed him the steaming ceramic mug and settled down on the floor across from him. He accepted it carefully, holding it with both hands, his large fingers dwarfing the cup and making it look like a child's toy. He held it up to his face, breathing in the scent of raspberry and honey.

"This smells amazing."

"It's one of the best things in the world," I agreed, and I took a deep sip, letting the warmth spread through me as I leaned my head back against the humming refrigerator.

Just then I heard claws scratching on the wooden porch outside.

"Oh, lord, here he comes," I muttered, picking up my cup so I could hold onto it firmly and try to keep the contents from spilling everywhere. "Brace yourself."

My small, mixed-breed, hyperactive fuzzball of a dog, Pip, threw himself through the doggie door and burst into the room. Completely unconcerned about the horned, furry man sitting on his kitchen floor, Pip pricked his ears forward and his whole body danced with the pure joy of not only finding me at home but also *sitting on the floor* where I would be both easier to jump on and more easily accessible for belly rubs. He hurtled toward us with a half-bark of excitement and a number of small yips which I interpreted to mean generally, *I'm so happy to see you— why didn't you tell me you were here—have you brought me any treats????*

Pip put his paws up on my chest and licked my nose, narrowly avoiding spilling tea all over the front of my shirt, before turning his attention to Rowan, who, for the first time in a long time, was wearing an expression that could almost be called a smile. He held his hand out, palm up, for Pip to sniff, but Pip did not seem to be interested in formality. Instead, he simply melted onto the floor by Rowan's side, resting his chin on Rowan's thigh and looking up with a blissful expression that clearly conveyed his expectation that Rowan would immediately scratch behind his ears. Rowan obliged.

"Well, you're a dog-whisperer," I said, stretching out my legs in front of me. "Usually Pip only has two modes: hysterical and sleeping. Getting him to settle down like that must really mean he likes you."

We sat without speaking for several minutes and, surprisingly, the silence wasn't awkward. The quiet of the kitchen was restful and warm, and after a few minutes Pip sighed with utter contentment and drifted off to sleep, his tongue lolling out of his mouth, his head still resting in Rowan's lap. I soaked up the feeling of peacefulness like a plant soaking up the sun. A voice in the back of my head wondered how many moments of happiness like this I had left, but I pushed that thought away, and sipped more deeply from my mug. The curse might have stolen most of my time away from me, but I at least had this moment. I was determined to enjoy it, to drain my cup of fragile peacefulness down to the very last drop.

"You fought well," Rowan commented, breaking into my reflections.

"Thanks, I guess." I grimaced at the memory of the creature's teeth snapping in the air, inches in front of my face. "I didn't have so many options."

"May I ask you something?"

I raised my eyebrows. Something about Rowan's tone made me think I wasn't going to like his question. "Sure."

"I noticed that you did not use your Truthsight to defend yourself, when the beast attacked."

"Ah." I set my cup down and rubbed the back of my neck.

"Why were you unwilling to use your magic to defend yourself?" He leaned forward.

My cheeks flushed hot, though I couldn't have said for sure why I felt embarrassed.

"It's isn't so much that I'm unwilling, although I don't really like the idea of using my abilities that way. It's more that I never learned how."

"I don't understand."

I sighed. "I didn't have an exactly conventional education as a mage, Rowan. My abilities came a little later than is normal for most clan children. They started to surface right before my parents died, actually, and Meri took me in not long after that. I had such a strong affinity for healing that Meri decided I didn't need to bother with learning other branches of magic. She knew healing was what I really loved. So, while the other mage children were spending their time learning how to affect the weather or make themselves invisible, I was learning how to save lives." I shook my head. "I can't deny that knowing some of the things I missed might have come in handy now and then. But I don't regret it. Sometimes you have to focus on what matters most to you, even at the expense of other things."

"Is that what Meri told you?"

"Yes." I smiled at the memory. "She told me I had a rare gift. Healing ability is always uncommon, but I had a real aptitude for it from the very first moment my abilities surfaced."

"But you could still learn how to use your magic for defense?" Rowan asked, his voice urgent.

"Well, theoretically, yes." I couldn't keep the distaste I felt from leaking into my words. To me, my Truthsight was a precious gift. A pure stream that ran through me, enabling me to do good, to ease pain. I was not unwilling to fight to defend myself, or those I cared about. But the idea of using my Truthsight to cause a living creature pain…it felt wrong.

It felt like a betrayal.

I paused, narrowing my eyes at Rowan. Time to change the subject. "But now you're being nearly as cryptic as Crinea. Why are you asking me these questions? And what was that creature that attacked me? Before you called it a trespasser."

"I am sorry, Asa. I fear your connection to me has made you a target." Rowan scowled. "The invasives crept in while the Earth-child slumbered, unaware. Beasts of the deep and the dark, driven from their homes when humans dug too deep, built too many structures and tunnels deep under the ground. Creatures of nightmare."

"Creatures plural?" I asked. "How many of them are there?"

"We don't know for certain," Rowan replied. "The Earthchild was dormant for a very long time. And during that time, the land was vulnerable."

"Vulnerable?" I thought of the Earthchild, of the way it had appeared to me when it had helped me save Rowan's life. The wild flash of its eyes, the raw power that rolled off it in waves, making my skin tingle when it came too close. I couldn't really imagine a being like that ever being vulnerable.

"It was unconscious for a very long time. For all of that time, it could not protect the creatures who lived here, much less fight off invaders." Rowan's voice deepened, his tone carrying a hint of a growl. "The invasives had the opportunity to burrow deep beneath the skin of the land. The native creatures here often did not even know they were being preyed upon."

One hand massaged the back of his neck as he looked up at the ceiling for a long moment. Finally, he went on. "The invasives were clever: they attacked in the dark, when there were no witnesses. They preyed on the young and the weak." Rowan clenched his teeth and swallowed hard. "And they left no evidence behind them. For a long time, even the centaurs were not sure what was happening. But eventually the invasives had claimed so many lives that not all the disappearances could be blamed on the harshness of winter or the nearness of man."

"Is this the reason the centaur's chief was so eager to have you try to bond with the land when he first met you?" I asked, and Rowan nodded.

"In part. He had realized that a threat was lurking, all the more dangerous because it knew so well how to hide its face."

"Okay, but now the Earthchild is awake again. Can't it root out these invasives and force them to leave?"

Rowan sighed. "Unfortunately, it is not that simple. The Earth-child has been...disoriented, since it woke up."

"How is that possible?" I cried, my mind reeling. "The Earth-child is by far the most powerful supernatural being I have ever encountered. How can a spirit like that be confused?"

"It slept for so long," Rowan said. "And it woke to a world catastrophically different from the one it had known. Many of the creatures that had been its companions eventually went into hibernation, much as it did—and most of them have still not awoken. The humans have built on much of the land that was once a part of it, deadening it with their asphalt and iron. And the preternatural creatures, whose lives are like the beating of its own heart, have thinned out, died. Been hunted."

"You're saying that it's been weakened."

"Yes, but that is just part of it." Rowan leaned toward me. "After centuries of silence, darkness, and peace, the Earthchild is now being bombarded at every moment with a thousand sensa-tions, sights, smells. Some of them are completely new to it. Others it simply does not remember how to understand."

"But how is it possible for the invasives to defy you? Doesn't your role give you authority over any creature that lives here?"

"Over any creatures that *lives* here, yes. But the invasives, being what they are, are outside my realm of power."

"What do you mean by that?" I asked, a cold shiver of fear growing in my belly. "What are they?"

Rowan paused, his eyes on the floor, and I wondered for a second if he was trying desperately to think of a plausible lie. He shuddered slightly. "I mean that they are undead."

It felt as though the floor I sat on was spinning round and round. I wanted to argue with Rowan, to tell him he was wrong – but I couldn't manage to say anything at all.

"They are monsters outside of life and nature," he continued. "They run counter to everything the Earthchild is. We cannot control them—we cannot even sense their presence clearly. The first time the invasives struck after the Earthchild awoke, we didn't even understand what was happening. It was the middle of the night, and the Earthchild woke me. Screaming."

Rowan shook his head, his eyes closing. His face creased as he remembered. "I tried to run toward the source of its pain, but the child's emotions were like a blaring alarm inside my head. Pain. Panic." Rowan swallowed. "Terrible, deadly rage. It was so intense I could hardly see. Lights kept popping in my eyes."

"Your connection to the Earthchild is that deep?" I asked, surprised. Rowan opened his eyes, and stared at me.

"Asa," he said slowly. "This you must understand, for it is truth, pure and simple. The Earthchild is a part of me now. As I am a part of it." He placed his hand over his chest. "Our lives are bound together, and that bond can *never* be undone."

The sentence hung in the air between us and, in the back of my mind, I began to understand. After a moment, he went on. "I did the best that I could, but I was too late." Rowan ran a hand over his face, rubbing his eyes. Somehow the motion made him seem more human. "By the time I got there, the pixie was too far gone for saving."

"A pixie?" My whole body stiffened, and Rowan held out a hand.

"It was not Grenalda or any of her kin," he said, and I felt a wave of guilty relief. Knowing my friend was safe calmed the sear of panic in my chest. But an innocent had still been killed. "How did I not hear about this?" I demanded. "Why hasn't anyone told me this is going on?"

"Many of the creatures in the forest believe them to be evil spirits," Rowan explained. "They think that to name them, or to even speak of them, will increase their power. And, based on what I saw that night, I cannot blame them for believing these creatures to be demons. I found that creature, gnawing on the pixie it held, still living, in its claws. You see, these creatures do not nourish themselves with meat." Rowan's face contorted. "They feed off pain."

The air froze in my lungs and, for a second, I couldn't breathe.

Rowan lay a hand against his chest, his face clouded with remembered pain, as though he was trapped in a memory. "I cannot describe what I felt in that moment, with the Earthchild's emotions coursing through me, as we realized these monsters had invaded our land. That they were slaughtering the ones we are meant to protect. My body was not big enough...not strong enough...to contain the fury inside me. It shook me like an earthquake and I threw myself on the creature, beating it, cutting it." Rowan's voice wavered. "But it would not die. No matter what I did, it kept fighting. I struck it, again and again. Nothing slowed it down, not even when its bones broke beneath my fingers. And the more it fought, the more enraged I became. I cut my hands open on its bones, and did not even feel the pain."

He looked at his palms, as though searching for scars, but the earth must have healed him of those wounds, too. His voice dropped. "It wouldn't die...so I ripped it to pieces with my bare hands."

There was a long beat of silence, and his words seemed to ring, over and over again, in the air between us. His eyes burned into mine, lit with some emotion that I could not name. "You wonder why I stopped coming to see you, Asa? Why I turned you away, when you came to search for me in the woods?"

I nodded, too overwhelmed to speak.

"This is why. That night, and everything I have learned and done since then, is why. If you could have seen me in that moment, Asa, with the gore dripping from my fingers, with unsated rage burning in my heart...you would not ask why we cannot be together. You would not invite me into your home, or let your friend sleep, so trusting and defenseless, at the side of a creature like me."

"You're wrong."

"I'm not wrong," he snapped. "This is why the Earthchild chose me, the reason I am so well-suited to this land." He spread his hands out in front of him in a helpless gesture. "It is a land in need of a warrior. A land that needs a long and bloody battle to be fought. I am suited to the task; it turns out that I am just as savage as the spirit of this land." He laughed, but the sound was bitter and harsh. "We are well-suited to each other. The Earthchild is the spirit of barren soil, soaring rocks, and brutal cold. And I am its champion." His eyes darkened. "That is why we can never be together, Asa. Deep in your heart, you must know that what I say is true."

I wanted to argue. To tell Rowan all the reasons he was wrong, all the ways that what he said did not change the way I felt about him. I opened my mouth to speak, but suddenly a bang echoed from the back of the house. All the lights were off and the curtains were still pulled tight back there. Rowan stiffened, and in a fluid movement he gently pushed Pip aside and rose to his feet, staying half-crouched, his fingers reaching behind him to brush against the weapon he wore strapped across his back.

"I thought your house was empty," he said in a low voice.

"I thought so, too," I murmured back, trying to think of a simple explanation for the noise and pushing away the image in my head of dozens of invasives slinking through my living room window, or a team of vengeful mages tiptoeing toward me down the darkened hall. Rowan nodded, and pulled his weapon from its holder. Moving on the balls of his feet with soundless elegance, he crept down the hall toward the darkened living room that the noise had come from.

"Some guard dog you are," I hissed, glaring at Pip, who smiled in his sleep and rolled over onto his side. Cautiously, I followed Rowan down the hall.

When I caught up with him, Rowan stood in the doorway of the living room. He had put his weapon away, and though I could see there was no danger, he did not turn around when I came up behind him. The lights in the living room were off. I reached over and flipped them on.

Jason sat cross-legged in the center of the floor. His eyes were bleary, his usually well-kept hair standing up in multiple directions, his face pale and drawn. All around him were the boxes of books that we had carried inside last night. Several of the boxes had been ripped open, their contents stacked in tottering, multicolored towers all across the floor. Several volumes lay open, as though he had flipped through them partway and then abandoned them for other, more promising tomes. One lay open in his lap—a slim, green volume I recognized vaguely.

Jason looked up, his eyes seeming to have trouble focusing as he looked from my face to Rowan's.

"Did you tell her?" His voice sounded higher pitched than usual, his words a little slurred. Rowan gave a small shake of his head.

"Are you all right, Jason?" I asked. If I hadn't known him better, I would have wondered if he had been drinking. "We didn't even realize you were here. Why are you sitting all alone in the dark?"

"I don't need the light," Jason answered, tapping himself on the temple. His eyes were unfocused, staring at nothing. "Night vision. Did I forget to mention that symptom? Sorry. And sorry for not telling you I was here. I didn't mean to scare you. I let myself in. I couldn't wait for you to get back. I had to see."

"See what, Jason?" I asked, keeping my voice gentle. His eyes were wide, and glittering as though he had been crying, though I didn't see any tears on his cheeks.

"There isn't much," he went on, as though he hadn't heard me. "Almost nothing, in fact. And what there is, is probably inaccurate. I was hoping for some pictures, maybe. Even drawings. Or some eyewitness accounts. But there was only this."

He held out the small green book that had been lying in his lap. I reached out and took it from him, staring down at it. I vaguely remembered buying it from a used book shop in Sioux

Falls several years ago. I had never done much more than flip through the pages. The title, *Aquatic Beasts of Myth and Legend,* had caught my eye, but hadn't seemed likely to be relevant to my patients. I had never gotten around to reading it.

"I don't understand," I said. "Why are you showing me this?"

"That's me, Amy," Jason said, rising unsteadily to his feet and roughly prodding the page the book was open to with his finger. "This is what I am."

For a second I stared at him, my heart stuttering in shock. Then I peered more closely at the open book's pages.

"No," I murmured, narrowing my eyes as I read. "No, that can't be right. You can't be a member of this species."

"Jason is correct," Rowan broke in, his voice a grave rumble. "I told him the truth of his origin this morning. After you refused to let me slay the beast that cursed you."

"But this can't be right," I insisted, my voice rising. After all these years of waiting, I cared too much about Jason to let him believe something that wasn't true. "I'm sorry Rowan, but you're making some kind of a mistake. Every account, every legend I've ever read agrees. Water nymphs are female. They're *always* female."

Jason's lips twisted in a bitter smile. "It would seem," he said, "that I'm breaking the trend."

EIGHT

For a second I just stared. Then I rounded on Rowan, holding the book out in front of me, trying to keep the accusation from my voice. "How can you be sure?" I demanded.

Rowan hesitated, his eyes flicking away from mine.

"Rowan? You've got to tell me. This matters too much to Jason for us to risk getting it wrong."

"I am not wrong," Rowan snapped, his eyes flashing. "I've known Jason's origins from the first moment I met him."

"But how?"

Rowan sighed heavily. "If you must know," he finally said, half-closing his eyes and speaking as though the words embarrassed him, "I knew from his scent."

"His scent?" I repeated dumbly, but it made a sort of sense.

"Yes. It is quite distinctive. Water nymphs are exceedingly rare, even more so now than when I was a boy and first encountered them. But there is no mistaking it."

I stared at Rowan for a long moment, finally starting to believe him. Then I turned to Jason. The expression on his face was just as lost and overwhelmed as I felt.

"Oh my God," I cried. "We know. After all this time." I put my hands on Jason's shoulders, not sure if I should laugh or cry. "I don't know what to say."

Jason lay his hand on top of mine, squeezing my fingers. "I know. I don't know what to feel," he admitted. "It isn't real to me. Not yet." He turned his head over toward Rowan. "Go on," he said. "Tell her the rest."

"What?" I asked, looking between them at the solemn expression they exchanged. "What more is there to tell me?"

"There is a reason I delayed sharing the truth with Jason," Rowan explained, speaking slowly and seeming to choose his words with care. "Water nymphs are not only rare...they are also exceedingly dangerous. They are one of the very few types of creatures my own father feared."

"*Your* father feared them?" I asked, dumbfounded. When I had met Rowan's father he had been old and on the verge of death. But he had radiated such strength and fortitude I found it nearly impossible to imagine him being afraid of anything.

Rowan nodded. "There were only a few who lived on the very outskirts of our land when I was young. My father was always very careful to give them wide berth, and went to great lengths to avoid encountering them. They were not only deadly and deeply secretive, but their connection to the water gave them so much power that they could do real damage to the land itself, if they desired to do so."

"And your father's own power flowed from the land," I said as the pieces clicked together.

Rowan gave a sharp nod. "Exactly. As a result, I learned only a few, basic things about them when I was growing up. I had hoped that, given a little time, I could learn more about them, so that I could prepare Jason to encounter them, or shield him if they rejected him and wished to do him harm. Unfortunately, my efforts have borne little fruit."

"He has been able to tell me a little," Jason broke in. "It seems that the water nymphs are water purifiers. They feed off impurities in the water, drawing those impurities into their own bodies and converting some of it into nutrition, and some into a toxin which they use as a defense mechanism."

"Their poison is very dangerous," Rowan warned. "It renders some victims utterly compliant. Other victims it kills, instantly. Since I do not know what kind of reception Jason might receive upon his return, I felt it my duty to prevent him from knowing anything which might set him on a dangerous course. But it seems we have run out of time."

"What does that mean?" I asked. "Why is Jason out of time?"

"I'm not the one who's out of time, Amy," Jason said gently. "You're the one who has been cursed. But there's a chance that I might be able to help you."

"Help me?" I said. Jason nodded, and a little bit of the light that usually shined in his eyes came back.

"Yes," he said. "The nymphs are purifiers—that's what they do. That's the reason that Lord Rowan decided to finally tell me. If I can learn how to use my abilities, I might be able to extract the curse—pull it out of your system. We can't know for sure that it will work. But it might. And right now, Amy, it's the best option that we've got."

"Jason," I said, putting a hand on his shoulder as I fought to keep my voice calm. "I appreciate you wanting to help me—of course I do. But Rowan just got finished telling us how dangerous these creatures can be. We don't know how they might respond when you suddenly reappear. We simply don't know enough for you to go back yet."

"Seems as though that should be my decision," Jason responded, color rising in his cheeks.

"We don't have any idea what might happen," I insisted. "They may see you as a threat. Rowan said that they're highly secretive. Once you've seen their home they may not want to let you leave. Or they might attack you on sight. It's too dangerous!"

"I know it's risky," Jason admitted. "But you've done so much for me these last few years, Amy. There's no doubt in my mind that you saved my life a few times over. And I couldn't live with myself if I had a chance to save you and didn't even try." I started to protest, but he cut me off with a shake of his head. "This isn't your call." There was no heat in his voice, no anger. And with terrible, terrifying clarity, I realized that, this time, I might not be able to change his mind.

"Jason, please," I said. "You don't have to do this. You don't owe me anything for the time I've spent helping you. I've just been doing what friends do."

"You're right," he said, his voice full of quiet resolve. "And it's my turn now."

Tears stung my eyes, and I blinked them back furiously. "I thought you said I was a hard woman to say no to," I protested. When had he said that? Had it been just this morning? It felt like it had been a hundred years ago.

Jason smiled and shook his head. "I've listened to you before. Maybe too much. When you were running from the mages, and wanted me to stay and keep the clinic open, I did. And this morning, when you told me to stay away from the hellhound and to leave—I did just what you said. But this time it's different. This time it's about me. My past, my abilities." He shrugged. "My choice."

"Damn it," I whispered softly. "I'll go with you."

"Can't." The shake of his head was sharp and definitive. "For one thing, you've already got that curse inside you, just waiting for the right moment to strike. For another, you for sure won't have any defenses against their poison. The fact that I'm one of them might give me some natural resistance, and I may be able to protect myself. But there's no way that I'll be able to protect you, too."

"I will accompany Jason." Rowan broke in, and I turned to stare at him.

"You, Rowan?" I asked, incredulous. "Is it even possible for you to leave here? Won't that...be painful for you? Strain your link to the land?"

"I will be weakened by the distance from the Earthchild, and by separation from this land," Rowan admitted, with calm indifference. "But not to the point of pain. Jason needs me to open a path for him, transport him, and then wait and bring him back when he is ready to return."

For a minute, I stood, shocked into silence. Though Rowan downplayed it, I knew how profoundly distancing himself from the land affected him. At the very least, it would weaken him, make him vulnerable. And I wasn't quite sure that I believed that it wouldn't cause him any pain. The fact that he would do that for me, even when he was so sure that we could never be together, made a lump form in my throat, and feelings swirl deep inside me that I didn't want to name.

"How do you even know where to go?" I asked, forcing myself to push those feelings down and ignore them.

"Apparently," Jason explained, "there's a pod of nymphs, not far from where my parents were living when I was a baby. Our best guess is that's where I come from. I'll go there, but even if that isn't *my* pod, it won't matter. I just need to learn enough about my abilities to be able to help you."

"I will hang back, and not approach the nymphs with Jason," Rowan went on. "As an outsider, my presence would almost certainly be objectionable to them, and might be all the reason that they need to turn on him immediately. But I will stay close. And I will do everything in my power to bring him home safely."

"Don't worry, Amy," Jason said, his voice full of false cheerfulness. "I'm a real fast learner. We'll be back before you know it."

"You don't have to do this," I murmured, barely noticing that my hand was clutching the sleeve of Jason's jacket until he reached up and gently pulled it away.

"Sure I do," he replied.

He hugged me, a short, hard hug that ended too soon. Then he turned and, without another word, hurried out into the hall. Rowan and I were left alone, staring at each other. I wanted to tell him to be careful, to hurry back. I wanted to tell him that I trusted him, and that the things he had told me earlier had not changed the way I saw him in the slightest. But my throat was too tight for words.

"Keep yourself safe, Asa," Rowan said, his voice urgent. "Stay out of the woods until I return."

I nodded, and started to speak. But in a swirl of gray and silver, Rowan was gone.

NINE

I was alone, and the house felt hollow and empty. I shook myself and ran my hands through my hair. I needed to sleep. But first I needed to talk to Meri. Baxin's information at least gave us a time frame for the curse's progression, and Jason's undertaking might offer her some hope, even if it was a slim one.

When I knocked on the mirror on my bedroom wall, it took Meri longer than usual to respond. I was just starting to worry when the silver rippled. I could see her standing on the other side, her hair disheveled, and a haunted, fretful look clouding her eyes. Her fingers kept creeping up to fiddle with her half of the clamshell hanging around her neck. I told her everything I had learned. She listened, but her eyes never lingered long on my face.

"Are you all right, Meri?" I asked at last, and her eyes flashed.

"Of course I'm not all right," she snapped. "Here I am, surrounded by a clan populated entirely by idiots and hangers-on, who can do nothing right and can't even follow the simplest of instructions. After so many years of having no one who could lead them competently, they cling to me like infants. I can't possibly leave them to come to you. And the one person I love and actually want to be with, the *one* person I want to keep close and safe from harm, is far away from me. Dying."

"I am not dying," I replied quickly. "The curse isn't a virus or an infection. It doesn't work like that..."

"Oh, spare me your doctor-speak," Meri groaned, rubbing her eyes with the heels of her hands. "I know the curse isn't a medical condition. If it were, you would cure yourself and be done with it. But it is there. Inside you. Biding its time. And I am reduced to such helplessness that my best hope for my own daughter rests on the shoulders of two inhuman animals."

I straightened up as my face flushed with heat. "Those are my friends you're talking about," I told her, not trying to hide the anger in my voice. "My friends who, right this minute, are taking terrible risks to try to help me."

Meri flicked her hand in the air as though shooing away an annoying insect. "Yes, yes, I know. You'll have to ignore me, Asa. I'm not at my best right now, and am having difficulty choosing my words with care."

She covered her face with her hands. All at once, she looked so fragile. Her hair fell, messy, around her shoulders, and I noticed she was barefoot and shivering a little. My anger melted away.

"It's all right," I said. "I don't think either of us is at our best right now. I need to rest, and you should, too. Things won't feel so hopeless in the morning."

"How can I sleep?" Meri asked, her face still hidden in her hands. "How can I waste even a minute, when I know you have so little of it left?"

I wished I could hug her, and promise that everything was going to be all right. Instead I forced a smile, and pressed my hand up against the glass.

"Hey," I called softly, and she looked up. "I love you."

She smiled back at me, and lifted her hand to meet mine against the glass. "I love you too, Asa," she murmured. "And there isn't anything I wouldn't do to keep you safe." She shook herself and pulled her hand away. "Sleep now, child," she told me. "You must keep up your strength."

Her image shimmered, then vanished. I pulled off my jeans and shirt, let them fall the floor, and pulled on the long flannel shirt I used as a nightgown before climbing into bed. It was almost twilight, and I hadn't eaten since morning, but I needed sleep more than I needed food. I pulled a blanket up over myself, and was deeply asleep within minutes.

When I woke, sunshine was creeping in through the windows. I lifted my hand to my forehead. I had the strangest feeling, as though, just a moment ago, someone had been stroking my hair. Had I been dreaming? I couldn't remember. My sleep had felt more like a deep coma than the kind of rest that lent itself to dreaming. I wiped sleep from my eyes and got up, shuffling around the room as I pulled on fresh jeans and my oldest, most comfortable sweatshirt. I found the clamshell Meri had given me, laid carefully out on the top of my dresser, and clipped it to an empty belt loop on my jeans. By the time I had tramped down the stairs, my stomach was rumbling.

Pip had settled into his favorite spot on the couch, but he rolled to his feet with a sleepy yawn when he saw me, and padded after me into the kitchen. I grabbed a piece of bread and started wolfing it down as I set the kettle on the flame.

I slipped two more pieces of bread into the toaster, and began to rummage through kitchen drawers. Pip watched me from under the table with drooping eyes, his ears flicking this way and that, following the sound of banging drawers and slammed cupboards. I liked the noise; it somehow made the house feel less empty. I pulled out the doggie kibble and filled Pip's bowl, but he just yawned and closed his eyes again. Ever since he had made friends with the clinic's centaur guards, he had lost interest in his dog food, preferring the treats they seemed to delight in giving him. But it made me feel better to know the food would be there waiting for him, if he decided he wanted it. Then I began my search. By the time the kettle sang and the toast was browned, I had found what I was looking for.

I set my food down on the table and spread the lunar calendar out. I took a bite of my toast and chewed slowly, refusing to acknowledge the cold fear that clamped down inside me as I counted off the days until the next full moon.

Baxin had estimated I had three weeks before the moon reached its zenith, but it turned out that guess had been a little generous. According to this, the next full moon would be on the twelfth. The small, silver crescent that suddenly had so much power over my life would wane and reappear, growing, it seemed to me, at a reckless, feverish pace. I only had eighteen days until it hung, full and swollen, in the sky. Then the curse would wake.

I finished the toast. I carefully drank the tea down to the dregs. I stared out the window, and watched the sky lighten slowly, Baxin's words spinning round and round in my head.

Live. Live as much and as fully as you can. Beat it by fitting a lifetime's worth of living into the next few weeks.

I stared out the darkened kitchen windows, and my own pale face stared back. I only wished I knew how to do that.

Finally, I shook myself and stood up. I opened the cabinet under the sink and filled a bag with cleaning supplies and paper towels. The clinic was dusty from all the old books Jason and I had been carting around. Maybe getting my hands moving would help my thoughts flow. It certainly couldn't be worse than sitting, doing nothing, and letting my mind drive me nearly insane. I hurried across the yard, and kicked the clinic door open with my foot, coming to a full stop when I found someone standing in the middle of my clinic, her long brown braids pushed behind one shoulder, her hoof once again pawing at my floor.

"Crinea!" I cried. "What are you doing here? Are Finar and the baby all right?"

"They are fine," she answered stiffly, folding her arms across her chest. "Which is more, I think, than can be said of you."

"Ah." I let the barn door slam shut behind me and stomped past her. I should have expected this. Rowan had been at the centaur camp when Jason ran to find him. Of course, Crinea would have found out about what happened. I should probably count myself lucky that she had come and not the chief. All things considered, I didn't quite feel up to having the chief clomping back and forth in my clinic and glowering at me today.

"I heard," Crinea went on, "that the clinic was open, on the very night we had agreed it was to be closed."

"It wasn't open, exactly." I pulled items from my bags and set them down on the table with a bang. I wished that ignoring her would make her go away, but Crinea was, hands down, the most stubborn creature I had ever encountered. "Do we really have to have this conversation now? I just got up, and my head is pounding. Couldn't you give me a stern talking-to tomorrow? Or maybe the day after that? I'm sure there are more interesting things you could be doing. Don't you have enemies to slay? Or a son to be getting out of bed?"

"I have done enough slaying for today. And between you and my son, you seem by far to need more looking after!" Crinea's voice rose as her outrage mounted. "We had an agreement! Yet you treated a patient, didn't you?"

"I was already cursed with death by then," I snapped. "It hardly seemed to matter at that point."

Crinea shot me a glare as sharp and cutting as the sword that swung from her belt.

"Okay. Okay! You're right. I admit it." I threw my hands up in the air. "How could I have known that the one night the guards were gone was the night a hellhound would come to my door? What are the chances of that?"

"I do not think it is chance at all."

I stilled. "What do you mean?"

She huffed in exasperation. "Asa, you cannot possibly be this thick-skulled. There was one night"—she held up a finger to emphasize the singularity of the occurrence—"ONE, during which you had no guard, and Lord Rowan would be certain to be delayed in coming to your aid. On that very night, a threat comes. Can't you see how clever they were?"

"There is no 'they,'" I insisted woodenly. "Rowan and I have already been over this. The hellhound was just an innocent beast."

"Beasts can be driven." Her lips pressed into a hard line. "And two beasts who could both do you the worst kind of harm were driven to your doorstep on the same night. When those animals should never have been in these woods at all."

I didn't answer. I remembered what Baxin had said. *What brought two of them here, of all places, and at the same time, is a question well worth asking.* So much had been happening that I hadn't really stopped to think about his comment, but now...

"The beast was a pawn, a piece moved by the hand of a skilled player. Think about it, Asa. Rowan is resistant to the mages' magic and you are an exceptionally talented healer. If they had attacked you physically, you would have had a good chance of healing yourself from any wounds they managed to inflict. But they found something you could not heal, and Rowan could not deflect. A way to strike that would slip under both of your defenses. Something that could pass for an accident, and not bring your foster mother's wrath down on their heads."

"He said it wasn't over," I said, my mouth suddenly dry. "Paul. He said he would wait for a moment when Meri was weakened, or distracted. And then he would come after me again."

"I have found," Crinea said, her voice quiet, "that it is best to do one's enemies the courtesy of believing them when they say that they intend to kill you."

"But Rowan told them to stay off the land, and I thought..." My words trailed off, and I pressed my fingers to my temples, trying futilely to soothe the headache that raged there. "Oh, I've been a fool. I thought that, even with Meri weakened, the mages would be too frightened of Rowan to try to come here and do me harm. But I forgot they don't see him the way that I do. I look at him and see this incredible, wise, brave warrior. They see him so differently, even Meri. They look at him like some kind of lesser being. As a beast."

"I know." Crinea's face darkened. "I remember."

I flinched, remembering the way that, the last time they had come to the forest, the mages had hunted centaurs for sport, taking Mattis from his tribe and leaving Natia a widow.

"I'm not sure what to do." I rested my hands on the cool surface of the clinic table. "Meri is already on edge, and her hold on the clan is fragile. If I tell her I think mages are responsible for what's happened to me...she won't be able think calmly. She won't formulate a plan; she'll just lash out. React. And Meri is awful when she's angry. She could do something that would cause her to completely lose control of the clan. And then all hell would break loose."

"That may even be their intention," Crinea pointed out. "If they wish to shake her hold on the clan. By coming after you, they can destabilize her, force her into rash and thoughtless action. And then seize power when she is too distressed to respond effectively."

"Even if I was sure mages were behind this, I couldn't tell her," I said, feeling numb. "It would just put her in danger. And the damage is done." I looked down at myself, half-imagining I could see a dark shadow blooming, like a wide, black bruise under my skin. "Maybe, if I can get through this, survive it somehow...then I could tell her what really happened—help her to think of a good way to respond. But not now. Have you told Natia what's happened?"

Crinea looked uncomfortable. "No," she admitted. "We've been working rather hard to keep her from hearing of it. We don't want her to worry. She is still early in her pregnancy."

I nodded. "And since I'm the one who's supposed to keep her

alive through her delivery, knowing I'm not likely to survive the new moon is bound to be stressful."

"You are not unlikely to survive." Crinea bristled, her tail swishing violently. "Lord Rowan and Jason will return soon, and they..."

At that moment Crinea's head whipped around. She hurried over to the barn doors, flinging them open and leaning out, her head tilted to the side, her eyes narrow with concentration.

"What's wrong?" I asked, and hurried over to the door, my eyes probing the trees, but I saw nothing. Crinea could hear something that my human ears could not. Her expression changed, setting into hard lines, as she pulled her sword from its scabbard.

"It's happening again," she hissed. She glanced in my direction. "Lord Rowan is away and can do nothing. I must go." Without another word, she galloped away into the trees.

I started to run after her, then halted. I had promised Rowan I wouldn't go into the woods. And besides, if Crinea was off to do battle, there was little I could do to help.

But then a sound split the morning air, a high-pitched keening that tore at my heart, and at once my feet were pounding across the forest floor after Crinea. I flew past the Earthchild's spear, still driven point-down into the ground behind the clinic, noticing as I sped by that it seemed to be sprouting small branches. A moment later I had entered the woods.

If I had ever wondered if a human could keep up with a centaur who is running at full speed, I would have discovered in that moment that the answer is simple: not even close. But Crinea had torn through the branches so quickly that she had left an easily identifiable trail behind her. Plus, I did not have to go far to find her. When I caught up with her, her tail was held high up in the air, and something red was splashed on her forelegs.

"Amy, stop!" Crinea cried when I ran up behind her. She held up her hands. "It's over. You don't have to see..."

But then I pushed through the leaves, and came to a halt beside her.

It was as though the small, oval-shaped clearing in the trees had been painted red. The tree trunks were splashed with it. The ground was so soaked that the toe of my shoe squelched in the grass. The deer were dead, but that was not the horrific part of it. The small herd lay with their legs sprawled at haphazard, unnatural angles, their eyes open and rolled back into their heads. Their mouths were white with foam. And their bodies...

"Are those bite marks?" I whispered, though really, I already knew. The animals' bodies were riddled with more puncture marks than seemed physically possible, every inch of their skin ragged and torn. Except, I noticed with a shudder, their throats. The creatures who attacked them had been careful to strike in a way that would prolong their victims' pain for as long as possible.

"There were five deer." Crinea commented, her voice carefully emotionless. "Three does, and two f...fawns." Her voice faltered a little on the last word. "Their attackers startled and fled when I approached." Her lip curled with disdain. "Cowards."

"The invasives did this, didn't they?" I asked, and Crinea shrugged.

"Yes, if that is what you want to call them." She slid her sword back into its holder with an angry push. "I call them demons."

We stood for a moment, just staring.

"They're getting bolder," I commented. "Rowan said they used to only attack at night, but this is the second day in a row that they have struck while the sun is up."

"They want to show that Lord Rowan has not cowed them," Crinea agreed, and then shook herself. "We cannot just leave these poor creatures like this. Even a simple animal's soul may linger and grow dangerous, when subjected to such savagery. We must bury them."

I felt it then: a building pressure in the air, a sensation that made my skin prickle and the hairs on the back of my neck stand up.

"Crinea," I whispered. "Wait. Don't move."

The leaves rustled, and a small figure stepped into view. The last time I had seen the Earthchild, it had helped me save Rowan's life. I had felt a certain kinship with it then, but still, despite its help...it had frightened me. And that fright was nothing compared to the cold, hard fear that sliced into me when I saw it now.

The Earthchild's black hair hung down almost to the ground, its thick tresses matted with mud and leaves. Red mud clung thick against its body, covering it like a second skin. Its teeth were barred in a silent growl, its eyes—one sky-blue and the other red as blood—flashed with fury. The air popped and sparked around it as it moved to stand in the center of the carnage, the blood on the ground matching exactly the mud that covered its skin. It made no indication that it had seen us. Its eyes were focused on the bodies on the ground. I felt the earth tremble a little beneath my feet, as though the soil wanted to buck and crumble with rage.

Crinea gasped and, quick as lightning, the Earthchild's eyes snapped over to look at us. I felt its regard like a stinging slap against my cheek, a heavy weight that turned the air around me thick and viscous.

"Back away!" I breathed, grabbing Crinea's arm with sweaty hands and straining to pull her with me. She seemed frozen in place, her eyes wide and slightly glazed, her chest rising and falling too rapidly as she stared dazedly at the child. "Crinea!" I hissed, desperation making my voice louder than I wanted it to be. "Please. Come with me."

Her legs moved, though she seemed shaky, and without turning around we backed away together, our steps feeling torturously clumsy and slow.

The Earthchild's attention moved back to the deer. It turned away from us as we moved farther away. The last thing I saw before leaves and branches hid it from view was the child, leaning over, running a finger along the muzzle of one of the slaughtered fawns.

We turned then, and moved faster, walking as quickly as we could without breaking into a run, like children afraid to be caught running in the hallway at school.

"I can't believe that I have seen the earth spirit with my own eyes," Crinea murmured, when we were far enough away to risk speaking. She ran a trembling hand over her face. She looked pale and bewildered, like someone waking from a dream. "I've heard the legends, of course. The stories. But still, it was nothing like I imagined."

"I thought it was going to attack us," I said, wrapping my arms around my middle and willing my heart rate to slow. "Are you all right?"

"Yes. I don't believe it would have done us harm." Her face creased with uncertainty. "Should we wait until the spirit has gone, and then go back and bury the animals?"

"No," I said with certainty. "The Earthchild came because of them. It will take care of them now." I looked at the trees around us, the swaying branches, and the light dancing on the forest floor. It chilled me to know that such cruelty and violence could happen in such a beautiful place.

Crinea nodded and shook herself. "I must go to my brother. He needs to know what has happened here. Let me escort you home first."

"I'll be fine."

Crinea opened her mouth to protest, but I raised my eyebrows and dropped my chin. She wasn't the only one who knew how to glare. "Really. The chief needs to know about this right away. You scared the invasives away, and the Earthchild is here now. They won't come back any time soon. And it isn't far from here to the clinic. I'll be fine."

Crinea hesitated, but I could see her instinct to be overprotective warring with her desire to alert her people.

"You're sure you'll be all right?" she asked, after a long, uncertain moment.

"Yes," I told her, "Go. And be careful."

"The same to you, my friend," Crinea said, her tail swinging back and forth widely behind her. She turned to leave.

"Wait!" I called out in a furious whisper, afraid to raise my voice too much, for fear of attracting the Earthchild's attention. Crinea stopped short and looked back. "You need to bring Natia to see me. Tonight. We can't afford to wait. If I can't be there for her delivery, then I at least need to do everything I can for her right now."

For a moment, I thought Crinea would argue, but then she nodded. "Very well. We will come once dark has fallen." Then she turned and galloped away, the rhythm of her hooves a staccato beat of alarm on the forest floor.

TEN

It had just gotten dark enough for me to turn on the outdoor lights when I heard Crinea's voice outside.

"You can do this," she was saying. "You know that Amy will do you no harm."

"There is no point," a second, fainter voice answered. "If the healer is cursed, then she will not be there to tend me when the time of birthing comes. The baby and I will join Mattis in the next world. Perhaps we were never meant to live without him, after all."

"You can't let yourself think like that," Crinea said, her voice urgent. "You know that isn't what Mattis would want. He was a fighter. He would want you to fight, too."

There was no response, but Natia must have given her consent, because a moment later the barn door creaked open, and Crinea entered, her hand clasped with Natia's, who trailed a step behind her and startled a little when the barn door swung shut behind their tails.

I had been hoping Natia would have improved a little from the last time I had seen her, when her grief was so fresh. But if anything, she looked worse, as though the mounting strain of going day after day without her husband's presence was quickly wearing her down. Now that the final rites for Mattis were done, I had expected to see her back in her regular attire, but she still wore the garb of a new widow. Instead of the tight-fitting leather vest most centaur women wore, she wore a long, loose, sleeveless shirt of roughly woven, beige fabric that hung down well past her waist. Statuesque, in sharp contrast to Crinea's slight form, Natia still seemed fragile. Her black curly hair hung down thick and tangled on her shoulders. As a mourner, she wore no sword.

Her nostrils flared as she approached me. I knew my scent frightened her, and I could hardly blame her. The mages who had hunted her husband down had given her good reason to fear my kind.

"Hello, Natia," I said, keeping my voice soft and making no move to step closer.

I had done everything I could think of to try to put Natia at ease. I had left my cell phone and Meri's shell in my house on the table next to my bed, so that no strange sounds would startle her. I had changed into fresh clothes, for fear that some of the smell of blood from the deer I had seen this morning might somehow still cling to me and frighten her. I had even closed a resentful Pip into a spare room in the house, so that he wouldn't run to greet Crinea and beg her for treats, as he sometimes did, and alarm Natia with his barking.

But I couldn't change what I was.

Natia's black eyes widened at the sound of my voice, and her hooves skittered restlessly on the floor. Her dark hair fell like a frame around her full, pale face. Her expression was a portrait of distrust.

Her sides were wider than the last time I had seen her, as the baby continued to grow. I wondered, not for the first time, whether the pregnancy that had become apparent only days after her husband's death was really the mercy it might seem. Though the child provided a connection to the husband she had lost, the truth was that in recent years the vast majority of centaur women had died in childbirth. Now she had to face all the fear and uncertainty of a dangerous pregnancy alone.

"I'm glad you're here," I told her honestly, continuing to hold myself perfectly still.

"I don't understand the point of this." Natia's voice was so low I had to strain to hear it. She sounded angry, but I recognized the emotion in her voice for what it really was: fear. Her eyes met mine for only a second before turning to anxiously probe the dark corners of the room, as though searching for some hidden threat. "Crinea tells me you are cursed. I am sorry for that news but, if it is true, then the same thing will happen to me that happened to Crinea, and all the others. And there will be no help for me. Why must I be here now?"

"You're right that I may not be there for your delivery," I admitted. "But that just makes it more important that I do everything that I can for you now. You know how much I want both you and your baby to be all right, don't you?"

Natia hesitated, then gave a reluctant nod.

"I just want to examine you," I told her. "Like the last time. You remember? We'll start simple." I held up my stethoscope so that she could see that it was harmless.

She stared at it suspiciously. I hated to think how she would respond in a few minutes, when I told her I wanted to take another blood sample. "Let me just check on your heartbeat, okay? And we'll go from there."

"It'll be all right." Crinea lay a hand on Natia's shoulder. "You know what Amy did for me. You can trust her."

Natia looked at me for a long moment, biting her lip. Then she took a deep breath. "All right." She closed her eyes, spacing her legs further apart, as though bracing for a terrible blow. "I am ready."

I approached her slowly, making sure my feet made noise on the floor so she could hear me coming. "This will be a little cold," I warned her, but she still jumped when I lay the stethoscope against her chest. Her heartbeat was fine, if slightly elevated. After a minute, she grew accustomed to my closeness and opened her eyes.

"The baby really is getting bigger!" I exclaimed, leaning over to prod her sides gently, and the apprehension melted out of Natia's eyes as a warm, broad smile spread across her face.

"I know," she said softly. She looked down, her hands moving to caress the growing bump. "This little one is growing quickly."

"Would you like to hear the baby's heartbeat?" I asked, and Natia's eyes grew to the size of saucers.

"Is that possible?"

"Yes, but I would have to use a different piece of equipment. It is electrical, but I promise it doesn't pose any risk to you or the baby. It will just make the baby's heartbeats loud enough that we can hear them."

Natia hesitated, but I could see her eagerness to hear her baby's heartbeat quickly winning out over her fear of strange human technology. After only a moment of indecision, she nodded, her cheeks flushing with excitement. Crinea paced closer, watching with interest as I pulled the mini-Doppler out. The small speaker was attached to a wand, which I pressed to Natia's abdomen. Both centaurs jerked their heads back a little when the machine started to hum, but soon their discomfort was replaced with fascination as I moved the machine around Natia's belly, searching. Then I found it, a steady, rapid beat like a small drum beating.

"Is that...?" Natia asked, and I nodded. She gave a wordless cry of pleasure.

"Your baby has a strong heart," I told her, and her eyes gleamed.

"I know," she murmured. "Just like its father." Her smile faded, and her face creased with pain. "I wish Mattis were here," she said. "He would have been so happy. To see the baby growing. To hear its little heart beat so strongly." She turned her face to the side, but there was no hiding her tears.

"Mattis *is* here," Crinea said, her voice fierce, her eyes glittering. "His spirit is with you still. A man as stubborn as Mattis wouldn't let a little thing like death come between him and his child. Or between him and his wife."

Natia laughed a little through her tears. "You are right," she said, wiping her eyes. "He was the most stubborn man I've ever met. I believe his spirit is with us—truly, I do. But still, sometimes…it is hard to not feel alone."

Crinea put her hands on Natia's shoulders and leaned over so that their foreheads touched. "You will never be alone," Crinea whispered. "The tribe will never let that happen. *I* will never let that happen. I promise."

Just then, the clinic door banged. At first, I thought the wind had blown it open, as an icy gust of wind swept through the room. Then I saw the figures stepping in from the night.

"Hey there, traitor," Paul drawled. "You knew we'd come pay you a visit sooner or later, didn't you?"

ELEVEN

ADRENALINE FLOODED MY SYSTEM AS A FLASH OF PANIC MADE MY ears ring. Through the darkness outside I could just make out two crumpled forms lying on the frozen ground: the centaur guards. I couldn't tell whether they were simply unconscious, seriously injured, or dead. My mind reeled as several other mages filed in after Paul, quickly fanning out into a loose semi-circle on either side of him, forming a wall between us and the door. I recognized their faces, though I did not know their names. There wasn't much point in distinguishing one from the other, though; their identical expressions of hate and gloating triumph made them all but interchangeable. Behind Paul, another figure skulked in the darkness—a large, hulking form whose face I couldn't see.

Crinea moved forward, maneuvering herself so she stood in front of Natia, shielding her pregnant friend with her body as much as she could. Natia gave a cry of alarm, her hands fluttering to her belly. Crinea's hand darted to the hilt of her sword, but she did not draw it. She and I exchanged a glance of understanding. The mages were powerful. If the confrontation came to violence, our chances were slim.

I flexed my fingers with frustration. Never had my limited

knowledge of magic felt like such a burden. For once, I wished that I knew how to use my Truthsight to protect my friends from this threat. But our best chance was to stay calm. Maybe we could talk our way out of this.

"You," Paul called out to the mage standing in the shadows behind him. "Look around. Check every patient room. Make sure nobody is hiding back there. I don't want any surprises." After what seemed like a moment of hesitation, the man stepped out of the shadows, and the sight of his face hit me like a blow.

"Greg?" I gasped. His step faltered, and he looked at me. "*You* brought them here?" I asked.

Greg was probably the closest thing to a friend I had in the clan. Or, I had thought he was a friend until now. Even as a girl I had liked Greg. He was always making jokes, and he had taught me all my first curse words. His easy, self-deprecating humor put me at ease, and his blunt, sometimes too-direct comments made it easy to believe he had nothing to hide.

Greg's greatest talent was making portals. But I wouldn't have believed he would have helped Paul come after me.

"Asa," he said, his voice low. "I'm sorry. I didn't..."

"Go!" Paul roared. Greg jerked his eyes from mine. He jogged off to do Paul's bidding, sticking his head into one patient room after the other.

His brown curly hair swung back and forth as he moved through the clinic, avoiding making eye contact with me. His ample girth was perhaps a little wider than the last time I had seen him, and he seemed to be sweating profusely, despite the cold.

"All clear," Greg announced after a minute. "But listen to me, man. This is a stupid idea. We should get the hell out of here. It isn't too late."

"Shut up, you idiot," Paul snapped. "You stuck your nose in where it didn't belong, didn't you? Wanted to know what I was up to? Well, now you know. And when this is all over, your hands will be just as dirty as mine, and I won't have to worry about you taking any tales to Meri." The other mages gave murmurs of agreement. "Unless, of course, you'd rather take the traitor's side?"

Greg didn't answer. He hung his head, so his brown hair hid his eyes.

"I didn't think so," Paul sneered. "Now be quiet, and do as you're told."

"What are you doing here, Paul?" I broke in. "Did you come to gloat? You sent a hellhound after me, I took the bait, and now you want to see for yourself?" I held my hands up, showing them my body as though they could see the curse lurking under my skin. "Here you go. Congratulations. You're one clever bastard. You got me. You've already won. Now you've seen it with your own eyes, and you can leave."

"I'll admit that sometimes I'm a pretty lucky bastard. Every once in a while, chance is on my side, even beyond my wildest hopes," Paul replied, his eyes dark and narrow. "But I don't think I've won anything quite yet. You're still breathing. And from what I've heard, you've got a possible cure on the way."

I closed my eyes. Meri trusted Paul. She must have told him everything I had told her about Jason and Rowan's plan. I'd suspected that Paul sent the hound, but hadn't said anything, for fear of her being so angry that she would do something unwise. I'd been a fool.

"I hear your overgrown goat of a boyfriend is out of town for a bit," Paul went on, his tone mocking. "I thought it would be an excellent time for us to pay you a little visit, as it seems unlikely we'll be interrupted."

"What do you want?" I tried to make my voice sound more exasperated than worried.

"Same thing I've been wanting for years." Paul smiled, baring his teeth. "Your head on a plate. You didn't really think you'd get away with it, did you? You took down the barriers protecting the Source, so that every renegade and half-breed who wants to use a little magic can just go and help themselves. The mage clan used to be a bastion of power. You've made us into a joke."

"All right." I swallowed, my mouth suddenly dry. "This is between us, then. Let the two centaurs go. Then we can talk."

"Nothing doing," Paul sneered, taking a step closer. Behind me, I heard Natia stifle a gasp. "You see, Asa, you're about to have an accident. It's a shame, really. Hellhound curses can be so unpredictable. We thought you had longer than this. Meri will be so brokenhearted when she hears the news." His face hardened. "And there won't be any witnesses to tell her different."

He turned his head to address the other mages. Greg flinched just from the look he gave him. "Remember," he said. "No one taps into the Source. If you do, Meri will know we've been here." He turned back to face me. "But don't worry, traitor. Even without magic, you and I can still have plenty of fun." And he pulled a knife from where it hung on his belt. "That's the thing about these old barns. They're such terrible fire hazards. And once this one goes up in flames, there's no evidence. No way to tell what went wrong." He stepped closer, and I fought down the impulse to back away from him. "But you and I will know that, after all this time, *I* was the one who ended you."

"I know you," Natia's voice rang out, suddenly sharp and clear. She stepped around Crinea, who was still trying to shield her from Paul. "I know who you are," she repeated, her face white as snow, her eyes burning. Her long black hair flowed around her shoulders like a shroud. Her voice did not tremble, and she stood perfectly still as she stared at him, her eyes riveted on his face. For the first time, I noticed that she was slightly taller than Crinea.

She raised a trembling hand to point at Paul's face. "That cut on your face. It hasn't quite healed yet, has it? You wear the mark my husband left you, when you ambushed him. You *coward.*" Her voice rose an octave, ringing with derision, and she took another step closer to him. "How many of you were there, mage, when you set upon him unprovoked and unannounced? When you hunted him like an animal?"

Paul's smile had been growing the whole time Natia spoke. "Holy hell!" he exclaimed, whistling through his teeth. "Is that fat mule talking to me?"

The other mages laughed, and my eyes darted to Greg, who still stood off to the side, half-hidden in shadow, as though trying to distance himself from Paul. His face flushed, and his eyes met mine for a second, full of wordless apology. Then a snarl from Crinea made me look away.

"Wait!" I muttered to her urgently as she reached for her sword, though her eyes were flashing so brilliantly that I wasn't sure she could even hear me through her growing fury.

"She's right, though," Paul went on. "I was so disappointed to lose that prize. Such a nice, big specimen, too. Would have been quite the trophy." His eyes narrowed as he stared at Natia, malevolence glinting in them. "I was going to stuff him. Stand him in my study, once I got him home. Maybe use him as a coat rack."

Natia was like lightning when she moved. Even later, looking back, I couldn't really blame myself for not being fast enough to stop her. Her hair streamed out, dark and flowing behind her. She made no noise at all, even her hooves were silent against the wooden floor, and for a second it was as though everyone else in the room stood frozen and gaping, held captive by the mixture of beauty and savagery as she flew across the room, her eyes burning, her face twisted with resolve. Her hand snaked out, grabbing a broom from where it leaned against the wall. In her hands, it twirled, spun, and morphed into something deadly.

A second later she reached Paul, and the silence shattered as she let out a howling cry and swung the broom wide, bringing it crashing into the side of Paul's head. He crumpled to the ground. Natia lifted her front leg, and with a deafening snap she broke the end of the broom off, leaving a spear of splintered wood, deadly, in her hand. With a practiced motion, she flipped the spear around and lifted it high, ready to drive it into Paul's chest for the death blow.

There came a flash of light, a burst of air pressure.

One of the mages threw his hands out with a twisting motion, and it was as though the air itself rose up, and casually batted Natia aside. She shot sideways, and for a second I saw her there: framed by the light, her hair billowing around her, her eyes narrowed and her hand still gripping her weapon, even as her equine legs kicked in useless slow motion in the air. There was something beautiful and heartbreaking about that single, frozen moment.

Then her body collided with the wall.

I heard bone shatter. A pained gasp sounded that cut off into a brief, bloody gurgle. She fell.

Natia lay twisted on the ground, one of her legs bent backwards underneath her. White bone poked through her fur. She moaned, and one of her unbroken legs kicked weakly in the air.

"Natia!" I cried, running toward her. I could see her face, slack and deathly pale. A thin stream of blood dribbled from her lips.

"No, dammit!" Paul shouted from the ground, his voice rough with pain. "I said no magic! Now Meri will know we were here."

But the two mages on either side of Paul didn't seem to be paying him much attention. Their eyes were wide and trained on Crinea, whose precise, controlled movements did nothing to obscure the absolute fury that filled her at the sight of her friend's body on the ground. She stepped closer to them, her lips pulled back from her teeth, her eyes blazing with cold determination.

She trilled a high-pitched war cry and wrenched her sword from its sheath.

The mage standing to the right of Paul threw out his hands, and the air pressure twisted around us, ripping the sword from Crinea's hands. It spun, end over end through the air, the light glinting from its long, silver blade as it whirled off to the side, and into the shadows.

I heard a wet, hollow thud. A muffled moan sounded in the darkness. Something fell, heavy, to the ground.

I reached Natia's side, and as I dropped to my knees beside her, my Truthsight sprang up inside me in an effortless stream, as though the power that lived inside me was as desperate as I to save Natia and her baby.

Meanwhile, the loss of her sword had done nothing to slow Crinea down. Her lips twisted in a grim smile as, with an elegant, fluid motion, she reached down and slid a curved dagger from a hidden sheath under her vest.

With my Truthsight pounding in my veins I saw her: eyes burning with rage, a crown of blood-red jewels on her head. Her arms were ringed with tight-fitting golden bracelets that covered her like armor. The dagger glinted, golden and red as it flew from her hand, so fast that the mages had no time to stop her. Before I even heard the impact, I saw the small spurt of red mist that clouded the air, as the dagger sunk into the eye of the mage who stood next to Paul. Instantly, I saw a tiny light inside the man's body flicker and go out. The blow was a fatal one, and he was dead before his body fell, before any magic could have hoped to heal him.

The mages gave a cry of shock, and Crinea used the moment of confusion to leap across the floor and plant herself squarely in front of the spot where I crouched over Natia. She had no weapons left, but if anything, that made her seem more ferocious. She held her arms out wide, as though inviting the mages to do their worst, bracing herself with a grim smile for what could well be her final stand.

The mages moved, closing ranks around us, their teeth bared, their hands sparking with blue and green as magic flew to their fingers.

"Stop, you idiots!" Paul shrieked from behind them. He struggled to his feet, one hand holding the side of his head. "Meri will know we were here! We can't touch the traitor now—she'll kill us if we do. We've got to get out of here."

The mages hesitated.

"Now!" Paul barked and, without turning their backs, they began to move away, keeping their eyes fastened on me, even as they bent down to pick up the body of the dead mage. Paul unlocked the door and waited in the doorway until they had rushed past him, out into the dark. He stood there, for a moment, his form silhouetted in the darkness. I knew what he was about to do only a split second before it happened, but even if I had realized it sooner, there was nothing I could have done to stop him.

"The cat's out of the bag now. And I owe you one. I might not be able to touch the traitor, but Meri won't care if I kill a mule."

His hand flew out toward Natia, whose eyes had just flickered open. She gazed across the room blearily, her glazed eyes focused to Paul's left as a deadly green orb formed in his palm.

"Mattis?" she whispered softly, her voice full of wonder, and Paul hurled the death curse straight at her.

Even with my Truthsight, I couldn't quite understand what happened next.

There was a blur, a haze to Paul's right that left an impression of emptiness and motion. It pressed against Paul, a quick, savage jolt against his shoulder. Paul stumbled, and the curse sailed off course, missing Natia widely. Paul stumbled back, swearing. Suddenly, the mostly-healed cut on his face split open. Fresh blood coursed from the old wound and he grimaced, clutching at his face. From outside the other mages called to him, urging him to hurry. With a growl of frustration, he turned and stumbled out into the darkness.

Crinea moved with desperate speed, throwing herself on the ground beside me, her face paler now than it had been at any time during the confrontation.

Natia looked up at Crinea, her eyes glazed.

"He was here," she sighed, her voice weak and rasping. "You were right." Crinea bent her head closer.

"Right about what?"

"Mattis." Natia's eyes closed, and a peaceful smile spread over her face. "He hasn't left us. He was here."

"Natia, try to stay awake! Stay with us," Crinea called, but Natia's head rolled to the side and she didn't answer.

"Can you save her?" Crinea asked, her voice almost pleading. She sounded, for the first time since I had known her, truly frightened.

"I'm not sure yet," I admitted, keeping my eyes focused on my work. "I'll do everything I can."

"Her leg!" Crinea moaned, her hands hovering uncertainly above the shattered limb, which was an absolute ruin, and bent the wrong way. Shards of bone had punctured the fur and stood out, gleaming red and white, above the skin.

"I know. But I'll have to deal with that later. She's bleeding internally. I've got to fix that first."

"What can I do?"

"Pressure. Grab a towel. Press down there and there." I pointed without looking up, and heard Crinea hurrying to follow my instructions. I bent my head low over my work, taking slow breaths between my teeth. I tried to force myself to work slowly, carefully. Without access to my Truthsight, I would have been able to do nothing to treat an injury this severe. But now my abilities let me see the damage done internally, and I moved cautiously, pushing together what had been torn, pinching it back together like dough that had been rolled too thin. It was delicate, painstaking work. And every second that passed, more blood pulsed out and over my fingers.

The baby was all right. I could see it, a tiny centaur female, floating in Natia's womb, its eyes open. Watching me. But although the baby had gotten through the incident unscathed, its health was wholly dependent on Natia. It was far, far too early in the pregnancy for the baby to have any chance of survival outside the womb. I forced those thoughts away. I tried only to think of my fingers working, of making progress, inch by measured, painful inch. Sweat dripped down the side of my face. The stitches in my chest grew angry and itched. Under my fingers, the bleeding slowed. Natia began to breathe more easily. Her eyes stayed closed, but now her face seemed more peaceful.

"Oh, thank God." I murmured.

The danger had passed. Her leg was still badly broken, but, comparatively, healing that would be relatively straightforward. I looked again at the baby, peering at her closely, making absolutely sure she was really all right, and in no danger. The little one looked back at me, her small black eyes knowing and wise. She reached out, and for a second, she pressed a tiny hand against the wall of her mother's womb in a gesture of thanks. I smiled back at her in wonder. The baby and Natia were out of danger. I breathed a small sigh of relief. Then I turned away.

"Crinea," I said. "Natia is stable now. I need you to stay with her. I'll be right back."

"But her leg…"

"Soon," I said firmly. "She's unconscious and not feeling any pain. The baby is fine and there's no sign that she's going into premature labor. She's stable. Just stay with her. Keep putting pressure where I showed you, and I'll be right back."

I turned, my eyes probing the shadows. I hadn't known for sure. I hadn't allowed myself to think about it while Natia's life lay in my hands, and the slightest mistake, the slightest instant of hesitation, could have cost her and her baby everything. But I had heard a muffled moan when Crinea's sword sailed across the barn. And I knew there was one mage who hadn't left with the others.

"No," I moaned, when I found him. "No, no, no."

TWELVE

I KNELT IN THE POOL OF BLOOD THAT HAD GATHERED UNDERNEATH Greg's body. The sword had sliced deep into his midsection, cutting through vital organs, leaving a great gaping wound open to the air.

"I'm here," I told him. "I'm so sorry I couldn't get here sooner."

"Asa…" The words cut off in a heart wrenching gurgle. The striped shirt he wore was brown and orange and soaked with blood.

"Just hang on," I told him. "I can fix this. You're going to be all right."

Seeing Greg in Truthsight made tears spring to my eyes. My abilities showed me his truest self, and before me I saw a boy of no more than eleven or twelve. Profoundly chubby, with a round, dimpled face and ruddy cheeks, reddish-brown hair that had been unevenly cut, and thick bangs hanging down into his eyes.

"I'm so sorry, Asa," he gasped, and I stopped my work for just a second to lay my hand against his face.

"Don't worry about that now," I told him. "Just breathe. I'm going to get you through this." My fingers left a red smear of blood on his check when I lifted them away.

"Paul..." he grunted. "...made me come. Said he'd kill me if I didn't."

"Shhh. You don't have to explain. Save your strength."

"Knew something wasn't right. So...strange. Wanted to figure it out."

He coughed, and his insides convulsed and twisted. I cried out in dismay, my fingers flying, trying desperately to repair some of the damage, to somehow piece him back together again. But the more I worked, the more I realized just how deep and extensive the damage was. The sword had cut right through him, and had even clipped his spinal cord. Fragments of bone swam around his torn, ruined organs.

"Asa. Listen to me." Greg lifted a hand, gripping my shoulder with surprising strength. "Listen!" he said again, and reluctantly I lifted my eyes from my work, meeting his steady gaze. "Paul..." he wheezed, speaking with tremendous effort, "didn't send the hellhound."

His eyes glazed over, and his hand slipped, limp and lifeless, from my shoulder.

"No," I told him fiercely. "You aren't going anywhere. I'm going to..."

Suddenly, when I touched him, I felt something smooth and hard under my fingers. I looked down and gasped in horror. My Truthsight vision morphed. His whole body changed...crystallized.

He had turned to glass. I looked down, and saw a tiny light shining deep inside him. As I watched, the light flickered, and went out. There was a sharp, screaming sound, like steam blasting through the top of a kettle.

The glass shattered.

He fell to a million pieces under my hands. I tried to catch the shards, to hold on to something, some hope I might still be able to save him. The ragged glass sliced my fingers and cut into my palm.

"Oh, no," I cried. An instant later, even with my Truthsight, all I could see was Greg's body, gray and lifeless on the floor.

I had lost him.

I was crying, but that didn't matter. I forced myself to my feet. Suddenly I felt the weight of everything that had happened over the last few days slamming down on my shoulders like a one-thousand-pound weight. For a second, I thought I could even feel the curse, unfurling slowly inside me. The entire universe seemed to be conspiring against me, as though it was determined to send me every type of trauma and pain it could muster in whatever small amount of time that I had left. Greg might have been an imperfect person. But he had died under my hands. I was a healer. I didn't know how to walk away from the death of one of my patients and not feel piercing grief. And I didn't want to learn. I stumbled back to Natia's side, my mind clouded with the heavy weight of exhaustion. But Natia still needed me. I couldn't fall apart. Not yet.

"Amy..." Crinea said uncertainly, and reached out to touch my shoulder.

"Don't." I shied away from her touch. If I accepted comfort now, I'd start crying and not be able to stop. "I've got to focus on Natia's leg."

Natia's bone had splintered. If I hadn't been able to use my Truthsight, it would have been an injury she would have never fully recovered from. At best, she would have limped for the rest of her life. With my abilities, I knew a few hours of steady work would put her to rights. I sank into the work gratefully. I couldn't think about Greg, and how my abilities had not been enough to save him. I couldn't think about his last, mystifying words. I pushed the questions away, pushed away all thought of the curse, waiting patiently under my skin. All I could think of was this: piecing back one piece of bone into another, like a giant jigsaw puzzle that could be completed by no other hand but mine. I could only care about giving this woman back her life again.

As I worked, I knew Crinea had stood up, and found a sheet to lay over Greg. I knew, in the very back of my mind, that she had gone out to check on the two centaur guards, and had found them unconscious but not seriously injured. I heard her speaking with them in hushed voices, the guards nodding as they answered in low tones. I was glad that the guards were not seriously injured, but right now I couldn't spare them more than a thought. Most of my mind was taken up with Natia, about the way her leg was taking shape again under my care. I thought about how close I had come to losing her. She had bled so much, almost bleeding out completely before I could stem the tide.

Something about that caught my attention.

I mulled it over, thinking carefully as I worked, and in my mind, some other pieces began to come together.

The sun was well up in the sky when I sighed heavily and leaned away from my work. Though Natia's internal injuries had been far more severe, the painstaking job of piecing her bone back together had taken far longer to heal. I finally let my Truth-sight fall away, closing my eyes as my head spun. I had had nothing to eat or drink in hours. My clothing was stiff with dried blood, and my hands ached.

Crinea hurried over to my side, leaning over to peer at Natia, anxiety plain on her face.

"Were you able to save her leg?" she asked, worry and hope warring in her voice. I allowed myself a weak smile.

"Oh," I told her, allowing myself a slow, satisfied smile. "I'm going to do a whole lot more than that."

Crinea wanted me to explain, but I refused. Natia would regain consciousness soon, and the best thing for her would be for Crinea to take her home, where she could be surrounded by her family and nurtured back to full health. I told Crinea to come back in the evening.

The clinic would be closed, I said. But I was still going to need her help.

"Can you wait with her until she wakes up, and then take her home?" I asked, "I need to...take care of Greg." Crinea nodded, her eyes wide and full of worry for me, but I couldn't think of anything to say to reassure her. I turned and staggered home.

I took just long enough to clean up and choke down some food that I couldn't taste. I needed badly to sleep, but there was no way I could rest with Greg's body lying unattended in my clinic. I would bury him by the old oak tree on the far end of my property, I decided. Everything else would have to wait.

I had never buried anyone before. I wasn't exactly sure how to go about doing it. But I found a blanket that the widow who had owned this house had knit to wrap around him. It seemed warm, and I felt certain the widow would have been glad to have it give someone a last bit of comfort.

I trudged out to the barn, determined, but overwhelmed by the task ahead. My steps slowed when I saw three centaurs who I did not recognize standing there. Waiting for me.

"Crinea told us what happened," one of them said. "We came to give whatever help you have need of."

"Thank you," I said, overwhelmed by the unexpected kindness. We did not speak at all as they helped me load Greg's body into the back of my truck. They cantered along beside me as I drove out to the old oak. Silent and solemn, they set to work, helping me dig a deep grave in the partially frozen ground.

As we worked, I thought of how the other mages hadn't stopped to help Greg when he had been injured. They hadn't even come back to claim his body as their own.

We lowered his body gently into the ground. He had been abandoned by the clan, I realized. Cut off, just as I had been. And as I pushed the dirt over him and patted it down, my every emotion as raw as my hands in the cold afternoon wind, I felt that I wasn't just burying him. I was burying any hope I had ever held, no matter how small, of one day being reunited with the clan. They had been my family once. No matter how much I had denied it, a part of me had always hoped that, one day, I would have a place among them once again. But that dream was dead now. Despite my love for Meri, the clan itself was full of violence and hatred. I knew now that I didn't want them, just as much as they didn't want me.

When our work was done, the centaurs nodded to me deeply and then moved off to a respectful distance, standing a little way off, in the shadows of the trees. I stood alone over Greg's grave.

The oak tree was beautiful, even now, when most of its leaves had fallen. It stood, bare arms reaching out into the sky, as though it could catch the sun's warmth in its branches, and hold it tight against the coming cold.

"I'll get you a gravestone," I told Greg. "A proper marker, just as soon as I can." I felt as though he was listening, and I felt sorely unfit to be the one to oversee this, the last chapter of his life. "I don't know what else to say," I sighed. "There ought to be more. Some prayers. People sharing memories. You deserve all of that, Greg, and more. You deserve so much more. You should have had a long, happy life. You were a good man. Not perfect—but kind and funny. You would have done good things, if you had had more of a chance. I'm sorry I couldn't save you. I'll remember you, though. I'm not sure how much that is worth. But I guess it's the only thing that I can do for you now."

I stood for a few more minutes, until I realized how deep the cold was cutting through my jacket, and how numb my fingers were. The centaurs watched over me while I slowly climbed back into my truck and drove away. As I drove, I saw them cantering off into the trees.

I pressed down on the gas and craned my head to the side, staring up at the sky. The sun was still up, but I found myself searching the skyline for the moon.

I had a plan now. For hours, it had been percolating, taking shape in my mind as though it had a will and a drive of its own. I knew what I *wanted* to do, but I wasn't sure if it was possible.

Suddenly, I felt very, very short on time.

When I got home I ran inside and thundered up the stairs to my room. I kept a journal, with notes about all the patients I treated, and I knew that I would need it now.

I opened the door of my room, and Meri stood in the mirror, waiting for me. The unexpected sight of her made me jump, and my heart skipped a beat.

"Oh, thank God." The moment she saw me, Meri sat down heavily, holding her head in her hands. I hurried over to the glass, inwardly cursing myself for my stupidity. One of the mages had tapped into the Source while they were attacking us—Meri would have realized that something had happened. I had been so caught up with caring for Natia and Greg that I had completely forgotten Meri would be desperate to see I was all right.

"I'm sorry," I told her. "I should have let you know that I wasn't hurt."

"Yes, you should have," she replied, not looking up. "And you should have had the clamshell that I gave you with you when they attacked. You would have been able to contact me. I would have helped you."

I tried to pick my next words carefully, knowing that she was exhausted, upset, and not thinking clearly.

"Even if you had known what was happening," I said gently, "making a portal takes hours, sometimes days. You wouldn't have been able to get here in time." Meri didn't say anything in response, but she looked up at me, and her eyes still flashed.

"I want you to keep it with you all the time," she insisted. "Promise me, Asa. I want to know if you're in danger. You can at least do that much for me."

"I will," I told her. "I promise." I took a deep breath. "And I need you to promise me that you aren't going to do anything rash in response to what Paul did. You've just returned to power. You mustn't do anything that might cause you to lose control over the clan."

Meri stood up in a sudden, fluid movement. She made a sharp cutting movement with her hand, as though pushing my words away. "I am never rash, Asa," she said, her eyes running over me one more time, as though checking me over for injuries. "I wouldn't have retained my position as leader here for so many long years if I did not know how to handle disobedience calmly and decisively. Don't worry about me." Her voice grew cold and distant. "I must go. There are things I must attend to."

I nodded a farewell as the glass shimmered and Meri's image disappeared. For a long moment, I stood and gazed at my own pale reflection in the glass, worrying about her, wishing I knew what to say to make her pain less intense. But no insights came, and soon I turned away, snagging the clamshell and notebook before heading back out to the clinic.

Crinea arrived just after sunset, and I was already in the thick of it, my hair pulled up into a messy bun that kept spilling out and falling into my eyes, a pencil tucked behind my ear, surrounded by piles of open books and pages and pages of paper thick with scrawled notes.

"How's Natia?" I asked without looking up.

"Better." Crinea closed the door behind her and approached with slow, cautious steps. "She is resting. Are you all right, Amy?"

I grunted in reply, leaning over to pull a discarded book closer, flipping furiously through the pages before tossing it away. "Useless," I muttered under my breath. "None of these people know the first thing about centaurs."

"Amy?" Crinea sounded really worried now. "What's going on? Don't you think you should rest? You look pale."

"How much do you remember?" I asked, ignoring her question. "From when you had your baby?"

The question stopped Crinea in her tracks. Her face clouded, and she bit her lip. "It is difficult to say," she answered, after a minute. "I remember moments. Feelings. But it is difficult to piece them together in a way that makes sense." She stepped closer. "Why do you ask?"

"When you went into labor, you became anemic. Severely anemic. The baby's growth was so complex it sucked all the iron out of your system." I stopped and looked up at her. "That's why you bled so much."

Her eyes went dark. "That I do remember," Crinea answered.

I picked up a stack of books, and began sorting them into piles on the tabletop. "I tested your blood throughout your pregnancy, and up until that moment I had never seen any sign that there was a problem with your iron. So, I assumed something had happened right at the last moment of your pregnancy. Something catastrophic. Something that could only be remedied with Truth-sight. But...what if I was wrong?" I set a book down a bang. "I was still in hiding during most of your pregnancy, which meant that I couldn't use my Truthsight to monitor your condition for most of that time. I only used it at the very last moment, when it was the only possible way to save your life. Up until then, I used standard medicine to try to monitor you. What if that standard medicine was just plain wrong?"

"Amy," Crinea said, speaking slowly. "I don't understand what you're saying."

"When Natia got hurt, she bled profusely. Too much. As though her body is being affected already. Even though her last blood tests came back normal."

"Isn't that a bad thing?" Crinea asked, her eyebrows knitting together. "You're saying she is sick...so why are you smiling?"

"Because. If her blood is already being affected, that means the condition develops gradually. Over time. And *that* means I have a chance to work out a treatment we can administer *now*. Something that will save her, and the baby. Whether I'm there for the delivery or not."

Crinea stood silent for a long moment. Her chest rose and fell rapidly, as though she had just run a great distance.

"You're saying you could develop a medicine," she said at last. "One that will save Natia. So she could live, even if the curse strikes before her time of delivery comes."

"Not just Natia." I leaned over the table toward Crinea, and dropped my voice. "If I'm right, and *if* I can develop a medicine to treat her successfully...we could send the medicine to other centaur tribes. Send runners all over the country with instructions about how to help pregnant centaurs survive. Centaur women have been dying while delivering their babies in terrifying numbers." I tapped the tabletop with my fist. "We can change that. We can *end* it, Crinea. I'm sure of it. I can feel it."

"Wait. Amy, wait." Crinea held up her hands. "Let's think about this for a second. I am...incredibly grateful for what you are proposing. But you do not have long left before the curse becomes active. You are a healer. Shouldn't you use your time to find a way to heal yourself? Once your life is safe, then you can still develop this medicine."

"A cure for the hellhound curse won't work," I told her bluntly. "This will."

"But..." Crinea's words sounded pained. "This is too much. Too great a gift for anyone to give. You are talking about spending your last few days on this Earth bent over a table, working on a cure for my people. You don't owe us that, Amy! If anything, then we are in your debt. Don't you want to spend your final days in some other way?"

I caught Crinea's hand in mine, squeezing her fingers. "I went to talk to Baxin the other day. You know Baxin, right?" Crinea nodded. "He told me that, if I couldn't undo the curse, that I should beat it by fitting a lifetime's worth of living into the time I have left. Ever since he told me that, I've been trying and trying to figure out what it could mean for me." I shrugged. "Now I know. It means this. This, right here, is what it means to make the most of the time I have. For me, *this* is living. I may not have much longer, but I have enough time to do this. If this is the last thing I ever do…"

I thought of the little centaur baby growing in Natia's womb, of all the centaur mothers and children I hadn't met, who I would never get to see, who might be helped if I could figure out how to make this work. I swallowed hard. "Well. Seems to me like a pretty good way to go."

Crinea threw an arm around me, pulling me halfway across the table, in a hug so tight it hurt. "This is what you want?" she asked in a voice rough with suppressed tears. "Truly?"

I nodded. "It is."

She let me go and wiped her eyes with the back of her hand. I pretended not to notice.

"Very well," she said. "If this is what you want, then I will help you in any way I can. How do we begin?"

I pressed my fingers to my temples. I couldn't remember the last time I had slept. My head felt heavy, like it was stuffed full of cotton balls. The smart answer to Crinea's question would be to say that we started by getting a good night's sleep, so we could dive into the problem well-rested in the morning. But I simply did not have the time.

"Coffee," I answered instead, rolling up my sleeves. "All great medical discoveries begin with coffee."

THIRTEEN

THREE NIGHTS LATER, THE BACK TABLE OF THE BARN WAS STREWN with printouts, and pages and pages filled front and back with scribbled notes. I had given up going back to the house to rest. Instead, between treating patients and my own frenzied research, I threw myself down on one of the clinic's cots for the occasional hour or two of uneasy sleep. I spoke only occasionally to Meri, through the clamshell. Our conversations felt forced, and Meri sounded preoccupied, but I was too wrapped up in my work to worry once our conversations ended. I was subsisting on a diet of Pop Tarts and Campbell's soup. I tacked up a lunar calendar on the wall, and each morning I crossed a day off. Once a night I would step outside, stand with my hands shoved deep into my pockets, and stare upon the slowly swelling crescent in the sky. Then I would go back into the clinic and throw myself headlong back into my work.

Natia returned to the clinic just long enough for me to take blood samples. Although she had lost all fear of me, she was more reluctant than ever to come into the barn, for which I could hardly blame her. So I brought my supplies outside. We stood next to the Earthchild's spear, which was still stuck deep into the ground in front of my clinic, and I took all her vitals and checked her over thoroughly. She had recovered well from her injuries and, when she left, she walked away steadily on all four legs.

Crinea left periodically to check on her family, but she was always back before too long. When I asked her with concern if she was getting enough rest, she responded with a glare so fierce that I dropped my eyes and quickly changed the subject. Part of her ceaseless energy, I reminded myself, might be due to her new favorite beverage. As I glanced at her discreetly out of the corner of my eye, I thought that on some level I could die happy, now that I had seen a centaur sipping coffee out of a battered paper cup.

My world became a blur of test results and scribbled notes, of ideas seized eagerly, only to be discarded as useless after a few hours of fevered investigation. Every book I owned on homeopathic medicine lay open on one surface or another, except for the ones I had flung across the barn in frustration.

Centaurs were infinitely complex, their dual human and horse-like natures interacting in ways that I was only beginning to understand. Most importantly, their metabolism was so high that their bodies would burn off almost any medicine I could administer before it could be absorbed into their bodies. I was convinced that there was some plant or oil that could be administered along with the medicine, that would keep it in their systems long enough to do them good. But figuring out what that would be was unbelievably difficult. I had tried mixing the medicine with devil's club, and tea brewed from the needles of a blue spruce. I had even tried juniper berries and dandelions. I tried everything I could think of, and used the samples I had taken of Natia's blood to run test after fruitless test, and still I found nothing promising. But I couldn't stop.

Every time I began to think of Rowan, or of Jason, to worry for them and to hope that they were all right, I forced myself to push the thoughts away. I had to focus. My worry would not do them any good, but I could do real good here, with this medicine—if I could only figure out how to make the damn thing work.

Several days later, Crinea stood peeking over my shoulder.

"Is it time?" she asked.

"Not yet."

"You said these test results were promising." She leaned closer. "What is that?"

"It's pulp, from a honey locust tree," I answered. "The Indians in this area used it as a painkiller. They also fermented it to make beer. But I think it may work as an additive to the medicine that I've made for Natia. Something that will help her body absorb the dose she needs."

"Is it working?"

"I'm not sure."

"You said that an hour ago." Crinea paced back and forth behind me, her tail twitching as her voice grew sharp. "You keep going over the same test results again and again. You're stalling."

"I am not stalling. I'm just reviewing my calculations." I turned to look at her. "You have to understand. The results may seem promising now, but I'm not at all sure things will go any better now than they did yesterday, or the day before."

"That is no reason to delay," she insisted. "It is a reason to push forward quickly, so we have time for more attempts!" She paced closer, her brow furrowing. "When centaur young learn to throw a spear, we hang a hoop from a tree far away, and tell them to throw the spear through the circle. It is very, very difficult to learn. You miss again and again, before you succeed. But each time you miss, you grow closer to your goal. You learn the heft of the spear in your hand, how to move your hooves as you throw. The misses are not failures. They are part of your eventual success. The only way to fail is to stop picking up your spear."

"Wow." I leaned back and crossed my arms, staring at her. "That was really deep."

Crinea's cheeks turned pink. "It is the same speech Finar gave to me," she admitted, not quite meeting my eyes. "When I broke a spear over my knee after missing for the fifteenth time." She shrugged delicately. "I was very young."

I couldn't help it; I laughed, more at her expression than anything else.

Crinea went on speaking, ignoring my laughter complete-ly."You are afraid this won't work. But failure is nothing to be afraid of. Being over-cautious can be dangerous." She put a hand on my shoulder, and dropped her voice. "Especially when you do not have a lot of time."

"You're right." I stood up and shook myself. "It's time." I lifted the vial and stared at it. The liquid was slightly blue, and glinted in the sunlight that poured in the open barn door.

"All right," I said, swallowing hard. "Here we go."

I leaned back down over the table, carefully adding a few drops of the medicine to a sample of Natia's blood. Crinea hovered at my elbow.

"What now?" she asked, when I straightened up. "How do we tell if the medicine worked?"

"Well, technically, we need more lab results and then years of careful medical testing."

Crinea's mouth dropped open. I winked at her.

"But don't worry. We get to cheat. I can use my Truthsight to gauge the results. If it's working, I'll know. If not..."

Crinea squeezed my shoulder. "If not," she said, "we will try again, and again. And we will make it work eventually."

I took a step away from her. At my call, silver flashed in the corner of my eye, like a lone candle in a window: a beacon of home. I let go of the world around me. With a feeling akin to stretching out my legs under a quilt and letting myself drift off to sleep, I sank into the silver mist and all the comfort it promised. I felt a shock of cold, and the air seemed to fill with a perfect symphony of ringing silver bells. I smelled lavender, freshly turned dirt, and the aroma of raspberry tea and honey. I stood at the bank of the Source and it glided past my feet, a silver river that laughed a greeting at me as it rushed along.

Then I looked down at the vial.

"Well?" I heard Crinea's voice calling out to me, although it echoed strangely and sounded very far away. "What do you see? Did it work?"

In my hand the vial glinted, then glowed. The light grew brighter and brighter, until I felt like I held a newborn star, clenched tight between my fingers. When the glow faded, the liquid in the vial still sparkled and shone.

I laughed and let my vision fall away. "It worked!" I cried, throwing my arms around Crinea's shoulders. "We did it!"

"You're sure?"

"Yes," I told her, and for the first time in a long time, I felt a true ray of happiness cut through all the darkness that swirled inside me. "It will work. And today—right now—I'm going to teach you how to make this medicine." I turned back to the table, and pulled out a sheaf of papers. "I'll explain everything, show you everything you need to know. I'll write everything out, and then we'll re-copy the instructions, as many times as we need to. The chief can arrange to have them sent to every other centaur herd he knows of. Then they will all know how to save their people, too."

"I...I don't believe it," Crinea stammered, staring down at the vial I held. "Do you realize what a gift you have given us? How many centaur mothers and their children can be saved?"

I didn't respond, just wrapped my arms around her in another fierce hug.

"My people will find a way to honor you for this, Amy," she whispered. "I promise you that." She leaned back to look at me, her eyes glistening. "Perhaps we will name all the babies after you."

I laughed. "Even the boys?"

Crinea smiled back at me. "We may have to number them

eventually, just to keep them all straight. Amy number eight. Amy number five hundred."

"It does have a nice ring to it." I grinned. And then we got back to work.

Figuring out what needed to go into the medicine had been terribly tricky, but once we knew the components, making more batches wasn't that complex. By the time Crinea galloped away late in the morning, she had successfully brewed a batch of the medication, start to finish, all by herself. We had copied and re-copied the instructions, and though all the components were herbs and plants that were commonly known, I had given her several samples of each of them to send along with the instructions, so that there could be no mistakes.

As she left, I caught a glimpse of one of the centaur guards the chief had posted around the clinic. He waved a solemn greeting to Crinea, before leaning down to feed yet another treat to Pip. I pulled the clinic door shut and began to clean the clinic. It felt good to put things in order, to wipe down the tables, to sweep the floors. I hadn't realized how much mess had accumulated while I did my fevered research, and I took real pleasure in making the clinic neat again. I paused to eat, then cleaned some more. Pip wandered in after a while, and after condescending to eat part of a hot dog, curled up to nap in the fading sunlight.

When there was nothing more to do, I turned off the lights and went home. I didn't feel happy, exactly. But a sense of accomplishment warmed me, and the hollow, aching dread that had been hanging over me for so many days had disappeared. I climbed the stairs to my bedroom. Putting on actual pajamas and crawling into my own bed felt like a lavish indulgence after so many days and nights of dozing on a cot in the clinic. My eyes strayed to the mirror on the wall, and for a moment I thought of contacting Meri. But I was so tired, and besides, I really didn't know what I would say. Instead, I rolled onto my side and fell into a dreamless sleep.

FOURTEEN

A SOUND LIKE A GUNSHOT WOKE ME. I COULD BARELY SEE THROUGH the thick darkness in my bedroom. I jerked out of bed, stumbling to my feet as I struggled to pull free of the covers.

"Aaaammmyy!" Jason's howl poured through my open window. "Help me! I need you!"

I shot down the stairs like a rocket, tripping over my feet in a blind panic, leaving the clamshell behind on the top of my dresser as I pelted heedlessly across the lawn and toward the clinic. The only light came from the large lamp hanging directly over the exam table in the center of the clinic. Jason stood next to it, his body half in shadow, the other half illuminated in a harsh light that revealed thick black and purple bruises running all along the right side of his face.

"Jason!" I cried, running toward him, "Oh my God! What happened? How badly are you hurt?"

Jason's eyes were wild. Tears and dirt stained his face. His clothes, what was left of them, were torn, ragged, and caked with mud. "Not me!" he choked. "Help him. I've killed him. He's fucking dying!"

My concern for Jason had been so intense that I hadn't seen

the lifeless form on the exam table. The man lay all but naked, and unmoving. His eyes were closed, his breath wheezing. When I leaned closer, I saw that his lips were swollen. I could see almost every inch of his skin. Hives rose all over his body, and thin, white scars covered his neck. His pale brown hair lay beneath him in a long, languid tangle that would have reached almost to his knees if he had been standing on his feet.

"What happened to him?" Automatically I leaned over the patient, my fingers seeking out a pulse as my eyes ran over him. The heartbeat that pressed against my searching fingers was faint and weak. His tongue and throat were so swollen that he could barely manage to suck in any air. When I pulled his eyelids up, vacant, pale blue eyes stared up at me, unresponsive and unseeing.

"I couldn't leave him there."

Tears streamed down Jason's face. He stood with his arms wrapped around himself, shaking. He didn't move to help me care for the unconscious man. He didn't do anything except stare with wide, horrified eyes as I started doing chest compressions.

"I told myself that, even if he didn't make it, he was better off dead than staying there. I didn't know what leaving would do to him—but I did it anyway. He seemed okay at first, just following after me. But then he started screaming." Jason wiped his streaming eyes with his shoulder, keeping his hands fisted and his arms tightly folded. "I had to keep dosing him, just to keep him quiet. If they had heard us leaving and caught us, they would have ripped us both to pieces."

"Dosing him?" I glanced up. "With what?"

He didn't answer, just stared at me.

"Jason!" He jerked a little, blinking as though he was just now waking up. "What did you give him?"

"Toxin. M...my toxin." His voice stuttered, his face burned with shame, and he clamped his arms down harder over his hands. "It's what he wanted. I...I didn't know what else to do."

I stared down at the man who lay, unmoving, under my hands.

"Who is he?" I whispered.

"He's...me." Jason stammered. "I mean, he's the one they took, when they left me in his place."

Shock slammed into me, and my hands stilled.

"What are you talking about?"

"When I was a baby." Fresh tears coursed down Jason's face, and this time he didn't wipe them away. "They stole him from my parents, and left me in his place."

"Oh my God."

I stared down at the unconscious man. Precious seconds bled by, my hands frozen in shock, my mind reeling. Then I realized I had stopped moving. Cursing, I forced my hands back into action, forced my mind to focus on the task at hand.

"Okay." I spun and began grabbing supplies, slamming them down on the table as I talked. "We don't have time to process this right now. First, we save him. Then, we think." I pulled out a shot of adrenaline, and jabbed it into his outer thigh. "He's in severe anaphylactic shock, and I'm not sure the adrenaline will open up his airways fast enough. Elevate his legs. I'll use my Truthsight and do what I can. You may have to administer CPR until I get him breathing regularly."

"No." Jason shook his head and took a step away. "I can't."

"What are you talking about?" I cried. "Of course you can. I need your help. You've got to keep him breathing. I can't save him by myself!"

"I think I've done more than enough to him already, Amy!" Jason shouted, his eyes wide and haunted. "I'm not touching him again!"

I took a gulping breath, and swallowed the shouted response that sprang to my lips. I forced myself to speak softly.

"You're not going to hurt him. You know how to do this. It'll be okay."

"I can't."

"Yes, you can. You can help me keep him alive. You're the same person you were a few days ago."

"I'm a monster," he whispered.

"Bullshit." My voice wasn't so soft anymore. "You're my best friend, and I trust you, and whatever species you may be and whatever hell you may have just been through, I know who you are. Now shake it off, and get the hell over here. Right the fuck now."

Jason blinked and shook his head a little, as though he had just had cold water thrown in his face. He stumbled forward and began to prop up the man's legs.

"Okay. I'll see what Truthsight can do for him. Where is Rowan?"

"He's coming. He stayed behind to close the way and make sure none of those...things...followed us through." Jason closed his eyes, shivering. "We really don't want any of them knowing where we are."

"All right, when he gets here, he can take over doing the compressions if you're too tired. You just need to tell him what to do. Everything is going to be all right," I told him, even though I wasn't sure that it was true. "Just hold it together a little bit longer. Okay?"

Jason glanced up at me, and his eyes were clearer than they had been moments before. He gave a barely perceptible nod.

I took a step away, and reached for the silver that glinted in the corner of my vision, pulling it toward me in a clear, cold wave. I wrapped the feel of it around my shoulders, draping it over my head like a cloak, like a shield I could pull between myself and the rest of reality. I closed my eyes for an instant, letting the feel of it settle inside me. There was a sensation, like cool rain falling on my face. For a split second, I drank it in. I let it comfort me. Then I opened my eyes, bracing for whatever I might find when I looked up.

I gasped when I saw him. I had been healing people for almost as long as I could remember, and I had seen countless injured people, with hundreds of types of injuries or disease. But nothing I had seen before had prepared me for this.

What had happened to him? I had thought that he was suffering from anaphylactic shock, but now I realized that the shock was the least of his problems, and was already starting to fade. The adrenaline had worked, and I could see his throat relaxing, see the air coursing freely to his veins. But the rest of him...

It was as though a huge part of him had been hollowed out, or somehow sucked away. I saw him in my Truthsight, the real him, the essence of what he was. His body was a candle that had all but burned away. His limbs were thin shells of yellow wax—motionless, lifeless, lying inert on the table beside him. His chest was sunken in, a cavity that held nothing but a thin layer of still-molten wax. His heart, which I saw as a tiny black wick, smoldered and flickered weakly. His face was the worst part of it all. He had no features, no eyes or nose...it had all melted away. Only a wide, gaping indentation where his mouth should have been remained. It looked as though he had been screaming once, long ago, when he was still alive enough to feel the pain. The wax had hardened as it ran in rivulets down his face and stood as permanent, silent tears.

As I watched, a small, thin wisp of smoke rose from the wick, as the final ember in his chest died. The last semblance of life and hope was falling away from him. I raised my hand and leaned in to help.

Then I hesitated.

Who would I be helping if I re-lit this flame, and extended his life? I had never seen anything as pitiful, as heartbreaking, as what this man had become. I was a doctor, a healer, before all else. My first obligation was to do no harm, to do everything and anything to keep from causing pain. Even if I could manage to keep that flame burning for a little while longer, what hope could I offer him? When I had healed Natia, her shattered bones had been like puzzle pieces in my hand, simply needing to be fit back together. If this man was a puzzle, then the pieces that were meant to make up the core of his life force were simply gone. Stolen away. There was nothing for me to put back together. Who he was, who he might have been…simply was not there. Wasn't letting him go the kindest thing that I could do?

My mind raced, and I remembered Rowan's father. He had needed my help. Not to extend his life, but to break free of the forest's hold on him, so he could pass on. Wasn't this situation the same?

But Rowan's father had been an old man, I told myself. He had already lived well past his time. And it had been his choice to let go, not mine. I had only eased his way, made it possible for him to let go when he was ready. The man lying in front of me was not making any choice. There was no one to decide but me.

I stood with my hand hovering over the man's hollow chest, trembling a little. Uncertain.

Then, from behind me, Jason sobbed.

It was just a short, gasping sound, the kind of sound you make when you are holding back tears, or when you've already cried so much that you have no more strength for crying, even though the pain is still sharp. I thought of Jason, of the guilt he would feel if this man died right now, on my table, with Jason's hands still trying to coax his unwilling heart to beat.

I held my palm up and stretched my fingers out and, with a whisper of will, a tiny, purple-blue flame leaped up between my fingers.

"I'm sorry," I murmured to the man.

And then I saved him.

I wasn't sure it was the right thing, or the kind thing. I wasn't even sure whose sake I was saving him for. But I leaned down and let the flame fall like a rose petal from my hand, and it tumbled down onto the still-smoking wick. An instant later the wick glowed, and a small, sad flame burned low. I straightened up, looking over his body, wishing I knew something else I could do for him—but for the moment I had done all I could. I brushed my fingers against his cheek, wishing I could brush away the wax tears frozen there.

"Don't give up," I whispered to him, hoping that somehow, he could hear me. "Give me a little time to try to learn how to help you. There's a light inside you. As long as that light's burning, there's hope. Hold on a little while longer. We'll figure something out." Then I closed my eyes and let my Truthsight fall away.

FIFTEEN

When I looked up, Rowan stood with head bent low over the scarred man's body, listening for breathing.

"He's stable," I announced, and Rowan's head snapped up, his eyes focusing in on me with burning intensity. "At least for now. It'll take me time to figure out what else I can do."

If I can do more, a despondent voice in the back of my head added, but I pushed that thought away.

"What happened here in our absence, Asa?" Rowan asked, his face creased with worry. "I smell blood, and magic."

"Some mages came. It was bad, but we got through it." I grimaced. "Most of us, anyway. I can tell you everything later."

I looked around, searching for Jason. He sat, half-hidden in shadows, leaning against the wall several feet away. I grabbed a first aid kit and a clean towel, and hurried over to where he huddled, knees pulled up to his chest. I crouched down in front of him.

"Let me look at your injuries," I said, my voice gentle. "You did everything you could for that man. You got him out. You got him here. Now let me take care of you."

"I'm fine." Jason wouldn't look up. "Just let me be."

"You're bleeding." I reached for the gash on his forearm, and he jerked away as though my fingers would burn him. He pressed his body tighter against the wall.

"Don't touch me, Amy! I'm serious."

I froze. I had known Jason wasn't human from almost the first moment that I had met him. But it had never been a barrier between us. He had been gone for such a short amount of time. Had I really lost his trust so quickly?

"I'm not going to hurt you. Don't you know that?" I couldn't keep the hurt from my voice. "I just want to take care of your wound."

"I'm not afraid of you, Amy," Jason exclaimed, scrambling to his feet. He scuttled away, moving until he stood behind Rowan, using the leshy as a barrier between us. He wrapped his arms tight around his middle and stared at the ground.

"Jason," Rowan's voice rumbled. "Let me see your hands."

Jason looked up at him, eyes wide with fear, and I could tell he wanted to refuse. Rowan gazed at him, imperious and waiting, and I watched as Jason's effort at resistance crumbled away. His shoulders slumped, and the stubborn expression on his face melted into shame and defeat. He hung his head, and held his hands out, palm up, to Rowan. Rowan reached out and, with extreme care, lifted Jason's hands up so he could examine them.

The last thing I wanted to do was embarrass Jason. But if I wanted to help him, I needed to understand what was going on. I moved closer, standing on tiptoe so I could get a better look. At first, I saw nothing at all. His fingers and palms looked completely normal. Then I noticed something on his fingertips glinting strangely in the light.

Hundreds of tiny needles were poking out of Jason's skin. Concentrated on his fingertips, the needles were quite short and clear, clustered closely together, and almost invisible to the naked eye. They reminded me of porcupine quills. They looked hollow, and each came to a sharp point.

"Do they hurt you?" I asked, my voice hushed.

Jason shook his head miserably. "I can't even feel them," he admitted.

"There is nothing to be ashamed of," Rowan told him. "These quills have always been a part of you. You simply did not know how to extend them. Now you must learn how to retract them at will. That knowledge will come. You only need time to learn control."

"I don't want to learn how to control it," Jason hissed, his face flushing as he pulled his hands away. "I don't want it at all. You don't understand, Rowan. You didn't see what I saw. Those things were monsters." His eyes flashed, and I could hear panic building in his voice.

"How about this?" I broke in. "I'll get some gauze, and wrap it around your hands. That way you won't have to worry about anything. Then you can sit down, and I can take a look at your injuries."

Jason hesitated, and then nodded reluctantly. He allowed me to maneuver him over to an exam table, and sat down heavily. He tilted his head back against the wall and stared at the ceiling with his hands resting, palm up in his lap. I moved swiftly, bandaging his hands as gently as possible. Without being asked, Rowan brought over some warm water, and I started to clean Jason's wounds.

To my surprise, the gash on his arm wasn't nearly as bad as it had seemed at first. In fact, as I cleaned more of the blood away, it seemed smaller.

I leaned in closer. I could actually see Jason's skin melding back together, re-growing at an incredible rate.

I swallowed an exclamation of surprise, and kept my tone casual. "Your injuries don't seem too bad," I observed. "How do you feel?"

Jason closed his eyes.

"Better than I have in years," he answered, "and I *hate* myself for it."

"What happened?" I asked. Jason didn't answer. I looked to Rowan, who raised his hands.

"There isn't much I can tell you," he said. "I could not approach the pod too closely, for fear that my presence would frighten or anger them. Perhaps cause them to turn on Jason. So I hung back. Jason and I devised a distress signal that he could send if he had need of me. I waited for days, but the distress signal never came." He paused and they exchanged a look.

After a long moment of awkward silence, Rowan went on. "Then, tonight, Jason suddenly appeared with this human in tow. I got them to safety as quickly as I could, then did all I could to ensure we would not be pursued. I do not know what Jason saw. And I don't know what happened to the man he brought back with him."

"They were feeding off him," Jason said, the words cold and blunt, his eyes squeezed shut.

My breath caught, and I swallowed a horrified gasp. Of course; that's what my Truthsight had been trying to tell me.

"That's why they took him, all those years ago," Jason continued. "They're all sick, you see." He opened his eyes. I had never seen him look so tired, so utterly defeated. "They used to get all the nutrition they needed from the water, but water quality has decreased so much…it just isn't enough to sustain them anymore. Hasn't been for a while. So Desinda—she's their queen—she found another way to keep the nymphs alive." Jason looked down at his bandaged hands. "The needles are like syringes. They can inject toxin. And they can extract things, too."

"Extract things?" I said. "Like what?"

"Life force. Pure life force, from humans' bodies. The nymphs can pull it right out of them, and use it to extend their own lives. He wasn't the only one." Jason looked over at the scarred man and shuddered. "There were other humans there, living together, in a herd of sorts. Dozens of them that the nymphs were holding captive. Too many for me to be able to get them all out. I wanted to, I really did. But there was no way I could. Even just taking him with me, I was pretty sure they would catch us, and we would both die. But I just couldn't leave him behind. Not when I know that everything that's happened to him has been because of me."

Jason ran a trembling, thickly bandaged hand over his eyes. He paused so long I didn't think he was going to go on, and then he did. "If they had caught us, they would have ripped us to pieces. They aren't sane, Amy. Feeding off humans has kept them alive, but it isn't how they're meant to get nutrition. I think it has been slowly making them lose their minds. Or maybe they've always been bloodthirsty and vicious. I've got nothing to compare it to, since they threw me away when I was only a week old."

"I'm sorry," Rowan said, shaking his head. "I would have told you all that I could learn about your origins sooner, if I had imagined the nymphs had stolen a biological child from your parents. It never occurred to me they would have done such a thing. I had no idea they would have any use for a human. With their persuasive powers, it would have been simple to tell a human couple you were their child, and have them believe it."

"It isn't your fault," Jason said. "You couldn't have known. And you got us out of there. They weren't very happy to see me in the first place. I keep trying not to imagine what they would have done if they had caught me stealing away one of their humans."

"Why weren't they happy to see you?" I asked, wishing I could hold Jason's hand. But I didn't think he would want me to touch him.

A bitter laugh came from Jason. "Because I'm an aberration."

"You mean, because you're male?"

"Because I'm anything." Jason sat up a little straighter.

For just a second I saw a flash of the man I knew, saw a shadow of the fascination at a new discovery that I had seen glimmer in his eyes so many times.

"They aren't really female, though they may look it. They reproduce asexually, Amy. Through spores. That's why they all look exactly alike." Jason shivered. "Freakiest damn thing I've ever seen, too. Sometimes they even speak in unison. Apparently, every year one or two 'abnormalities' are born. Like me. Whether they're male or female, the nymphs don't want them. They want to keep everything the way it is. "Harmonious," they called it. "Consistent."

"And sexual reproduction causes variation," I murmured. "I've actually heard of something like this before. I think there are some jellyfish who go through a cycle, first of asexual reproduction, and then sexual reproduction after that. It could be that the nymphs go through a similar process, only over the course of generations, rather than in a single life-span. And that, for whatever reason, they are trying to suppress the next stage of their evolution."

"They believe they are absolutely perfect," Jason said in a bitter tone. "And they sure don't want anything to change. Apparently, aberrations like me don't usually live for long once they're abandoned. Not when they're away from the water, with no one to teach them what their body needs. I think they might have killed me outright, if they hadn't wanted to figure out exactly how I had kept myself alive all this time. I wasn't supposed to survive in the care of humans."

He pressed his lips together into a tight line, and a touch of pride glinted in his eyes. His sudden willingness, or need rather, to speak so much encouraged me. It reminded me of the old Jason.

"They wouldn't have assumed I'd die so quickly if they had actually known my mother. If they had known how stubborn she was, or how hard she would fight to keep me alive. Or you, Amy." He looked at me, and smiled just a little. "First you took down the barriers to the Source. Then you fought like hell to figure out what my body needed." He slid off the table, and stood, slightly shaky, on his feet. "I think it's about damn time I returned the favor."

"Can you do it?" Rowan's voice was suddenly rough with emotion. "Can you extract the curse from her body?"

"There's only one way to find out," Jason said, with a confidence I could tell he didn't really feel.

"You don't have to try right now, Jason," I told him, each word rushing out. "You only just got back, and you're injured. You need to rest. Let's take care of you first."

"I think you've been taking care of me for long enough, Amy," Jason said, and there was a decisiveness in his voice I didn't quite recognize.

"It cannot wait, Asa," Rowan agreed. His voice was low, but edged in steel. "Your condition is dire. You do not have much time left." He turned to gaze at me, and his eyes burned. "Do you forget that I can see the curse? Did you think I would not notice how it has grown since the last time I saw you?" He shook his head. "There is no time to waste. And Jason is stronger than you know." He turned his eyes back to Jason. "He's shown me that over the last few days." He shook his head. "I'm sorry to ask this of you. But there is a chance you can help her. I do not think that we can risk waiting even a few hours."

Jason turned to Rowan, standing so his back was to me, and dropped his voice to a low tone I could barely hear. "I want to do this," he told Rowan. "But you have to help me. I...I can't be trusted. I'm dangerous. I don't know how to control this yet. I don't want to hurt her—you know I would never want that. But I'm afraid of what I might do if I lose control."

Rowan lay a heavy hand on Jason's shoulder. "Do not be afraid. Do you remember I told you, once you left my territory, the weight of my authority would fall from your shoulders? It happened just as I said it would, didn't it?"

"Yes," Jason answered.

"And then, as soon as you returned, you felt that weight return?"

"Yes," Jason said, his eyes clouding with confusion. "But I don't understand what that has to do with this..."

"Moments like this are the reason that my authority exists. Creatures like you and me...we cannot always be trusted." Rowan smiled, and in his expression I glimpsed his sympathy for Jason, and a burgeoning respect. "We are too powerful; there is too much we might do in a moment of carelessness or anger. I answer to the land; it checks my power. In turn, I exist to act as your protector, your guide, and to place a limit on your actions. I will help to ensure you do no harm, when you are not able to. I promise you." Jason lifted his eyes to Rowan's, surprised by the sudden fervency of Rowan's tone. "I would never let you harm her. Trust me, if you cannot trust yourself."

For a second, Jason just stared up at Rowan, and I saw the panic that glinted in his eyes lessen. He nodded once, and turned to me. "Let's try this, Amy. Quick, before I lose my nerve."

I wanted to protest that Jason was too tired. To tell him to rest, to take a shower. To convince him to at least let me heal the wounds that still lingered on his face and neck.

But Jason had called himself a monster. His fear of his own nature was so great he had been afraid to touch me. If I protested now, Jason wouldn't think I wanted him to rest, and take care of himself. He would think I feared him.

So instead of arguing, I walked toward him, keeping my steps slow and measured, just as I would have done with a patient who was new to the clinic, and wasn't used to a human's touch. I stood in front of him, so close that I could see his hands trembling. I wanted to throw my arms around him and promise him everything would be okay. Instead I looked deep into his eyes.

"I trust you," I told him softly, and held my arms out a little from my side, silently inviting him to do whatever he needed to do.

Jason looked over at Rowan, as though to reassure himself that Rowan was close enough to intercede if something went wrong. Could that be respect I saw growing between them? It certainly looked like it. Rowan came closer, positioning himself so he stood right at Jason's shoulder. Jason pulled the gauze, slowly, away from his hands.

"Okay," Jason said, his voice shaking. "I'm going to touch your face, Amy. All right?"

"Sure," I answered easily, but still Jason hesitated.

He lifted his hands toward me slowly, moving and then stopping before moving again, as though testing himself with every inch he moved closer. Finally, his fingers touched my temples, and his palms lay against my cheeks. His freezing fingers made me shiver. The hair on my arms and the back of my neck stood up.

"Are you all right?" he asked.

I smiled at him, willing him to feel how much I trusted him. "Of course I am," I started to say, but the end of my sentence was lost in a gasp of pain-filled surprise.

Tiny, sharp pains, like beestings, pierced my temple, right where Jason's fingers touched my skin. My whole body stiffened, my head snapping back as something like electrical current radiated through me. A buzzing sound filled my ears, making it impossible for me to understand the tense words Jason and Rowan began exchanging. Normally it would have bothered me to be left out of their conversation, but the sensations coursing through me were all I could think about. The stinging feeling started to change, and instead of pain, I felt a sweeping numbness course down my neck, spread across my chest. It seeped through my entire body. It was like being given a huge dose of Novocain. My limbs grew rigid, my arms stretching out at my sides, but that didn't bother me, either. The constant ache from the stitches in my chest disappeared. I felt relaxed. At ease.

"I can feel the curse," Jason cried, his voice echoing strangely in my ears.

Rowan said something, but all I could make out was the deep rumble of his voice. I didn't try to respond. A new feeling distracted me.

Something was pinching me.

Deep in my belly, something stirred.

Baxin had told me that the hellhound's curse was patient. That it would wait until it was at its full power to strike. But what if we did something, now, to rouse it?

A sensation started as discomfort and built steadily, second by second, into a bright and blistering pain.

I wanted to move away, but Jason's powers held me immobile. The curse knew what we were doing. It was starting to fight back.

But I couldn't speak.

My body grew still, stiff as a board. The pinching pain in my belly spread, radiating down my hips. Sharp, jabbing, red-hot flashes of pain shot down my legs, pooling in the bottoms of my feet. My breath grew ragged. A battle raged inside me. Jason's power pushed, and the curse held on. I realized in a sluggish, half-conscious sort of way, that the low, keening sound I could just hear over the buzzing in my ears was the sound of my own moaning.

Rowan held me up, or I would have fallen. He was calling to me, but I couldn't understand him. Time slowed down, each pained second feeling like an hour. Each breath I pulled in through my teeth took incredible effort as I tried to force my lungs to expand in a body locked into utter stillness.

I felt the moment when Jason's magic broke, shattering as the force of the curse pressed up against it, and won. The numbness that had filled my body suddenly gave way. In its place a tingling coursed through me. The pinching pain in my abdomen stopped as suddenly as it had started. I could move again. I gasped for air and struggled to feel my feet under me so I could stand without support. Oxygen and blood flooded my head. Suddenly my vision swam and tiny lights seemed to burst before my eyes.

"Asa?" Rowan cried, his voice loud and panicked, as though he was calling to me from across a great canyon.

"I'm all right," I answered, though I wasn't entirely sure it was true.

The tiny lights danced, coalescing into one, forming a bright, burning golden haze that clouded my vision, blocking everything else out.

"I may pass out for just a second here," I added, for the sake of honesty. And then my legs gave out beneath me, and the world was gone.

SIXTEEN

IT IS IMPOSSIBLE TO MEASURE DARKNESS, ONCE YOU HAVE FALLEN into it. Nothingness cannot be counted or quantified, or even felt at all. The world and everything in it is there...and then it simply is not. You aren't even present in the nothingness. You are just something that it once consumed. You can't fight it, because you are nothing, too. You can't grieve what you have lost; there is no one left to remember. There is only falling, and then, if you fall through darkness and back into life, you have to sit up, and remember, and try to find yourself again.

The first thing I felt was softness. Incredible softness, wrapped all around me, warm where it pressed against my face. It was dark, but I recognized it as a lesser, fainter kind of blackness than what had pressed against me just a moment ago. My eyes were closed— but I had no strength to push them open.

"You are all right now, my Asa." Rowan's voice thrummed in my ear. I felt his arms, pulling me tight against his chest. "Do not be frightened. I am here, holding you. I will not let you go."

Awareness crept back inch by uncertain inch. I could feel my legs, my arms. I could feel a slowly fading ache, deep inside my abdomen. My cheeks were wet, though I didn't remember crying. A soft, steady rhythm vibrated against my side.

Rowan was purring.

With a shudder of effort, I forced my eyes to crack open. He held me cradled in his arms, his face leaning down close to mine, his sky-blue eyes intent, waiting for me to waken. I stared up at him. For so many weeks he had avoided my gaze, always turning away, always putting up walls between us. But now, something had changed. The walls had fallen. I looked up into his eyes and, even without Truthsight, I could see right into his soul.

"You've been crying," I murmured. I reached up, my hand a little unsteady, and touched his cheek. The moisture on my face was not my tears, but his.

Rowan's arms tightened around me at the sound of my voice. Relief flashed hot in his eyes.

"I thought I was going to lose you," he said, his voice rough and strangely vulnerable.

"Lose me? Wait…what happened?" I tried to remember, and the effort made my head ache. All I could remember was darkness and pain.

"The curse fought back," Rowan answered with a grimace. "When Jason tried to remove it, it hurt you. Badly." He smoothed the hair from my forehead. His fingers were warm and rough when they brushed against my skin. "Your heart stopped beating."

"That…that's not possible." Any feeling of comfort I had felt in his arms evaporated, as I strained to remember. Cold shot through me. Could it be? Had I really come so close to death? My recently re-started heart began to hammer in my chest, as though trying to make up for the beats it had missed. Wasn't there supposed to be a bright light? A tunnel…a staircase? Something? Something other than a dark so deep and sudden that you don't feel it coming, and once it's left you, you can hardly even remember it was ever there? Shock rolled through me like a hard, icy wave, and my breath came short and ragged.

"You are all right now." Rowan's voice was warm and insistent in my ear, his breath hot against my cheek. "Do not be frightened. Jason tried, but he could not save you. So I brought you here, into the forest. Close to the earth, where my power is stronger. And I did the best I could."

For the first time, I looked away from the burning pull of his eyes, and gazed around us. We were outside, deep in the forest. The blue of the sky above was so dark that it was almost black, and the stars still shone. The moon stared down from above, silent and implacable. Above us, treetops waved, their forms green-tinted shadows in the dark. The press of winter air swirled all around. If Rowan's arms and fur had not encased me, I would have been shivering with cold. But the blue of the sky and green leaves above were not what caught my attention. I straightened up, pulling myself to sitting so I could stare around me.

"W...what did you do?" I gasped.

We sat on the grass in the middle of a small clearing—but all the grass beneath us had withered. Died. Gray, lifeless ground spread out all around us. We sat in the center of a circle of death that stretched for...my mind stuttered as I tried to guess...fifty feet in every direction? Where the clearing gave way to forest, the trees had died, and now towering evergreens stood gray and inert, their color drained from them as though they were cutouts from a black-and-white picture. Their branches drooped sorrowfully, shedding brown needles like tears. Hesitant, I reached out and brushed the ground with my fingertips. The gray grass broke and crumbled to dust at the barest touch.

"I pulled life from the earth, and siphoned it into you." Rowan's hand tightened on my shoulder, as though he feared I would slip away. "It was not enough to cure the curse. But it pulled you back from the brink."

"I…I'm so sorry," I gasped. Rowan was the land's protector. His own life force was rooted in it. What had doing this cost him?

But Rowan only shook his head. "Do not be sorry, my Asa. I would have done much worse than this, to preserve your life. The ground will recover. New trees will grow. You…you are irreplaceable. Worth any sacrifice this world can give."

"But won't the Earthchild be angry with you?"

"The Earthchild is linked to me." Rowan brushed a hand against his chest. "It knows how badly I needed to heal you. It will not begrudge me this. Please, Asa. Don't worry about anything right now. Let yourself rest."

I wanted to argue…but I was so tired, and I found myself sinking back into his arms. Once I had lain back, it was easy to let my worry slip away. His warmth seeped into me, and I felt more at peace than I had for a long time.

I remembered this. The way our bodies seemed to fit together so perfectly, one against the other. His smell: fresh grass and wood-smoke. His fur was thicker than the last time I had nestled against him, in what felt like another lifetime. I let my fingers run through the thick gray and silver hairs.

"You've grown a winter coat," I observed, and Rowan chuckled.

"Yes. I would not last long here without one. Though I must admit, I've come to like the cold."

"Really?" I could feel his skin, like warm velvet, just beneath his fur. "Why?"

"The cold makes everything clearer. Crystallized. You can see things you couldn't see before. The frost on the ground. Your own breath in the air. Even the birds are easier to see in the trees, once the leaves have fallen. When the water has frozen solid, lakes and creeks that used to be barriers become their own kind of pathway."

"Pretty slippery paths," I laughed, craning my head around to see his answering smile.

"Yes," Rowan conceded, his lips twisting up at the corners. "But they are pathways none the less."

We fell silent then, and after a minute his chest began to vibrate again, with a satisfied, thrumming purr. I rested my ear against his chest, relishing the thrum of his heartbeat, the steady rise and fall of his chest. After a while I reached up to touch his cheek. He leaned his face into my hand, nuzzling my palm as he sighed deeply. Longing and regret in equal portions swelled inside me. It was lovely to be held. To feel wanted. To luxuriate in his touch. But he could never be mine...not now. It was best to remember that, and save myself what pain I could. I forced myself to pull my hand away from his face.

"I'm sorry," I whispered.

He stilled.

"For what?"

"That we missed our chance. It's for the best. I know that now." I tried to force some false brightness into my words, but couldn't make it stick. "Still, a part of me wishes..." I let the words trail off.

"Wishes what?" Rowan's nose wrinkled in genuine confusion, and despite the sadness that pierced my heart, I almost laughed at his expression. He looked as though he were about to sneeze.

"That we could have been together," I admitted, ignoring the burn in my cheeks. "It seemed, for a little while there, that things might work out for us. I would have liked that."

"You don't mean that." Rowan's eyes clouded. "Not really. You are a healer, Asa. A gentle spirit who delights in making those who are broken whole again. I am a savage." His words dripped with bitterness. "You could never have paired yourself with me."

"You're wrong," I told him, sitting up. Rowan began to turn his face away, and I dared to grab his chin and force him to look back at me. "First of all, you aren't a savage. I know you. You aren't some rampaging beast. You don't take pleasure in violence for its own sake. You are a protector—and, yes, a fierce protector at times. You use your strength, your magic, everything you have, to safeguard the ones you care about. That is nothing to be ashamed of."

"You only say that because you do not understand."

"Don't tell me what I do or don't understand," I shot back.

His eyebrows climbed a little at the flare of anger in my voice. That suited me just fine, if it surprised him out of his moroseness.

"Believe me, Rowan, I do understand. I've seen so much as a doctor, not just for the creatures that come to my clinic, but for humans, too. I know the damage that cruelty can do to the innocent. The shattered bones, the deep cuts. The horrible, irreparable injuries that I've had to try to somehow piece back together. Wounds given out of viciousness, to those who couldn't protect themselves."

I swallowed hard against the lump in my throat. It took a moment before I could get words out. "I *know* what brutality looks like; I've seen it in the ER a thousand times." I laid my hand against his chest. "And it doesn't look like you. Your anger is on *behalf* of the innocent. Your temper is what makes it impossible for you to sit by, idle, while someone you could protect is suffering. That isn't something to be ashamed of. It's something beautiful. Noble, even."

"Asa." Rowan rubbed his eyes, his expression pained. "You see only what you want to see. You refuse to see the parts of me that are dark and broken. Dangerous."

"Wrong again," I told him. "I see you. But sometimes I'm not so sure you really see me. At least not all of me. Do you really think I'm any different than you?" I demanded. "I've done things that have made everyone who used to be my family wish I were dead. I lost my parents, and my home."

I didn't expect him to answer, but I paused anyway. I had to. The memories were too vivid, too painful. Seeing the stubbornness lingering in Rowan's eyes, I steeled myself against the memories and went on. "I spent so many years hating myself that when the mages came to kill me, I walked out to meet them. I was almost grateful to them. I know all about darkness and being broken. But at my core, I'm a fighter. Like you."

The incredulous expression on his face made me shake my head. I poked him in the chest with a finger. "What? You don't believe me? I fight disease. Infection. Death. I stand in the doorway between the light and the dark, and try to hold life in. We aren't as different as you think we are." I took a deep breath. "If things were different, I'd argue more with you. I'd...fight for you. If it's true you cut off contact with me because you didn't trust yourself..."

"It is true." There was such heat in Rowan's voice. His words were at once wonderful to hear, and exquisitely painful. I kept my eyes down, avoiding his gaze.

"Well, then. Like I said, if things were different, I'd fight to make you understand. It's okay to be broken, Rowan. Because our broken pieces fit. Like this." I laced my fingers through his, and enfolded his hand with my own.

"You can't mean that."

"I do. But it's too late for us. I'm sorry." I let go of his hand and I rubbed the heels of my hands over my eyes. "I shouldn't have said anything."

Rowan didn't move, didn't speak. He held himself still as a statue, staring at me with a searching gaze that I did not want to meet. When he finally spoke again, his voice was a whisper.

"Then...why?" he asked at last. "Why is it too late?"

"You know why, Rowan." I rubbed my hands together, trying to warm them. Without Rowan's fur to shield me, the cold was difficult to bear. "Because leshies mate for life, and I've got a death curse swelling inside me. We can't be together now—not when it would mean you would be alone forever after I was gone. I could never do that to you."

"Asa." Rowan's voice was rough. "Asa, look at me." Reluctant, I turned my eyes to his. His face was pale. When he spoke, he sounded out of breath. "I have chosen you for my mate already," he choked out.

"No." I held up my hands, pushing him away. "You haven't. That's not possible. Don't talk like that, Rowan! Don't even say it. It isn't too late for you to pick someone else after I am gone. You're going to live a happy, full life, after all of this is over. We've never been...together. You haven't chosen me. That isn't true."

"It is true." He stretched out his hand, but I stood up, my heart pounding, filled with an irrational desire to run away. He reached out and caught my hand in his. "Asa. Listen to me, please. It is true that our bond is not complete—because you have not accepted it. But my choice is made. It has been made, since almost the day I met you. I will never choose another."

"No," I said again, though I was close to shouting. "Undo it. This isn't right, Rowan. I'm dying. I don't want you to be alone for the rest of your life." My voice broke, tears welling up no matter how hard I tried to blink them back. "You can't tie yourself to me!"

"It is already done." He rose to stand in front of me. "I am yours. I have been, for a long time. I stayed away—all those weeks —because I believed you would reject me when you knew my nature. I didn't want to tell you what I really was. I was not strong enough to watch the love die in your eyes. It was easier for me to stay away. I was a coward. Forgive me."

"Oh, God." I turned away from him and hid my face in my hands. "What have we done?"

"Don't cry, Asa. Please." Rowan lay his hands on my shoulders, pulling me against him. "Don't grieve. No one knows how much time they will be given, and loving someone is always the gravest kind of risk. I do not regret loving you, and I never will. No matter what the future holds, or what the past seemed to promise. You have already given me so much."

"What have I given you?" I demanded, spinning around, not

caring that he could see the tears coursing down my face. "What have I *ever* given you, Rowan, but heartache and injury?"

"You gave me your trust," Rowan crooned, his eyes soft, his voice full of wonder. "When I did not even trust myself. You looked at me and saw someone you would want to link your life to. I don't know what I did to earn that faith. But I swear to you, Asa, I will spend the rest of my life endeavoring to be worthy of it."

"But we've lost all this time!" I wailed. "If you had told me why you were pulling away, or if I had marched into the forest and *forced* you to really talk to me...we might have at least had these last few weeks. At least a little bit of time when we could have actually been together. Now..."

"Now we have today," Rowan growled. "Let us make the most of it, and waste no more time with regret."

I started to respond but he cut off my words by pressing his lips to mine. His arms wrapped tight around my waist, one of his hands clutching the back of my shirt while the other reached into my hair. After a second of surprise, warmth blossomed inside me. I leaned into him, standing on tiptoe so I could wrap my arms around his neck while his hands slipped under my shirt. I didn't even notice when, a few minutes later, he lowered me to the ground. I was too busy letting my hands explore the hard curves of his chest, finding the places where his fur thinned and gave way to rough, warm skin.

"You are certain?" he asked, a while later, his voice a little breathless. "This will change everything."

"Yes," I murmured. "I'm not afraid. Life is change, Rowan. I want it. And I want you."

And then his hands were everywhere, and his mouth was everywhere; the lifeless grass and fallen leaves were softer than a blanket beneath me.

Loss and uncertainty were all around us, and the moon still hung, ominous, in the sky. But as I pressed myself tighter against him, snow began to fall. Light and gentle, it melted where it fell against our bare skin, and seemed to glow as it caught and held the moon's light. The dark seemed lighter, and night birds began to call, their voices wise and ancient. Something almost triumphant sounded in their song.

And when I cried Rowan's name out into the night, it didn't matter what the future held, or what darkness swirled around us. Together, we were light and love. Together, we were alive.

SEVENTEEN

WE DIDN'T SLEEP; TIME FELT TOO PRECIOUS AND FLEETING FOR that. Instead we lay together, intertwined, and watched as the stars faded and the sun rose. The sky lightened to a muted blue-gray, and the snow stopped falling, leaving only a few slight patches of whiteness here and there on the ground.

The air felt different. Charged, somehow; colder and sharper against my skin. I snuggled deeper into Rowan's arms. He sighed contentedly, his fingers twining in my hair.

"Are you well, my Asa?" he asked gently. "Are you too cold?"

I leaned my head against his chest and smiled up at him. "I feel wonderful," I told him, and he smiled back.

"Are you hungry?" he asked. "If you would like, I could get something for us."

"I'd like to say no," I told him, reaching up to run my fingers across the rugged bristle of his cheeks. "In fact, I'd like to stay here, tangled up with you, just like this, forever."

"And yet..." he prompted, obviously hearing the "but" coming in my words.

"But I'm starving!" I admitted with a laugh. "I guess almost dying can do that to a person."

Rowan bent closer to me, nuzzling my neck and breathing in deeply, as though he wanted to take my scent so deeply into himself that he could never forget it.

"I will fetch us some food," he said.

He stood, and I lay back, drinking him in with my eyes while he retrieved his trousers and strapped his weapon across his back. He crouched down beside me and leaned in for a final kiss.

"I will not be gone for long," he said, his words a caress. Then he rose and loped off into the trees.

Without Rowan's arms to warm me, the chill pressed, biting, into my skin. I dressed quickly and settled back onto the ground. Soon I found that, in the harsh light of day and without the happy glow that came with Rowan's company, the withered circle of dead grass and trees felt lonesome and foreboding. I stood, yawned luxuriously, and hurried over to the shelter of the trees.

The circle was wide, but I walked quickly and soon came upon a wide tree, the ground beneath it smooth and moss-covered. I sat down and leaned my back against its trunk. I felt deliciously relaxed, and when the sun pushed through the branches and made a patch of yellow on the smooth ground in front of me, I stretched out to my full length, relishing the sun's warmth like a cat on a windowsill. I rested my cheek against the dirt as though it were a pillow, spread my hands out against the earth, and shut my eyes.

I did not know how long I lay there, just that a deep feeling of contentment uncoiled from inside my belly and swept over me as I rested. A sound stirred me. I opened my eyes to see a snake in the grass, not too far away from me, slipping along the surface, weaving over the tree roots as it went on its way. I knew it was harmless, and watched it go, feeling a light breeze ruffle my disheveled hair. The earth warmed to my body, embracing it, more comfortable than a feather bed.

I let my mind wander, almost dozing. I thought of the dirt, of all the things within it. Everything within it, really. Because there is nothing that does not come to the earth, sooner or later. And there is nothing that does not come from within it. All the creatures in this wood that scurried here and there, hunting for food, for water, so busy and anxious and caught up in their needs...all would come here, eventually. I thought of how close I had come to death just the day before, but the thought didn't trouble me at all. I thought of it with only curiosity.

I thought of all the things that lived in the soil beneath me, all the lives that had been and then sank back into the warm and the brown, broken down and wiped away. Later, it did not really matter how much later, plants would sprout from the good, brown soil they had become. How beautiful those plants would be! How colorfully they would blossom, for a day or a month or a year. Then they, too, would return. Everything did. That did not seem so bad to me now. In fact, it was so true and so right that life should be that way.

Every life arching back to the earth that it came from—to this —the great brown womb of the world. All life pulled in, accepted, all differences ground away, everything one. No matter who we thought we were when we arrived, we were all together in the end. No matter who we thought we might become, we would all be welcomed home again, after a while. There was no sadness as I thought of this. There was only certitude. Serenity. I, too, would be accepted here. Loved. Pulled inward, wrapped up and hugged tight.

A slow, calm, feeling spread through me. A feeling that I was exactly where I was meant to be. I had never meant to be anywhere else. Never meant to *be* anything else. The simplicity of it all, the plain poetry of it, was achingly beautiful. But I felt no surprise or excitement. It seemed odd that there had ever been a time I had not realized it. I would never forget it again.

I sighed and sank deeper.

How pleasant it was to stop. To rest. What reason had there been for all the struggling? I couldn't quite remember anymore. Trying to call up the memory would have been so hard, required so much effort. Effort like that seemed silly to me now. I could feel some fresh, young grass as it pushed up slowly from the soil. How green and tender it was! How lovely! I could watch it for days, and be completely mesmerized. I would watch it grow tall, see it blow gently in the wind, and then reach out lovingly to it, when it grew old and gray, and ready to return to me.

"Asa?"

There was a buzzing in my ears. Did I have ears, after all? I couldn't remember.

Strange sounds interrupted me as I listened to the grass. I shifted, stretching out more comfortably. All I wanted was to lie here. But it seemed, now, almost, as though I had once wanted something else. What was it, again? Hard to concentrate, when I would so love to watch the earthworms that pushed so gently all around me.

"*Asa!* Wake up. *Pull away!*"

There was something to that, now. Something jogged in my mind. I loved that voice. It wanted me to open my eyes—but I did not remember having had them. Still, habit asserted itself.

My eyes fluttered.

Pain ripped through me—staggering, bewildering pain. Terror followed closely on its heels.

"What?" I mumbled, suddenly realizing I had lips, that I could speak.

But my mouth was full of dirt.

Panic stricken, I tried to pull back, pull away. Why was I doing that? Why did it hurt so much? I started to feel afraid. The serene calm vanished, replaced by a blind struggle against what I did not understand. I could hardly remember my name. I didn't know where I was. I was lying on the ground, surrounded on every side by walls of earth. Deep brown, beautiful walls. Instinct took over. I thrashed and pulled and strained away. The ground seemed to hold onto me, as though it didn't want to let me go. Even as I fought to free myself, I still longed to reach out and press myself against the dirt. The sun was far away; the ground beneath me had sunk so deep that I couldn't possibly climb out on my own. The walls themselves seemed to convulse around me, shuddering as though they could hardly contain themselves. At any moment they would wrap around me, bringing me back in, as though in an embrace.

A hand was thrust down toward me, and the voice called out to me again.

"Take my hand! Climb!"

Without thinking, I reached out and grasped it, surprised to see that doing so smeared it with blood. The hand pulled and yanked at me, and I scrambled ineffectively, not sure whether I kicked my feet in an effort to find some leverage on the smooth sides of the hole, or to pull away and return to the bottom.

And then I was sprawled on the grass, looking up at Rowan, his eyes wild and frenzied as he stared down at me in horror.

"Rowan?" I choked out.

Confusion rushed in on me, along with the consciousness of pain. I reached up to touch my cheek. Where I had rested my face on the ground, the flesh had been torn away. Blood trickled down my neck. Both my palms, too, were ravaged and gory. Rowan swept me up in his arms, collapsing on the ground as he held me to him, ignoring the smears of blood that covered his chest and his hands.

"My Asa!" he choked out. "What were you thinking? Look!" He stared with wide, haunted eyes over my shoulder and I turned to see. "You have made yourself a grave!"

Then I saw.

Where I had lain down on the earth only hours, or maybe moments, before, the soil had sunk, caved in, forming a deep hole on the ground's surface. I was covered in mud and blood, and the earth had begun to collapse in, on top of me. I had felt nothing. Even now, I was too dazed to feel anything but pain.

Pain of so many kinds welled up inside me, and the strongest was grief. A feeling of loss so intense that, though I could not understand why I did it, I pulled away from Rowan's embrace and leaned over so that I could spread my bloody palms out lovingly on the ground.

"But, Rowan," I cried, my head pounding with confusion, tears stinging my ravaged cheek. "But it loves me so much!"

EIGHTEEN

ROWAN HELD ME IN HIS ARMS, EXCLAIMING OVER MY INJURIES. I couldn't think of how to respond. Shock clung to me like a thick woolen blanket, muting the world to a dull haze.

"You must heal yourself, Asa," Rowan urged me, though my eyes would not quite focus in on his face. "Simply sending power from the earth into your body will not heal these wounds —they are too complex. You must use your Truthsight to mend them."

He tried in vain to stop the blood that still leaked from the wound on my face. But the worst part of waking wasn't the blood, or the wounds, or realizing just how close I had come to dying. Again.

The worst part was having to be afraid.

I had worked so hard not to feel the fear. Ever since the curse had struck me, I had refused to let the raw emotions surface. I had drawn thick borders around the corners of my heart, and insisted that my fear stay deep and hidden. There had been no other way to keep functioning, and I had so very much to do. I couldn't let myself feel, and even if I could, what good could possibly come from it? Fearing death would not make it any less likely to find me. Mourning over the shortness of my days would only spoil the little time that I did have left.

I didn't stop to think that the emotions might someday have to surface, and that pushing them down and ignoring them might force them to fester and rot.

When Rowan pulled me out of the earth, the serenity it had offered me was ripped away. All the borders in my heart fell. Now I felt it all: fear and grief and dread. Panic, like a hand slowly closing, tighter and tighter, around my throat.

I tried to speak, but my mouth was too dry, my throat too sore. The words came out as a faint whisper.

"What is it, Asa?" Rowan asked anxiously, crouching closer and moving so that his ear was right by my mouth."

"Peaceful," I sighed. "In the earth, it was so peaceful. And now..."

"I know." Rowan's hands tightened on my shoulders. "Believe me, Asa. I know the loss you feel right now. But you must fight back against it. Heal yourself." Panic leaked into his eyes. "You are losing too much blood."

I nodded jerkily, turning away from him a little as I called my Truthsight forward and fell into it like a rock into a stream.

When I opened my eyes, I knew something was different. The Source was close by, a river of molten silver that coursed along, shining and bubbling as it went. But usually Truthsight transformed me more fully. Looking down at myself, I realized I was still dressed in my jeans and bloody tee-shirt. Although my skin was the silver bark of a weeping willow tree, I couldn't feel any roots stretching beneath the surface. Too weak to stand, I crawled on all fours toward the Source, realizing as I did so how terribly thirsty I was. My throat felt like sandpaper, and it seemed to take me hours to reach the water's edge. I sank down onto my stomach and reached out. The flow of water slowed, as though the Source sensed my closeness and understood my need. A small eddy formed just below my outstretched palm.

The water rose to greet me, a small fountain forming as it jumped up to fill my cupped hands. The silver water was a shock of cold against my skin, but after an instant of discomfort the sensation was immeasurably soothing. Wherever the water touched, my skin mended itself, smoothing over the wretched, bloody patches of missing flesh. The pain melted away.

Moments later I was strong enough to move closer and lower my face into the water. I splashed it on my cheeks, cupped my hands and poured it over my hair. When I finally rose, I stood steady on my feet. Silver dripped from my hair and trickled down my neck. I took a deep breath, and a renewed sense of purpose filled me. I still had a limited amount of time, and so many things that I wanted to do.

I looked down at the water's constantly moving, silver surface and smiled.

"Thank you," I whispered to it. The river laughed gently and continued on its way.

NINETEEN

"I'M ALL RIGHT. REALLY," I PROMISED ROWAN YET AGAIN. BUT THE words did no more to reassure him this time than the previous three times I had said them.

"You can't imagine what I felt," he murmured, his eyes clouded, "when I saw you down there, partially covered in earth. Not moving."

"I'm sorry," I said, also not for the first time. "I still don't understand what happened."

Rowan had brought me food just as he had promised, and refused to answer any of my questions until I had eaten something. He seemed to need to constantly reassure himself that I was really all right. He touched my shoulder, my back. He cupped his hand around my chin and stared anxiously into my eyes.

"I wish I understood and could explain it to you," he finally told me, when he seemed confident that I wasn't on the verge of collapse. "I have never heard of an earth spirit doing such a thing." He shook his head. "I knew the Earthchild was confused. Disoriented after so long spent slumbering, and by the way the world has changed. But it is even worse than I feared."

"What do you mean?"

"Though the Earthchild can be hurt and feel pain, a state of stasis, like the one it had fallen into before I came here, is as close to death as it will ever come. I think it is…confused about you. It is happy we bonded, and wanted to welcome you. To pull you closer to it."

"And it didn't realize doing that would hurt me," I finished the thought, and Rowan nodded.

"I knew that life and death do not mean the same thing to the child as it does to us mortal creatures. It sees life more as a continuous cycle, like the ebb and flow of the tide." Rowan spread his hands. "It is natural that, now our bond is solidified, the Earthchild would want to reach out to you. But to do something like this? Endanger your life?"

I forced a smile I didn't really feel. "I'm sure you can help the Earthchild understand," I told Rowan. "But for now, we should go." I stood up. "When you ran off, there was no knowing if I was going to make it or not. Jason must be out of his mind with worry. And I want to check on the man he rescued from the nymphs."

Wordlessly Rowan glided to his feet and reached out to enclose my hand with his. We walked, our shoulders brushing against each other, not speaking, but our fingers wound together, tight.

As we walked, I tried to brace myself for what we might find when we got to the clinic. I knew perfectly well that the unconscious man's condition might have worsened during the night. A small, fearful voice deep inside me whispered that perhaps the man that Jason had rescued had already died, the small light that burned inside him too weak to have lasted…and I had not been there to help. When the barn came into view, I saw that the door had been left open.

Jason stood in the doorway, his arms folded tight across his chest. Even from a distance I could see the tension that held his back rigid and his head ramrod straight. He was turned a little to the side, gazing out at the tree line. Watching. We were approaching from the opposite direction, so he didn't see us right away. I saw the exact moment when our movement caught his attention. His eyes snapped toward us and he stared at me, frozen. Then his whole body sagged with relief, and he braced a hand against the door frame to steady himself. He hung his head, and it wasn't until we were just a few feet away from him that he straightened and walked forward to meet us.

"Amy." His face was paler than I had ever seen it. "Thank God. I have never been happier to see anyone in my entire life."

He reached out for me—his hands cocooned in fresh gauze—and with extreme care, wrapped his arms around me in an embrace so gentle and tentative I could barely feel it. I wasn't sure if he took such care because, despite the wrap around his hands, he was still afraid of touching me, or because my near-death experience had left him with the impression I was fragile as glass.

He looked up at Rowan, his eyes wide and red. "Thank you," he said, his voice rough with emotion. "For saving her when I couldn't."

"We both did all that we were able," Rowan told him. "And it still has not been enough to undo the harm the curse is doing to her."

That seemed like a dangerous conversation to launch into, so I broke in and changed the subject before Jason could respond.

"How is our patient doing?" I asked, and from his expression I knew the answer would not be good.

"He's slipping away," Jason answered, his voice dropping. "I think the strain on his body has just been too much. His heart rate is slowing, and his breathing is shallow. He's losing body temperature no matter how I try to warm him. He opened his eyes, but he's completely unresponsive. I've done everything I can think of. But I don't think we can save him." Jason swallowed hard. "All of this happened because of me. It's my fault."

Rowan spoke first. "The blame for this does not lie with you. You are just as much a victim as he is. You had no idea what had been done, and once you discovered the truth, you risked your life to give your brother a chance at survival."

"He's not my brother!" Jason choked. "Didn't you listen to any of the things I said? I'm an impostor. I stole his life!"

"You may not share blood with this man, but there is no denying that your lives are linked. The parents who gave birth to him raised you. You have risked your life to save his. Clearly, your lives are bound up with each other. That is as close to family as most will ever come."

"But all of my medical training, everything I know"—Jason ran a hand over his face—"after everything we went through to get him out of there. I ought to be able to save him."

A gravelly voice from a few feet away answered him before I could.

"That's no fault of yours, son," Baxin said. "There's not much that can undo the kind of harm that's been done to that one."

Jason and I both startled, and spun to see Baxin comfortably settled, his legs crossed and a smoking pipe in his hand, leaning against the side of the barn. I blinked rapidly, trying to figure out how I could have possibly missed seeing him up until now. He was sitting in plain sight. A cloud of smoke hovered above him, the smell of it in the air so strong it tickled my nose. But a second ago there had been no trace of him. I glanced at Rowan, my eyes narrowing in suspicion. He had not seemed at all shocked by Baxin's sudden appearance. Had he been able to see through whatever power Baxin had been using to hide from our sight, but refrained from giving the old gnome away before he decided to reveal himself?

"Who is that?" Jason exclaimed.

"Baxin?" I cried out, "What are you doing here?"

"Waiting for Lord Rowan to return," Baxin answered, none of the usual levity in his voice. He tapped his pipe out on the ground and got heavily to his feet. "What I've got to say concerns him, too."

"What do you mean?" I glanced back and forth between him and Rowan, but Rowan's forehead was wrinkled with confusion. He seemed to have no more idea what the old gnome wanted than I did.

"First things first," Baxin said, as he tucked his pipe into an empty belt loop. "Let me see the boy."

"The boy?" I answered, not understanding, but Jason immediately realized what Baxin meant, and he moved to block the door of the barn with his body.

"Why do you want to see him?" Jason demanded, his voice full of suspicion.

They'd never met before, so I had to be sure to handle this carefully.

"Do you think I mean him harm, lad?" Baxin asked, his eyes softening, "What harm do you think I would want to do him, heh?"

"Jason, it's all right." I put my hand on his arm. His whole body hummed with tension. "Baxin is a friend."

Jason hesitated before giving a sharp nod, but even as he moved aside and let Baxin enter, his eyes stayed riveted on the gnome, tracking his every move.

Baxin walked into the clinic and, without bothering to ask for permission, he dragged a chair over to the scarred man's bedside. Climbing up onto the chair, Baxin studied the man's vacant eyes, slack expression, and the painfully slow rise and fall of his chest. Baxin nodded, as though finding something exactly the way that he had expected to. He touched the scarred man's forearm, his eyes narrowing in an expression of extreme concentration.

"What is it?" I stepped closer, but Baxin gestured at me to be quiet. Unused to being shushed in my own clinic, I waited impatiently, shifting my weight from one foot to the other until Baxin turned around.

"Ya can't save 'im." Baxin gave a bitter shake of his head. "He's lost too much of his life to those creatures. Why, they've nearly drained him dry. You've done everything that can be done for his body. But the worst of the harm wasn't done to his body; it was done to his soul. That's what they needed—what they took their strength from. He hasn't much time left, now."

"You're wrong," Jason said, his face flushing. "There's no way you can possibly know that."

Baxin held up his hands. "Calm down, lad. I know it isn't what you want to hear. Let me say my piece. What I'm telling you is true; I've seen this before. That's how I know. You think that pod of yours is the first one to ever go rogue? Did ya think humans are the only ones they ever prey on?" Baxin tsked and shook his head. "We gnomes are their favorite victims. We live longer than humans. Some of us much longer." A cloud passed over Baxin's face, and his voice hitched for a second, but he kept going. "I've seen others like him—snatched away from the nymph's grasp. And let me tell you, we learned the same lesson you're learning now. Hurt to your body, that's one thing. But harm to your soul… there's no quick fix for that. No medicine or magic in this world can simply undo what's been done to this poor boy. But souls have their own kind of magic." Baxin smiled a little. "Souls heal. They thirst for life. They fight for it, long after the body has given up and the mind has turned away. He's still in there. And if you don't think he's fighting tooth and nail for every breath he takes, then you aren't really paying attention. What's his name?"

Jason blinked.

"I…I don't know," he stammered, "I'm not sure that he has one."

Baxin grunted. "Well, he'll need one soon enough if we are going to do this."

"Do what?" Jason asked, looking as lost as I felt.

"Save him, of course," Baxin exclaimed. "Haven't you been paying attention?"

"You just told us we couldn't save him!" I broke in. Baxin sighed and shook his head at my slowness.

"I said *you* can't save him, child. But I can. I've seen this before, and I know what needs doing to keep this boy alive."

"Well, what are we waiting for?" Jason cried, sudden hope lighting his eyes. "Whatever he needs, we don't have time to waste. He's getting weaker every second!"

"Keep your britches on," Baxin snapped. "You still aren't listening. And as yer about to make one of the most important decisions of your life, I suggest you calm yourself down, and mind what I say."

Jason stilled, staring at Baxin with confusion.

"First thing ya need to know. This only happens if Lord Rowan says he'll allow it." He looked over to where Rowan stood, watching the whole encounter with eagle eyes. "What I'm about to offer...well, some would think of it as a blessing, others a curse. Either way, I've got no intention of angering the Lord of the Land and getting tossed out on my ear. I like it here. I'm awfully fond of my burrow. I spent decades hollowing it out and getting the dimensions just right. So, if he says he won't let this happen in his territory, then this is all over before it's begun, and that's all there is to it."

Rowan's eyes narrowed. "You offer a bargain?" he asked, and Baxin bobbed his head.

"Could another pay its price?"

Baxin grimaced. "It's got to be this one," he replied, jerking his head in Jason's direction, "You said it right before. Their lives are already jumbled up together. He's the only one who can do what needs doing."

Rowan nodded, as though Baxin's answer did not surprise him. "Then tell Jason how your bargain would work," he ordered.

Baxin nodded and hopped down off his chair to step closer to Jason.

"All right, son." He folded his hands in front of him. "Now we come to the hard part. The first thing you've got to know, is that everything in this world comes at a price. I'd apologize for it, but it's the way the world has built itself, and really no fault of mine. You say you want to save this man. Now you have to decide how much you're willing to sacrifice to make that happen."

Jason swallowed. "I don't understand."

"I may be able help you save his life," Baxin explained. "But the cost will be twofold. One price you pay to me, for my help. The other price you pay to the universe. The universe has rules, its own way of doing things. Now, it is possible to get around those rules. To bend them. But the universe takes notice, and it demands a cost. Do you understand?"

"Not really," Jason said. "What would I owe? If you helped us?"

Baxin rocked back on his heels. "To me, you'd owe one service." He held up a finger. "A single service of anything I ask that is within your power to do, at a time and place of my choosing."

"What does that even mean?" Jason asked. "What kind of service?"

Baxin shook his head sharply. "Sorry, son, but that isn't how this works. You agree to provide me the service, and I tell you what it is when the time is right. It'll be of equal weight and cost to what I offer—which means what I ask of you won't be easy for you to give." Jason started to protest, but Baxin held up his hands to silence him. "The second price is not of my making, so don't blame me if you don't like it. You see, this man's life force has been drained away. We can't replenish it, at least not fast enough to save him. The only thing we can do is link him to the life force of somebody else. You see what I'm saying? We can bind his life force with yours. Like this." Baxin clapped his two hands together and interwove his fingers. "Like hitchin' a wagon to a horse."

For a moment, we were all perfectly silent.

"What is the price of that?" I asked, though I had a terrible, sneaking suspicion.

"Oh," Baxin answered quietly, with a nod in Jason's direction. "I think our young man has already guessed. We bind your life force to his. Interweave your fates. And that'll mean you and he'll share the same fate. Forever."

"The same fate?"

"Aye. It's like re-aligning your stars. His fate becomes your fate, and your fate becomes his. If one of you dies..." Baxin shrugged. "Then that's the end, for both of you."

"Wait," I said anxiously. "What if you do this thing, and bind their lives together, but it isn't enough to save this man? What if he dies anyway?"

Baxin looked up at me helplessly. "Once it's done, it can't be undone," he said. "For better or for worse, their lives'll be linked. If one of them doesn't make it, then neither of them will."

"This is crazy," I sputtered, and Rowan stepped forward to address Jason.

"I will not forbid this," he said, his face solemn. "I will let the choice be yours. But know that you do not have to agree to this. The misfortune that has befallen this man is not of your doing. You do not owe him your life."

"What other choice do I have?" Jason's face was pale and drawn. "I can't do nothing, and just watch while he fades away. How could I ever face my mother? How could I tell her she had another son, and I had a chance to save his life, but didn't think it was worth the risk?"

"Wait a minute," I said, my heart pounding. "We have to think about this from every angle. Jason, I understand you want to do everything you can. But what Baxin is suggesting is radical. Dangerous. It's like trying some kind of experimental surgery, that will have lifelong consequences, even if it is successful. Do we even have the right to attempt it without getting this man's consent?"

"If you want to know what the lad thinks about all this," Baxin called out, "I suggest you ask him."

We all spun around. Before, the scarred man's eyes had been

open but vacant. Now his eyes were clear, focused. Closely tracking everyone in the room.

He stared at us, and for a long moment, we stood frozen, staring back.

Jason took a hesitant step forward. "Hi," he said, his voice painfully uncertain.

The scarred man's eyes snapped to Jason's face. "I remember you," he said, his voice weak but clear. "Thank you. For getting me out."

We all moved to stand around him, Baxin stroking his beard as he studied the man.

"Have ya got a name, son?" Baxin asked, and the man grimaced.

"No," he said, his lips pressing together. "To the nymphs, we were just food. None of the humans that they kept to feed off were allowed to have names. As far as they were concerned, we didn't need them."

"Did ya hear what we were talking about?"

He swallowed hard, and nodded.

"And what do you have to say about it?" Baxin prodded.

"Any chance is better than no chance at all," the man answered. Emotion flashed across his face, making his cheeks flush and his eyes flash. "I want to live," he said, his voice gaining volume and strength. "I want to live, despite everything they did to me. And, someday, I want to make them pay for every day they took from me. For every single moment that they stole."

For a minute, no one spoke. Then Jason straightened up, and stood a little taller.

"I'll do it," he declared. "I'm in." He turned to Baxin. "I'll pay your price, and any other price I have to." And in that moment, I didn't have the heart to try to change his mind.

TWENTY

AFTER THAT, BAXIN STARTED FIRING OFF A STRING OF ORDERS, AND we hurried to gather everything he needed. He told us to build a bonfire outside, as big as we could manage.

"We're changing their fates, you see," he explained to me. "Aligning their stars. We have to do it out where the stars can see us."

I peered up at the night sky uncertainly. Heavy clouds were gathered above us. Not a single star was visible. Even the moon was little more than a vague smudge of luminescence behind the gray-white haze. But I didn't argue with Baxin.

It took almost an hour to move everything Baxin said he needed to the grass outside the clinic, and get the bonfire started. The sun was starting to set, and the air grew even colder. Outside the clinic doors, the spear the Earthchild had made for me was still firmly planted in the ground. It had started growing short, thin branches. Tiny buds were pushing their way out of the bark. We carried two cots out of the barn and set them next to each other in front of the bonfire. Rowan carried the scarred man out of the clinic in his arms, and gently settled him onto one of the cots. Jason sat down on the edge of the other, face pale, his fingers picking at his sleeve.

Baxin settled himself between the two cots. He had a bag slung over his shoulder, and now he opened it, spreading a variety of items out on the ground, humming as he got his supplies in order. I went over to the scarred man, crouching down and leaning close to him to check his heart beat. Jason was right—it was slower.

"I recognize your voice," the man said to me, and I looked at him in surprise. "I couldn't place it at first." He leaned his head back and closed his eyes. "You were the one who was there. In the darkness. Talking to me."

"You were able to hear me?" I asked in surprise, and the man nodded.

"You said I had a light, burning inside me." He cracked his eyes open to look at me. "Do you really think that's true?"

I found his hand, lying limply on the cot beside him, and squeezed his fingers. "I know it's true," I told him, and he flashed a weak smile in return.

"All right, everyone," Baxin called. "Let's get down to business. Jason, stop sitting on the edge of your cot like you're about to take off and run into the woods. Put yer feet up, boy. Try to at least look like you trust me a little."

After a second of hesitation, Jason swung his feet up onto the cot and leaned back gingerly.

Behind them the bonfire was a tower of flame. The smell of smoke and burning wood filled the air. Baxin picked up his bag and took out a small bundle of herbs, a braided cord, and a piece of parchment and an old style ink pen. He also set out several vials, what looked like a long metal nail, and two small flasks.

"What happens now?" Jason asked.

"Both of you roll up your sleeves and give me your arms," Baxin said.

Jason and his brother did as he said. Jason's brother sweated freely, the heat from the fire making his face flush bright red.

Baxin took Jason's right arm and his brother's left arm. He rested them, side by side, on a small table he had put between the cots. He took the braided cord of rope and loosely tied their wrists together. Then he picked up one of his flasks.

"This here is powerful stuff," he said, a mischievous glint in his eye. "It won't fix all your problems. But it'll make sure you don't worry about them too much for a little while." He laughed and held the flask to Jason's lips. "Drink up, son," he said. "You're going to need it."

Jason leaned forward and took several long gulps. Then Baxin offered the flask to Jason's brother.

"Wait a minute." I darted forward. "He's pretty weak. I'm not sure that's a good idea."

Baxin waved a dismissive hand. "Don't worry so much, healer. It's all a part of the magic."

I looked at Rowan, my eyebrows raised, and Rowan lifted his hands. Jason's brother drank, Baxin coaxing him to take a longer drink when he pulled back from the flask with a grimace. Then Baxin brought the flask to his own lips, and drained it.

"Part of the magic, huh?" I commented darkly, and Baxin grinned.

"Now," he said, sitting and pulling the parchment closer. "Jason, I need your name. Your full, true name."

Baxin hadn't been lying about whatever had been in that flask. Jason's eyes were foggy and his voice relaxed when he answered.

"Jason Brandon Falk," he said dreamily.

Baxin nodded and carefully wrote the name. Then he turned to Jason's brother, who was also clearly feeling the effects of the drink. His eyes glinted bright in the firelight as he met Baxin's gaze.

"Now, lad," Baxin said, "I know you told us you didn't have a name. But there must be something that they called you."

Jason's brother smiled bitterly.

"They called me 'meat,'" he said, "Or sometimes 'slave.'"

Baxin's teeth ground together, and I saw stark anger flash across his face. But when he spoke his voice was calm and soothing.

"Well, you are neither of those things any longer, son. You get to pick a name for yourself now. How would you like to be known?"

Jason's brother leaned his head back. For a second he looked utterly bewildered. Then he laughed a little to himself.

"Flint," he said, his eyes darting over to me with a smile. "Call me Flint."

"Ahhh," Baxin said, leaning over to write the name with a flourish. "Now that's a proper name. A strong name, for a strong young man who's about to beat the odds."

He was done with the parchment now, and he picked it up and tied it tightly to his bundle of herbs. He stood, and looked over at Rowan and me.

"It is very important," he said, "that from now, until I am finished, no one speaks to me. Whisper to each other, if ya need to, but don't disturb me. The image isn't one of my choosing. It'll come, but I've got to hearken to it. If I lose hold of it, or put it down wrong, then the bond won't be strong enough to hold 'em."

"What image?" I started to ask, but then shook my head. We didn't have time to waste with questions. Jason's brother—Flint— was too weak. "We understand," I said instead. Baxin looked over at Rowan, and for a second the mischievous grin I knew so well was back on his face.

"Not that our Lord Leshy here tends to prattle on too much," he chuckled. "But it is still worth saying."

Then he walked closer to the bonfire, and, lifting the bundle of herbs and the parchment up over his head, he threw them both into the fire.

Immediately, the air filled with waves of incense. The aroma rolled out of the fire and cascaded over us in heady, gray smoke. Hyssop, sandalwood, lavender. The scent was delicious, and so strong that it overpowered even the pungent scent of burning parchment. The incense swam in the air, filling the sky. Baxin stayed where he was in front of the fire, his eyes clenched closed, dragging in deep, hard breaths. When he finally turned and walked back, his face was flushed, his gait unsteady, and he was humming a low tune to himself. He sat and picked up the long metal nail, dipping it into one of the little jars he had brought with him. Then he leaned over, and pierced Jason's arm.

I gasped, but held myself still, watching as Baxin rotated slightly and pierced Flint's arm as well. I realized after a moment what was happening; Baxin was imprinting an image on their forearms. He bent over his work, occasionally dipping what I now realized must be a needle into one of his jars.

I leaned over and stood on tiptoe to get my mouth as close as possible to Rowan's ear.

"That," I whispered, "is the single most unhygienic thing I've ever seen."

Rowan raised an eyebrow. "It could be worse," he murmured. "He could have bled them both into a goblet, and then had them drink."

I blanched. "People do that?"

Rowan shrugged. "I have heard tales."

I shuddered, and wrapped my arms around myself. "You're right. That would have been worse."

It was difficult to see what Baxin was doing, but I had expected the process to take a long time. I'd never gotten a tattoo, but I knew it was careful, painstaking work. So I was surprised when I caught a glimpse of him, leaning low over their arms, his hands flying at top speed. His face was flushed, sweat dripping from the tip of his nose. Then I saw Flint's face, and understood why Baxin was rushing.

Flint's eyes were glazed and rolling back into his head. His mouth had fallen open. I rushed over to him, but then stopped myself before I reached out to touch him. Anything I did now might interrupt the ritual, and the ritual was Flint's only real hope.

The fire cast strange shadows. Baxin's face, bent over his work, was obscured by the darkness. Half of Jason's face was sharply illuminated; the other hidden in gloom. He stared up, dazed, into the sky, not reacting in any way to the repeated puncturing of his skin. The harsh light seemed to wash the last of the color from Flint's face, and he lay with his eyes open.

I looked down at the twin images taking shape on their arms. Baxin's work was amazing—artistry, really. The tattoos covered the inside of their arms from elbow to wrist in swirls of black and red and green. I stiffened.

The image was of a two-headed snake.

Though the snakes shared a body, the two heads were not the same. One was green, its mouth open and hissing, revealing fangs dripping with venom. The head of the other was made up of red, swirling flame; a burning forked tongue pushed out of its mouth.

I couldn't have said exactly why the image disturbed me so deeply. It was beautifully done, but also somehow...threatening. I looked at Jason's face, bathed in light and shadow, and hoped he would come out of this whole experience alive, still the same person that I knew and trusted.

Baxin panted as he continued at a feverish pace, humming a disjointed tune now and then under his breath. The tattoos looked nearly complete. Rowan came up behind me, and we waited together.

Baxin's hum got louder and louder. Suddenly he stood. He grabbed the second flask that lay on the ground and pried it open.

"Done, done, and done!" he cried loudly. "What once was two, now is one!"

And he emptied the flask out over Jason and Flint's arms. I could practically hear the alcohol sizzling in their still open wounds. They both gasped with pain, waking from their trance-like state, their wrists still bound together.

Jason coughed, and a second later Flint was also coughing. The sound was deep and painful, as though all the smoke from the bonfire had somehow gotten trapped in their lungs.

Then Jason wheezed, like someone in the throes of a terrible asthma attack. Flint echoed the sound. Jason's eyes bulged. He strained for air, fighting against a barrier I couldn't see. Tears streamed down his face. Beside him, Flint's body jerked, like a fish on hook, flopping weakly on the shore.

"Steady, boys," Baxin murmured, rubbing his hands together anxiously. "Steady. Just breathe through it."

Jason gasped again, and again. The sound hurt my heart. He wrenched his body to the side so he could look at Flint. Flint's eyes were clear again, and he gazed back at Jason.

Their eyes locked.

Jason reached over, and with his free hand clasped his brother's shoulder. Flint lifted his hand and hung onto Jason's wrist.

They took a deep, shuddering, synchronized breath. And another. It was the sound a drowning man might make when he finally managed to break his head from under the water.

"That's it, boys." Baxin wiped his sweat-drenched brow with the sleeve of his shirt. "You've got the hang of it now."

They breathed again, and again.

Rowan tapped my shoulder. "Look up," he whispered in my ear, and I lifted my eyes to the sky.

A soft wind had blown a gap in the thick clouds above us, and a constellation of stars shone, their brightness sharp in the pitch-black sky.

"Gemini," I breathed in awe, and then a fierce pang of triumph ran through me. I looked back over at Jason, who had collapsed onto his cot as he drew in one deep breath after another. "They're going to make it."

Flint sat up, his face pale but his eyes wide and clear. He looked from Baxin to me.

"What happened?" he asked. "Am I going to live?"

Baxin chuckled. "It surely looks like it, my boy."

"Will they always breathe at the same time like that?" I asked in an undertone, and Baxin shook his head.

"I don't think so," he answered, as he began to gather his things. "Once the newness wears off they won't feel quite so strongly linked together. And when Flint has had time to heal, and grow stronger, he won't need to lean on the connection so heavily. But still, it's hard to say exactly how the bond will affect them. It's unique to them, just like the symbol they wear."

"Now, if you'll excuse me, healer. And Lord Leshy, of course." Baxin nodded in Rowan's general direction. "But my wife will be snappish enough with me for being gone all night. I've no desire to keep her waiting any longer." With a nod, he slung his bag back over his back, and strolled off into the trees.

Rowan carried Flint back into the clinic, and I slung Jason's arm over my shoulder and supported him as he walked. Once we were back inside, Rowan and I both did everything we could to make them comfortable.

We gave them two cots next to each other to rest on, as Flint's heart rate spiked and his breathing grew labored whenever Jason was out of sight. Jason didn't want to eat, and after a few minutes of worry I decided not to press him. Flint, at least, was eager for food, and drained three bowls of soup before he'd had enough. He was jumpy, often craning his head to the door as though needing to reassure himself that he really was safe. It wasn't until late in the afternoon that he relaxed enough to allow himself to fall into a deep and, as far as I could tell, restful sleep. Jason did not sleep, but soon after Flint drifted off he settled into a calm, restful state. By then the sun was dipping low in the sky, and another sunset was descending.

Rowan came up behind me, and wrapped his arm around my waist.

"Come," he whispered, his breath warm on my ear. The stubble on his chin brushed against my cheek, making the hairs on the back of my neck stand up.

I shivered, leaning back against him, and nodded. We left as quietly as we could, pulling the barn door shut behind us. Our hands intertwined as we walked, silent, toward the trees.

I glanced up to the sky and my feet stilled, my hand pulling Rowan up short. He turned, concern plain on his face.

"Only two nights left." I pointed up at the moon, now on the verge of fullness. I tried to swallow the grief and fear rising in my throat. "So much has happened. But nothing has changed that."

Rowan took a quick step toward me, so his body pressed close against mine. His warm hand slipped up my neck and tilted my chin back so he could stare into my eyes.

"Do not give up hope," he urged, though I could hear fear in his voice. "Today we found a miracle for Jason and his brother. Who knows what miracle we might yet find for you?"

"I don't know." I wrapped my arms around his waist and let my hands slide up to his wide back. "I'm not sure how many miracles one person is entitled to. And if I only get one..." I stood on my tiptoes and pressed my lips to his neck. "Then I choose being with you." He moaned softly and leaned into my touch.

"I cannot accept losing you," he murmured. "I want to fight. To keep you safe beside me. But I don't know what to do."

"Neither do I," I admitted, laying my hand against his cheek. "But I do know what I want to do right now."

At that the melancholy in his eyes receded a little. He growled low in his throat, and leaned down. His lips were warm against mine, soft and insistent. Soon my breath was coming fast and ragged. He lifted me and I wrapped my legs around his waist, unwilling to stop kissing him for even a second as he carried me deeper into the privacy of the trees.

It was the darkest part of the night when my eyes snapped open later.

For a moment I lay unmoving, trying to remember what had

woken me. It hadn't been a dream, exactly. A noise, perhaps? But one that hadn't come from the trees around me, but had seemed, somehow, to issue from the ground below.

I looked over at Rowan, who slept soundly with his arm resting on my waist. The moonlight on his face made him look younger, more vulnerable. I had never seen his face look as relaxed as it did now, when he was lost in dreams. My heart ached as I wondered if life would ever be kind enough to him to let him feel so free during his waking hours. I was just starting to drift off when I heard the sound again.

My heart pounded as I sat up and looked around me. The sound reminded me of a baby's cry, at once pitiful and imperious as it called out, demanding to be answered. I stood, my legs a little shaky. I knew why the sound, that I had felt more than heard, had woken me and not Rowan.

The cry was a summons, meant only for me.

For a moment, I stood. Uncertain. The cold winter air pressed against my skin. I looked up at the sky, at the moon, so close to fullness. And suddenly, I knew what I wanted to do.

I was done with being afraid. Done with running, with hiding. With all of it. I might not be able to stop feeling my fear. But I wouldn't let it control my actions.

I left Rowan sleeping in the moonlight, and walked quietly off into the night.

I didn't try to retrieve my clothing, because the sound might have woken Rowan. I knew he would try to change my mind. So, I sneaked off as stealthily as I was able, risking breaking into a run only after I was some distance off in the trees. I would have expected to feel exposed and vulnerable with nothing but the cold night air between my skin and the surrounding trees, but the darkness clung to my skin like clothing, and the forest seemed empty and silent all around. No night birds stirred. No leaves rustled.

I knew there was no way I had run far enough, but after just a few minutes, I found myself back at the pit Rowan had hauled me out of the day before. The hole looked even deeper than I remembered it, and in the darkness, it was a pool of impenetrable black.

I stood, staring down into it, trembling. The moment of clear resolution had faded, and now I stood, fully aware of the risk I had determined to take, my mind racing with all the things that could go wrong. There was no easy way to do this.

I closed my eyes, gritted my teeth, and stepped forward.

The fall hurt more than I expected. The impact knocked the breath out of me, and for a minute I lay motionless, gasping for breath. After a while my breath came easier, but the gloom all around me would not let my heart rate slow. I stretched out on the soil. It was rough and scratchy on my bare skin. I extended my fingers and dug them into the dirt.

"I came back," I whispered. "I trust you. I'm not afraid." That last part was a lie. I was terrified. But somehow saying the words made me feel braver.

The ground warmed beneath me and the darkness softened, changing from the dark of a blindfold to the comforting dim of a familiar room. The euphoria I had experienced last time reached toward me like a hand outstretched.

I took a deep breath, and pushed it away. This time, what was about to happen to me was a choice that I was making.

I kept my eyes open as I sank into the ground.

TWENTY-ONE

THE LIGHT CAME BACK IN A BURST OF PINK AND PURPLE. I STOOD ON
soft green grass, and though I was still naked, it hardly seemed to
matter: my skin was made of silver bark, my hair of leaves. I
wiggled my bare toes in the grass, and stared around, my head
swimming with confusion. I had opened my eyes to a reality that
was at once foreign and intimately familiar. I could see the Source
out of the corner of my eye, though it was much further from me
than it usually appeared when I entered a Truthsight vision. It
flowed, molten silver that caught and held the light. But it was
quieter than usual; I couldn't hear it laughing. It seemed to be in a
great hurry to get to wherever it was going.

The more I took in my surroundings, the more I realized that
what I was experiencing now was radically different from any
Truthsight vision I had ever had before. Truthsight did not show
me an alternate reality—it showed me the real world as it truly
was, peeling back the layers to reveal the deepest truths, and
giving me the power to alter the things around me. The place I
found myself in now reminded me more of the way Rowan's
magic worked. His magic gave him access to a reality that was
wild, dreamlike, and utterly different from the real world.

It was as though I had woken into a place where Rowan's magic and my own were somehow overlaid, interacting in a way that I had never dreamt possible.

I didn't see the Earthchild coming. It simply appeared, standing in front of me, looking much the same as it had the last time I had seen it in the woods. Black hair, tangled and matted with leaves and mud, hung down its back and trailed against the ground. Red mud clung, thick, against its body, like clothing or a second skin. Its eyes, one sky-blue and the other red as blood, gazed up at me with the frank, unabashed stare of the very young.

Its gaze had weight, and force. I felt those eyes diving into me, an awareness prying inside me that was at once childlike and ancient. As I gazed back at it, I felt I stared into the depths of a dark, still pool that had no bottom, in which any number of unknown, threatening creatures might hide. I could not read the expression on its face. I noticed, for the first time and with a jolt of fear, that its teeth were slightly pointed.

It was then that I realized I couldn't move.

My feet were not my own. Neither were my arms. I could still move my head, but other than that I stood, frozen in place, my arms stretched out as though in a permanent offer of embrace.

The child stalked closer. There was something unsettling in the way it moved, its foot rolling toe to heel, silent on the ground. It walked with the wide, noiseless gait of a predator.

Fear churned inside me.

I swallowed, and realized that, at the very least, I could still speak. My voice failed me the first time I tried to use it, but the second time I managed a "Hello?" that was more question than greeting. It was a useless thing to say, but I could think of nothing better. It seemed not to matter, though, as the child gave no sign of hearing me.

It came to stand, so close that I could feel the way cold radiated from its body. The chill pressed against me, making me shiver. I smelled the wet dirt that encased the Earthchild, could feel the power that seethed in the air all around it, like static electricity snapping against my skin. It was slightly taller than I remembered, its head coming up to my elbow.

The child stared at my side intently, its eyes zeroing in on something only it could see, its gaze as sharp as a razor blade. It tilted its head a little to the side, reminding me of the way a bird of prey moves its head, perching motionless, waiting until its prey comes close enough to strike. My heart pounded. I tried to think of something, anything to do.

Then the child pounced.

It jumped forward, and slapped its small palms flat against my side, its fingers just below my rib cage. Immediately, cold began to pour into me.

I had never felt anything like it before. It was as though my insides were freezing, my organs turning to ice. Fierce cold spread across my body like ice unfurling across the surface of a pond. My teeth rattled. Frost formed in my eyelashes, clouding my vision. The cold deepened.

Then it burned.

I imagined the blood in my veins crystallizing, the pain beyond agony. It did not stop. The cold seemed to have no measure, no limit. It streamed from the child's touch and through my pores.

"Wait..." I managed to gasp out. "You don't understand. You... you're hurting me!" The child did not look up at my face, its eyes still intently focused on my side, but a tiny smile turned up the corner of its lips.

I had lost sensation in my feet, my fingers. Shock would set in soon, and I knew death would follow soon after.

"Please," I pleaded. "I'm your friend. Please don't do this."

The child ignored me. With a quick, tearing motion, it pulled one of its hands away from my side. I craned my head down. Where its hand had been, there was a small but deep crack in my skin, like a fracture in a thick layer of ice. A second later, black began to leak out of the rupture.

I screamed.

The substance was like tar, thick and gelatinous. It bubbled to the surface of my skin, like fat rising to the surface of soup as it boils. Black seeped out of my pores and began to take form. The tar became a thick, congealed mass that writhed and moved and grew. Helpless, I watched as it doubled, then tripled in size.

It began to take on a form, morphing into something that had two black, beady eyes. Scrabbling, spindly legs, jerked frantically when exposed to the frigid air. The creature was like a giant black tick, the base of its body still embedded deep in my side.

The Earthchild gave a grunt of satisfaction. Then it wrapped both its pudgy hands tight around the black creature, and pulled.

I screamed as the creature ripped out of me, taking with it wide strips of skin and fragments of bone. After a minute my cries died, and the only sound I could make was a wet, hacking cough. The force that had been holding me paralyzed suddenly evaporated, and my body collapsed. I lay on the ground, bleeding freely onto the frost-crusted grass, staring up at the Earthchild, who clasped the still-wriggling black creature in its hands. The creature's body was slick with my blood. Its legs flailed. Its beady eyes bulged.

The Earthchild smiled broadly. It brought the creature up to its mouth, and bit its head off with one snap of its pointed teeth. The creature's body burst, and black blood dribbled down the Earthchild's chin like filling from a blackberry pie. The child ate the whole thing, smacking its lips with enjoyment, devouring the creature in three giant bites.

Then the child looked down at me. Too weak to do anything but bleed and shiver, I stared back.

I was not even in much pain at this point. Shock had already set in. I didn't try to look down at the gaping wound in my side. The child's expression was unreadable, but as I gazed up into its uniquely colored eyes and wondered what would happen next, I felt an odd sort of detachment, as though I was really somewhere far away, watching something happen to someone else.

The child crouched down beside me. With one tiny hand, still wet with my blood, it reached out and patted me gently on the cheek. Then it stood and grasped one of my feet tightly with its hands. With a grunt, it began to drag my body across the ground.

I had no strength left, and I didn't try to resist. The child tugged me by my leg, and as I slid over the grass, I could see the thick, wide track of black blood that my body left behind on the grass. I should have been in agony. But the ground felt smooth as silk underneath my ravaged skin. On the verge of hallucinating, I imagined the grass as hundreds of tiny hands with waving green fingers, reaching up, gently lifting me, and pushing me along. The Earthchild didn't stop until it had brought me to the bank of the Source.

It leaned over, and with two hands, shoved me over the side and into the water.

TWENTY-TWO

I GAVE A WEAK CRY AND FUMBLED USELESSLY AT THE BANK AS I FELL, trying to find something to grab hold of. But the riverbank was smooth sand, and the most I could do was suck in a huge gasp of air before going under. I tried to swim, but I was so weakened by blood loss and trauma that my limbs were little more than weights at my side.

I sank.

I tried to calculate how long I could go without oxygen before I passed out. A distant, detached part of my brain made an evaluation of my injuries and calmly concluded that there was almost no chance I would survive. But the larger part of my brain was screaming at my body, trying to punch through the shock and pain. *Swim. Fight. Do something.* Pain clouded my eyes. I couldn't see. I managed to kick my legs a little, to rotate my body just enough so that, when I sank to the bottom, I landed on my back, staring up at the water, instead of face down in the dirt.

But there are some levels of hurt that no amount of willpower can break through. My body was done. The need to breathe built and built inside me. I knew that breathing water into my lungs would be the beginning of the end. I would drown. But after a certain point, the body stops caring what the mind is saying.

I breathed in.

Relief flooded me, as though I had filled my lungs with morning air. In an instant, the pain that had been wracking me evaporated. I felt fine, and whole. The Source filled my lungs, coated my insides. I breathed in again, and again, and the more that I took the Source into my body, the more profound the feeling of relief became. The wound in my side stopped hurting, as though it had never been there at all. My vision cleared. It was only then that I looked around me and realized: everything was *so* beautiful.

The Source wound around me, its water the color of molten silver. The Source was alive, aware and, more than that, it was…joyful.

I had often stood on the shore of the Source and thought I could almost hear it laughing as it hurried along. Now, submerged into its very heart—I could hear it *sing*.

The wordless song was surprisingly discordant, but somehow it was lovely all the same. The Source hummed and chuckled. It crooned trilling notes to itself, and made small cries of delight. It knew me, and welcomed me. The water was a soft hand against my skin, a gentle embrace wrapped around my limbs. I always tried to use a deft, gentle touch when treating a badly injured patient, and I recognized the gentle, delicate pressure against my side for what it was. The Source healed me swiftly, with no pain, and a touch like silk, far gentler than any I had ever managed, even in my best moments as a healer.

Part of me felt guilty for not paying more attention to the healing as it happened. I felt as though I were in the presence of a master doctor, and ought to be taking notes. But the beauty of the silver swirling before my eyes was so entrancing I could not look away. I lay on the bottom of the river, my hands now pillowed beneath my head, watching the Source in all its beauty as it coursed by, letting its power heal me. After the first, fearful breath, I gave almost no more thought to breathing in the water. It felt normal, and the Source was so cool and refreshing that I took lungful after lungful, letting the feeling of cool relief and the calm that followed close on its heels course through my entire body. The liquid was sweet and cool, and it slid down my throat and filled me from inside with a sense of comfort and peace.

I felt so good. Not just healed, but whole, inside and out. My body had been through so much in the last few hours; my soul had been through so much over the last few years. But lying there, I felt at peace with all the things that had happened to bring me to this moment, good and bad alike. I stretched, pushing my hands out into the cool liquid, kicking my feet. Slowly, I began to rise.

For a second, I felt a sense of loss. I didn't want to leave this moment of being so cocooned in love and safety. But the Source comforted me, and I didn't fight it as I moved closer to the surface. I couldn't understand the words it crooned, but I knew I wasn't meant to. The song was not to help me understand an idea, but a feeling. I felt healed, and the Source was glad of it. There was nothing else that needed to be said.

The Earthchild stood on the shore. Watching. It made no move to help me as I caught hold of the river bank and scrambled inelegantly back onto land. For a second I lay face down on the sand, panting. The serenity and strength that I had borrowed from the Source while I lay in its embrace vanished. Like an infant cast from its mother's womb, I lay trembling on the ground. I felt shaky, unstable. But I wasn't bleeding anymore.

I stumbled to my feet, and looked down at myself. My body was whole again. I pressed a hand to my side. New flesh had formed seamlessly over the gaping wound that, just a few minutes ago, had seemed to be a fatal injury. The pain was gone. My fingers darted to the place on my chest, where my stitches had pulled open again—but that deep, stubborn wound was gone, too. In its place was a long, silver seam that ran between my breasts, curling a little as it reached my chest. It looked like a long curl of silver ivy, and was cold when my fingers pressed against it.

I held up my hand up in front of my eyes. Tiny icicles dangled from my fingertips. Silver liquid still dripped from my body, pooling at my feet, where it quickly turned to thin patches of ice. The cold the Earthchild had poured into my body hadn't left me yet.

I looked up, and it was only then that I realized the Earthchild and I were no longer alone. A man stood by the child's side, his appearance so strange that all my instincts immediately screamed in warning. My body tensed, as though to run away.

Truthsight is supposed to show you the essence of people, the unadulterated truth about who they are and what their character is. I looked at the tall, thin man standing at the Earthchild's side, I knew that, without a doubt, that everything I was seeing was a mask. He wore a tuxedo and a black bow tie. Taller than I, and bone-thin, he wore his blond-white hair precisely parted down the middle, combed so that every hair was perfectly in place. Bright green eyes watched my every move, and I had the immediate sense that I was being evaluated, and found wanting. His long fingers were folded primly in front of him, and his thin, dry lips were quirked in an expression of disapproval and distaste. He stood towering over the Earthchild, the differences in their height so extreme as to be almost comical.

"Who are you?" I asked, my voice raspy and weak.

The stranger sneered at me, but didn't deign to answer.

The child smiled broadly up at him, its teeth flashing sharp and white, and reached out, grasping the stranger's bony fingers with its small, pudgy hands, and tugging him over to a sandy spot beside the Source. A part of me wanted to call out a warning to the child to be careful, though I wasn't sure why. I hurried after them. My legs were unsteady beneath me, like a sailor struggling to remember what it is like to walk on solid ground after many months at sea. I lurched a little as I walked.

By the time I caught up with them, the child had found a stick and had crouched down, its tongue sticking out a little between its teeth, squinting with concentration as it scratched symbols into the sand. After a moment, the child looked up at the stranger, and motioned urgently toward the markings it had made. The stranger sighed heavily, and turned his eyes up to the heavens with exasperation. Then he hiked up his pants, holding onto the fabric as though to keep it from dragging in the damp sand, and crouched down, his eyes narrowing as he studied the markings the child had made.

"The earth spirit wishes you to know that you are fully healed now," the man in the tuxedo said. "The curse is gone. The cold it used to drive the curse out will remain with you for some time, but will fade away eventually."

I sucked in a deep, hard breath, my hands instinctively flying to my sides. I was going to *live*.

A second realization followed close on the heels of the first one.

"Wait a minute," I gasped, stepping closer. "Those are the Earthchild's words? It's…speaking to me?"

The stranger looked up at me coldly, his eyes running from my face all the way down my body, disapproval radiating from him like heat. In that moment, I was fully aware of how I must appear: breathless and trembling, naked, my body encrusted with ice and sand.

"The words are certainly not my own," the stranger sniffed. "I agreed to translate. Not to engage in conversation with the help."

"Can it understand what I'm saying now?" I asked, my eyes flicking back and forth between the two of them. The Earthchild bent back down over the sand, its stick scratching something that looked to me more like hieroglyphics than any written language I had ever known.

The stranger kept his eyes focused on the sand as he spoke. "The Spirit says that he can understand some human speech, but

not all. Being so close to the Source makes you easier to understand, apparently. It wants you to know that it could not have
acted sooner to attempt to cure you. It had to wait until the darkness had collected itself into one place, so it could be forced out
all at once. Otherwise, the earth spirit would have had to do this
multiple times, and you could never have survived that. Even now,
the spirit itself could only remove the curse, but could not heal
you. Conversely, the Source could heal you, but could not have
removed the curse."

"So they worked together," I murmured.

The child still held the stick grasped tight in its fist, and its
hair had fallen over part of its face so that only its blood-red eye
looked back at me, steady and bright.

"Thank you," I said, "for saving me."

The Earthchild smiled broadly in reply.

"I was right, wasn't I?" I went on. "Rowan thought that the
other day, when you pulled me into the ground, that you didn't
understand what death meant. That you might have hurt me accidentally. But he was wrong. You were trying to help me, even
then. Weren't you?"

The child's smile faded. It blew out a sharp breath, and then
looked down at the ground, scratching furiously. The man leaned
closer, his brow furrowing, and when he read this time the trans-
lation was slow and a little halting, as though he had to struggle to
decipher each word.

"My leshy is green-bark young," the stranger read. "He does
not know how to trust me yet. He thinks me young, but I am old,
old, old. I slept long, and forgot much, but not so much that I
could harm you. My leshy is right that I do not fear death." The
child looked up at me as the stranger's voice read out his words.
"But I understand it."

"His mistake almost killed you," the child went on, with a
shake of its head. "He pulled you away before I could fix you. He
told you not to come back to me. I would not have pulled you to

me against your will. If you had listened, the curse would have run its course. He and I...we both would have lost you." The child's eyes flashed.

The anger in its expression made me nervous. "Rowan didn't mean any disrespect." I licked my lips nervously. "He was just confused, and frightened."

The stranger gave a sharp, derisive laugh. "Oh, yes. Now that you've explained it, things seem so much better. A leshy who is both craven and a fool. Delightful."

I didn't see the Earthchild's hand move; it flew too fast for my eyes to see more than a blur. All I did see was that, suddenly, the child's fingers were fastened tight around the stranger's throat. The stranger choked and gasped for air, his face quickly growing even paler than it had been a moment ago. He didn't struggle, or try to pry the Child's fingers away. Instead, he went limp, throwing his hands out to his side, and tilting his chin up, baring his neck.

"My...most...abject apologies," he wheezed. "I meant no insult to your...valued servant."

The Earthchild stared steadily at the stranger for another long moment before releasing him and turning back to the sand, and beginning to write again as though nothing had happened. The stranger rocked back on his heels, panting. With a shaky motion at odds with his elegant appearance, he jerked a pearl-white hand-kerchief from his front pocket. He pressed it against his neck, but not before I saw a line of red, where the child's fingernails had broken through his skin.

"My leshy does not understand," the stranger read out after a moment, his voice uneven, and a little breathless. "He fears me, and himself. But he is strong and noble and wild. And he trusts you."

"Yes," I breathed. "Yes, I think he does."

"I feel danger coming, but I cannot see its face. We need you." The child was not smiling now. It stared at me. For the first time, I saw uncertainty in its eyes. It dropped the stick it had been using to write and stood up. For a second its eyes were focused on the distance, as though probing something I could not see. Then it turned and ran away, down the banks of the Source, its flight so sudden and fast I had no chance to call after it before it had disappeared in the distance.

The stranger stood up, brushing the sand off his pants and hands with a grimace.

"Well," he muttered. "That was unpleasant." He turned and began to walk away.

"Wait!" I called. He looked over at me. "Who are you?"

He smiled widely, an expression that made his face look wide and hollow, like the cold grin of a jack-o-lantern when no candle lit it from the inside. "That is the pertinent question, isn't it?" he responded, a laugh in his voice that didn't reach his eyes.

And then he was gone.

No flash of light, no movement. One moment he stood, leering at me, and the next thing I knew, I was alone beside the Source.

My legs gave out, and I knew consciousness was slipping away. But even as I lay down, I fought to keep my eyes open, to commit everything about this place to memory. The way the Source reflected the purple color of the sky. I didn't know what exactly, but I knew something about this place was crucial to remember.

I didn't know the moment my eyes finally closed, but I knew when I was waking back up to reality. I could feel myself being carried in strong arms, cradled against soft, warm fur. We were still in the forest. The winter air was sweet and fresh against my bare skin.

"Rowan?" I asked, cracking my eyes open, and immediately I felt his lips pressing to my forehead.

"I am here."

I opened my eyes. I was being carried through the forest in Rowan's arms. I was dressed again; Rowan must have found my clothes and pulled them back onto me, to shield me from the cold. I looked up, into his face.

"I'm better," I told him, pressing myself closer against his warmth. "The Earthchild. It came and..." I tried to remember, but my memory was foggy and my head ached.

"I know." I could hear the deep timbre of restrained joy in Rowan's voice. His eyes were glowing. "As soon as I found you, I could see that the curse was gone." Rowan pulled me tighter against him. "Now you need to rest." He lowered his mouth to my ear, so that the stubble on his chin tickled my cheek, "Later, we will celebrate together. Just you and I."

"That sounds wonderful," I murmured, and tried to let myself relax into his arms. But there was a nagging worry deep in my gut. As though there was something important I couldn't quite remember, or something in plain sight I couldn't see.

"I woke and you were gone," Rowan went on. "But I could feel you were close. When I found you, you were covered in snow, but no snow had been falling. I was so frightened, but then I saw you...saw that the shadow of the curse was gone, and that your body was whole and undamaged. And I knew the Earthchild had come to our aid."

"I need to contact Meri. To let her know that I'm all right." My fingers fumbled at my waist, searching for the clamshell. But I had left it at home again.

"You can contact her soon, Asa," Rowan said, his voice soothing, "But you won't have the strength to do anything until you have rested."

We moved out of the trees, and my house came into view. With Rowan's long strides we were almost there already.

"So," I asked him. "Are you going to yell at me now?"

"Yell at you? For what?"

"Um, you know. Leaving you asleep while I ran off naked into the woods? Risking my life on a hunch?"

"You mean, yell at you for being both braver and wiser than I?"

Rowan climbed the wooden steps to my back porch and eased the door open. "No, my Asa." He looked down at me, an unfamiliar twinkle in his eye. "I will not yell at you for that. Although I will admit to being disappointed."

"Disappointed? Why?"

Rowan laughed, and carried me up the stairs to my bedroom. "I would have liked to see you running naked in the woods."

We were in my room now, and Rowan gently lowered me onto the bed.

"Well," I told him dreamily, "Now that the Earthchild has gotten rid of the curse, I'm sure we could arrange a repeat performance." I would have kissed him then, but my eyelids were so heavy they snapped shut of their own accord. I tried to push back against the darkness, sure there was something I needed to tell him. But the weariness was too strong, and I felt myself sinking into sleep.

Rowan pulled a blanket up over me. "Rest now, my Asa," I heard him murmur. "We can talk more later. Now, we have all the time in the world."

TWENTY-THREE

LATER, I WOULDN'T BE ABLE TO REMEMBER EXACTLY WHAT WOKE ME. Had I heard a strange sound from outside my window? Something falling? A cry of distress? All I would remember was lying in the dimness of my room, eyes suddenly open wide, every instinct screaming in alarm.

A thin layer of frost had formed on top of my quilt; the Earthchild's cold still swirled inside me. I rolled out of bed and looked around.

Rowan was gone. Something wasn't right.

Though the room was dark, sunlight crept around the edges of the thick curtains. It was day. I had no way of guessing how long I had been sleeping.

Instinct told me not to pull the drapes and look outside. I tiptoed out of my room in the semi-darkness, turning back at the last second to grab my half of the clamshell, and clipped it to my belt loop.

I went down the stairs and out my back door as quietly as possible and crossed to the clinic, my bare feet quiet on the grass. I glanced back, and could see frost forming on the ground wherever my feet had touched it, leaving a faint, white trail of footsteps behind me.

It was quiet, but that didn't reassure me. My heart rate sped up, as though my body was aware of a danger that my mind still hadn't registered. The back door of the clinic was unlocked. I eased it open, and stepped quietly inside.

The front barn doors were thrown open, and Jason and Flint stood there, side by side, gazing out at something I couldn't see. Jason had his hands clamped down on Flint's shoulders, and at first I thought Jason was supporting him so that he wouldn't fall. Then Flint jerked and tried to pull away. Jason pulled him back, and with a sinking feeling I realized that Jason was restraining him.

I walked through the darkened clinic and came to stand next to Jason. He didn't look over at me. His eyes were wide and locked onto something in front of him. I followed his gaze.

A group of water nymphs stood in the field between the clinic and the woods, like a ring of hungry wolves closing in for the kill. Though I had never seen creatures like this before, there was no doubt about what they were. Their long, pale faces were framed by auburn hair that hung well past their hips. They wore gowns that seemed to be made from seaweed or algae, and the green, sticky fabric was full of holes, and clung to their skin. Their eyes, which seemed too big for their faces, were sharp and full of menace. Their skin seemed nearly translucent in the sunlight.

They all looked exactly the same. It was like a visual illusion, the kind that gives you a mild headache and makes your eyes sting if you look at it too long. Their bodies were shapely, the symmetry of their faces flawless. But their faces were too savage to be beautiful.

When I looked at them, I could only see raw hunger staring back.

Rowan stood in front of the barn, his legs braced in a wide

stance, his face and shoulders completely relaxed. His scythe was drawn, but he held it loosely by his side.

Jason turned to me, his face pale. "I don't know how they found us," he whispered. "We were so careful to keep them from tracking us here. It should have been impossible."

"What do they want?" I whispered back.

It was Flint who answered. "Me." His face flushed and his teeth clenched as he stared out at the nymphs. He was shaking with fury. "They couldn't let me get away. They sucked the whole first half of my life away, but that wasn't enough. But I will never go back to them. Never." His voice rose. "I'll make them kill me first. I'm not a piece of meat anymore."

"No one is taking you anywhere," Jason said, and he gave Flint's shoulder a reassuring squeeze. But I could hear the slight tremble of fear in his voice.

One of the nymphs stepped forward, her movements smooth and languid. The rest of the nymphs moved along with her, as though pulled by some invisible cord, closing in closer around us.

"That's Desinda," Flint told me in a whisper. "Their ruler."

"Greetings, Lord Leshy," she said, her voice like a gentle bell ringing, and she dipped her head in Rowan's direction. "Pray forgive this intrusion into your territory."

After a second of hesitation, Rowan inclined his head slightly in return. A ripple of unease ran through me. Rowan didn't show deference to anyone lightly. How powerful were these creatures, that they could give him cause for caution?

"Welcome," Rowan responded. "There is no need to apologize for your presence. However, I am curious. From what I know of your kind, it is unusual for you to travel even short distances. You are highly accustomed to your warm home climate, are you not?"

Rowan gestured broadly with his left hand. It almost seemed a coincidence it was the hand that held his weapon, and that the razor-sharp scythe cut the air between them. "The harsh cold here cannot be comfortable for you." His eyes narrowed. "I fear you may find your visit damaging to your health."

"This land is savage, and, yes, the cold insufferable." Desinda agreed. She shivered. "But we will not be here for long. We have come only to reclaim our property. Once it is back in our possession, we will depart."

"I am not your property!" Flint cried.

Both Desinda and Rowan turned to look. An expression of surprise and concern washed over Rowan's face, when he saw that I was no longer safely in bed, but standing shoulder to shoulder with Flint and Jason. But the expression of worry was gone before anyone else could have seen it.

Desinda tilted her head, her eyes zeroing in on Flint. "Oh, how charming," she purred. "The cow is speaking." She straightened back up and looked at Rowan. "That slave has no value to us. He is merely a dried-up piece of meat. That one, however," she pointed a long, thin finger at Jason, "belongs to us. We insist that you return him." Her lips curled back from her teeth in a deadly smile. "Now."

Jason and Flint's breathing went abruptly still, and I could almost feel the shock rolling through them.

"But...but you didn't want me," Jason stammered. "You abandoned me when I was an infant. Why do you want me now?"

Desinda gazed coolly over at Jason. "We thought, perhaps foolishly, that left with the humans you would simply wither and rot. Now we realize our error. Alive, you are a threat to our species. We must learn more about you and how you have survived this long. Then you will be destroyed."

Jason let go of Flint's shoulders, a look of dazed confusion on his face. "A threat?" he asked, taking a small step forward. "What possible threat could I be to *you*?"

Desinda glowered. "Your very breath is a threat," she hissed, color rising in her checks. "Every step you take on this Earth is an affront to our entire species."

She took a deep breath, in an apparent effort to calm down, and turned her attention back to Rowan. "You see here"—she gestured behind her, to the ranks of identical nymphs—"arrayed before you, the best, the absolute pinnacle of our species. And here"—she gestured at Jason without looking directly at him —"is a deviation from that perfection. An aberration that must be eradicated before it can take root. If he has somehow managed to cling to life, then others like him might also still be living."

"Others?" Jason echoed. "Like me?"

Desinda ignored him, and spoke only to Rowan. She seemed to think him more worthy of her attention. "And if they were to locate each other and somehow…" She closed her eyes, as though the thought was so nauseating as to be nearly impossible to verbalize. "Somehow…*breed*…it is conceivable they could spawn a lesser branch of our species. They would be a threat to us. We cannot allow that to happen."

Without any visible cue, every single nymph standing behind Desinda took a long step forward. Their movements were synchronized perfectly. Their message was clear.

"As I said before, Lord Leshy," Desinda went on, "that which is ours must be returned to us. Instantly. I'm sure you understand."

Rowan smiled broadly, showing all his teeth.

"And I'm sure you understand," Rowan answered, "that I would never simply hand over someone who is under my protection." The earth began to tremble, and I reached out against the clinic's door to steady myself.

"You are powerful creatures," Rowan admitted with a nod. "But you have made a mistake. You overstep yourselves. You are out of your element here. This is our home." Thorn bushes began to push themselves up out of the soil, creating a barrier between Rowan and the nymphs. "Leave," Rowan told them, "Before I am forced to do you harm."

Desinda tilted her head back, silent. For a second she studied

Rowan. "I thought you might say that," she murmured, and then nodded sharply.

A clatter came from behind me. I started to spin toward the sound, but a heavy weight shoved against my back. I stumbled and fought to stay on my feet. A strong arm wrapped around my waist, clamping my arms to my sides. I struggled, kicking out with my legs, and wrenching my body side to side.

Then I felt the icy cold of a blade press against my neck.

I stilled.

"Don't move." I couldn't see the man who held me, but I recognized Paul's voice hissing in my ear. "My new friends thought they might need a little help handling all of you. We were more than happy to help out."

Straining my eyes to the side, I could just see a pair of mages wrestling Jason to his knees. Flint lay on the ground, already unconscious, the side of his face bright red and swelling from where a heavy blow had stuck him.

I could see at least four mages: Paul, who was holding onto me, the two subduing Jason, and the one who stood over Flint with his arms folded, looking bored.

The nymphs stood, watching with identical, triumphant smiles stretched across their faces.

We were surrounded by nymphs on one side, and renegade mages on the other.

Between them Rowan stood, his face pale with fury, his hand white-knuckled where he held onto his scythe.

Paul's breath was heavy and uneven in my ear. He smelled like old sweat, and his body pressed behind mine. I wanted to fight, to kick and bite and break free. But the knife against my throat forced me to stillness.

Rowan turned away from the nymphs and started to move toward me. "Stop right there," Paul shouted. "Don't test me. Slitting her throat would be a dream come true for me. All you have to do is give me an excuse."

Rowan froze, a mixture of fury and horror on his face. "Don't be a fool," he said, his voice low and dangerous. "If you hurt her, I will rip you limb from limb."

"Then don't make me do it," Paul said. "Drop your weapon."

Rowan hesitated. His eyes flicked as he measured the distance between himself and Paul, trying to gauge how quickly he could close the space, compared with how many milliseconds it would take Paul to slit my throat. He glanced over his shoulder at the nymphs who seemed to inch a little closer to him, every time he looked away. I could see the indecision, the panic, in his eyes.

Paul pressed the blade tighter against my throat. It stung as it broke the surface of my skin.

Rowan's nostrils flared at the scent of my blood. Instantly, he threw the scythe away from himself with so much force that it slid across the grass, nearly hitting Flint's unconscious form.

I thought of Meri's shell, hanging from my belt. If I could break free from Paul's hold and reach it, I could call her for help. But even if I could reach her, she wouldn't be able to get to us in time. My heart sank.

"Do you have them subdued?" Desinda asked, her eyes fastened on Paul.

"Yes, just like we promised," he answered. "We did everything we said we would. We helped you find them, and now we've got them under control." The sound of him licking his lips so close to my ear made me cringe. "Now it's your turn to keep your half of the bargain."

I stiffened, realizing the nymphs had not tracked Rowan and Jason. The mages had brought them right to us. But why? They couldn't have done it just to get to me. As far as they knew, I was already dying.

Desinda smiled. "With pleasure." She turned and beckoned to her people. "Do as I instructed," she called to them. "And do it quickly." She crossed her arms and rubbed her hands up and down her shoulders. "This place is excruciatingly cold. I wish to be gone."

At Desinda's command, the nymphs broke ranks. Though no words were spoken, they moved with perfect coordination, forming two long lines facing each other. They bent down, touching the soil as though they were searching for something. It reminded me of a doctor, pressing her fingers to the throat of a patient, anxiously searching for a pulse.

Jason, still held by two mages, strained to turn and watch them, his eyes narrowed with a mixture of confusion and concern. The nymphs movements were like a dance; each of them adjusting their positions slightly, responding to something in the earth that only they could sense. After a few minutes, they seemed satisfied with their positions. Moving like one body, the nymphs knelt on the ground and plunged their fingers deep into the earth.

For a second nothing happened, and I exchanged a confused gaze with Rowan. Then water began to simmer to the surface, obeying what must have been a summons from the nymphs. At first, it came so slowly that I wondered if my eyes were playing tricks on me, but what had seemed just a trickle soon became a long, narrow puddle.

The nymphs had found an underwater stream, and coaxed it above ground. Gradually, a shallow, muddy creek took form, and the nymphs sank their hands deep into the water, their eyes closing, identical expressions of satisfaction on every face.

Rowan grunted with pain.

My eyes snapped over to him, but he wasn't looking back at me any longer. His face flushed bright red. He ground his teeth together, and braced his hands against his knees. His back arched with pain.

"They're poisoning the ground water!" Jason cried, struggling vainly to break free from the hands that held him.

Cold fear shot threw me. Rowan's life was linked to the land, and the nymphs were pouring poison into it...into him.

"They're hurting him!" I screamed. "Rowan!"

Desperation gave me strength I had not found before, and I wrenched free of Paul's hold. A voice in my head told me to round on him and fight, that simply running away from my enemy was a foolish thing to do. But the louder voice in my head chanted *Rowan's hurt, Rowan needs me*, over and over again. I lurched over the grass, reaching my hands out toward Rowan's hunched form, Paul hot on my heels. He caught up with me after just a few steps, delivering a shattering blow to my temple with the hilt of his knife. Everything swam, and my arms and body went limp. I crumpled, and Paul threw his weight on top of me to hold me down.

When my vision cleared, I was lying on the ground with my hands pinned to my side. Paul's knife was pressed against my throat, and I was staring up into a face I could barely recognize.

Shock rolled through me like a hard, cold wave.

Before, Paul had grabbed me from behind and I had recognized his voice. Now I realized that I might not have recognized him at all, if I had only seen his face.

"What happened to you?" I gasped, horrified, as Paul glared down at me with his one remaining eye.

The right side of his face had been mutilated. Where his right eye should have been, there was a red canyon of ragged, ruined flesh. The wound had been magically healed, but it was still terrible to look at. It was as though a large claw had torn part of his face away. Deep wounds, like those left by a knife, stretched from his right temple down to his chin.

"This?" Paul grimaced, gesturing toward his face. The movement made his tortured flesh contort grotesquely. "This is Meri's mercy."

"What?" I replied dumbly. "What do you mean?"

"She spared my life, after finding out I tried to kill you." Paul's lips curled. "Even made me thank her for her kindness, after she was done."

"You're lying," I told him, with a furious shake of my head. It couldn't be true. "Meri would never do something like that. Ever. And if she had, you wouldn't be here again, defying her."

Paul pressed his knife harder against my neck. "You're a stupid, naïve child. All the insight that Truthsight gives you, but you've always been blind."

Rowan made a pained sound. I forced myself to look away from Paul's ruined face. Rowan was staring at something only he could see. He began to shake. He held one hand up unsteadily.

"No," he whispered. "Don't. Stay away." But I heard a howl from in the distance, and knew his warning would do no good.

The Earthchild burst out of the trees, and the air seemed to shimmer all around it, light and ice sparking where its feet touched the ground. Its mismatched eyes were wide and full of fury as it ran toward the nymphs. Its hair streamed out behind it, and its movements reminded me of a wildcat running, great leaps flowing like water, feet only seeming to touch the ground for a bare second before it was in the air again. Its mouth opened in a long, high-pitched howl, its face twisting in a savage war-cry.

Many of the nymphs stayed where they were, fingers still submerged in the water, eyes narrowing with increased concentration, and I realized they were siphoning poison into the water with even more intensity than before. Others rose. Their faces showed no emotion as they stepped forward to confront the child, no fear, no viciousness, just a vague, dim, malice.

The child stumbled.

My breath caught in my throat. It seemed to happen in slow motion—the child's eyes widening with surprise, its legs giving out beneath it.

Only then did I realize what a fool I had been. This attack was not just an attack against Rowan, or against me.

The nymphs were attacking the Earthchild.

TWENTY-FOUR

THIS WAS WHAT THEY'D BEEN WAITING FOR, AND THEY DIDN'T hesitate. The instant the Earthchild's steps faltered, the nymphs sprang. Dozens of nymphs threw themselves on top of the Earthchild, their fingers stretching out, eager to pour their poison into its system and steal its life-force for themselves. They pressed their fingertips to the child's neck, its legs, any place they could reach, hooking themselves onto it like leeches.

Rowan had told me the Earthchild could not die. But it could be forced back into dormancy. They had managed to hurt Rowan and the earth, and infuriate the child so much it had run right into their poison-laced hands. If the nymphs drained enough of the Earthchild's life away, and forced it to go back into stasis, its connection to Rowan would be severed.

Rowan would die.

And this land and all its creatures would be left with no one to protect them.

The Earthchild froze under the weight of the nymphs' attack. Its eyes widened and bulged. It looked up, and for a second I saw it lock eyes with Rowan. Then it collapsed.

Rowan howled. Sweat dripped from his bright-red face.

Tremors ran through his hands. I could almost feel the pain wracking through him.

But, somehow, he straightened. He took a step closer to the nymphs attacking the child. And another.

Paul was shouting, but I couldn't really hear his words. One of the mages holding Jason sent a curse billowing toward Rowan in a stream of red and blue. It crashed against Rowan's body and dissipated like mist, doing him no harm.

Rowan took another step.

The mages threw another curse at him, and another. The air around Rowan was stained with bright colors that hung in the air like fading fireworks, but nothing they could throw at him did him any harm.

"Do something!" Paul yelled at Desinda. "Our magic won't work against him!"

She snapped her head around. "We cannot subdue both him and the child at the same time," she cried. "They are too strong!"

Hope soared in my heart.

And then, like a mirage, like a dream, Meri appeared. I didn't know where she had come from or how she had gotten here, but suddenly she stepped out from behind the barn and strode across the grass, like an actress on cue.

"Oh, Meri. Thank God," I choked out, tears of relief sliding down my face. "They're hurting him, Meri!" I cried as she reached Rowan's side. He staggered, still moving toward the Earthchild, his eyes bleary and his body shaking.

Meri rested a hand on his shoulder.

Then she pulled a knife from her belt, and stabbed Rowan deep in the chest.

I saw everything as though from a great height, like I was a spectator at some terrible movie. Saw the knife sink, up to its hilt, into Rowan's flesh. Saw his knees give out as he crumpled to the ground.

His body lay, motionless, in the dirt.

Meri crouched down and pulled the knife from Rowan's body.

The skin on his chest shivered. The wound closed, just a little, around the edges, as a bit of healing seeped from the ground into Rowan's prone form. His connection to the land was healing him.

Calmly, Meri lifted the knife, and stabbed him again.

I screamed, and screamed, and screamed.

I clawed at the ground, trying to get away from Paul's restraining hands, trying to get to Rowan's side. Rowan's connection to the earth ought to keep him alive...but if the Earthchild was incapacitated, how could it heal him? But even through the horror and the grief, a numb corner of my brain kept saying none of this was real...it couldn't be. The cries were ripping from some primal part of me. My heart shattered like ice into a thousand ragged shards.

Meri let the bloody knife fall from her hand, and turned to Desinda. She didn't seem to notice that her fingers were dripping with red.

"There," she said. "Now he is subdued. But we won't be able to really finish him until the spirit is fully neutralized. How long?"

"Soon," Desinda answered. "Then we will take what is ours, and be gone."

Meri nodded in agreement, then turned and took a step closer to me.

"Oh, child," she whispered, reaching out toward me with a hand that dripped with Rowan's blood. "I'm so sorry that I could not shield you better."

"Meri?" My eyes burned with tears. What was left of my heart was so cold it burned. "Why are you doing this? I love you. I've always loved you."

"My sweet child." Meri smiled at me, tears in her eyes to match my own. "I love you, too. I did everything I could to keep the worst of the hurt from you. Today, I sent only a few mages here to assist the nymphs, hoping they would appear to be a small, renegade band. Just as I did when I sent the hellhound. I didn't want anything to threaten the bond between us."

"You sent the hellhound?" I echoed numbly. I couldn't look at her. I could only stare at Rowan's slack face. Paul had let go of me, and he stood over me, rather than holding me down, now that Meri was so close. I wasn't sure if it was because he thought Meri would be upset with him if he was too rough with me, or if he thought me too defeated to need restraint.

"Only because I thought it could be safely directed far away from you!" Meri hurried to explain. "The hellhound was meant for the leshy—not for you. If that had only gone as I intended, then all of this unpleasantness could have been avoided."

"But Paul came to kill me," I murmured, trying to fit all the pieces together. My head spun.

"That was his terrible error," Meri said, her face flushing with still-fresh anger. "And nearly the last mistake he ever made. He knew you had been cursed and did not want you to be saved. He thought he could manipulate the situation; attack and make it appear that the curse that claimed your life. I almost killed him when I found out."

"Then why do this?" I sobbed. "If you care for me so much, why would you want to kill the man I love?"

Meri's eyebrows drew together. "Because that *thing* is not a man at all, Asa. He is a beast, who has seduced you away from me. And I love you too much to stand idly by while he pollutes you with his feral magic." Her lips pressed together into a hard line. "There was only one way to keep him away from you, sweet one. I could not do it by myself, but I love you too much to let that deter me. When you told me what had happened with the nymphs, I knew I had found a way to save you. They were eager enough to go along with my plan, once I spoke with them."

I felt dizzy, and the whole world felt insubstantial and surreal. "Are you trying to tell me," I asked, "that, in some sick way, you think you're doing this for my own good?"

Meri's countenance fell. "Not just for your own good, Asa." She crouched so she could look into my eyes. "For the good of all of us. The whole clan. I knew that if you were with him, sooner or later his magic and yours would merge. That cannot be allowed. It would sully the purity of the Source, and it would give you access to vast, untamed, and dangerous power."

Her words hit me like a physical blow. I gasped, wanting to scream and rage at her, but unable to speak. And yet, at the same time, I didn't care. I only cared about Rowan.

She went on as if she didn't even notice the pain she caused me. "It's my duty to protect the clan—and you, even from yourself. I waited. With the curse infecting you, I could not bear to do anything which might darken your last days. I was willing to stand by, and let you find what happiness you could, even if the thought of it made my skin crawl. But now that the curse has been removed, I had no choice but to act."

"But how did you even know about that?" I started to ask, but the words died in my throat. Of course. My eyes flicked down to the clamshell still fixed to my belt loop. All this time, she had been eavesdropping on me.

"That's why I made the mirror in your room into a portal," Meri went on, "So I could take care of you." Meri reached out, and stroked my hair. "Watch over you while you were sleeping. I had no choice but to do this, Asa. Someday you'll understand."

Meri straightened up and turned away, as though there was nothing left to say.

I reached up to swipe the wetness from my eyes with the back of my hand. When I touched my face, I realized my tears had frozen as they rolled down my cheek. The Earthchild's cold still churned inside me. For a second I stared at the frost and ice that had gathered on my fingertips.

When I looked up, Flint was watching me.

He lay on the ground, perfectly still. But his eyes were open and burning. A mage stood behind him, but no one was bothering to pay him any attention.

Rowan's scythe lay on the ground in front of him.

I gave him the barest of nods.

Flint never should have been a match for a mage. But the thing about power is that you have to realize that you need to use it. Flint had been lying unconscious for some time, and the mage standing over him wasn't even looking in his direction. He didn't have a chance to see the scythe flying in the air, until it connected with his throat, and slit his neck cleanly.

The mages standing over Jason were more attentive, but they didn't know what he was. They didn't understand the significance when he tore away the gauze wrappings from his hands. In the exact same instant Flint struck, Jason rose, threw off the hold of the two mages restraining him, and pressed his fingers to their necks.

Tears streamed down his face. "I'm sorry," he gasped as venom surged into their bodies. They stiffened, their eyes widening in mute terror. "I don't want to hurt you, but you've left me no choice."

Flint held Rowan's scythe with both hands, out in front of his body, as a stream of nymphs abandoned their attack on the land and instead moved toward him. He lifted the curved blade high above his head, and swung it like a baseball bat into the first nymph's side. She cried out as she dropped to the ground. Flint gave a strangled cry of victory, and moved on to the next.

He was not a trained fighter; there was no elegance or calculation to his motions. He had the strength of desperation, the almost unstoppable force of someone filled with fury, someone who had endured pain beyond his capacity to bear. He threw himself among the nymphs, and soon blood stained his face and clung to his clothing.

Meri and Desinda both turned toward the noise and chaos, and in the confusion, I managed to struggle to my feet and break away. Every instinct I had screamed for me to hurry to Rowan's side, but I forced myself to turn my feet aside. Instead, I ran a few paces, to the very spot where the Earthchild's spear was still planted in the ground.

Paul's hand closed on my arm. I stumbled and grabbed the small sapling in front of me, as if for support.

The Earthchild's gift had been growing since I had planted it, spear-tip down, in the ground. Small branches stretched out from the top of it, with tiny budding leaves and even a few tiny, blood-red flowers.

"Stay down, traitor," Paul growled from behind me, his hand clamping down on my shoulder, painfully tight. "Don't tempt me."

In one fluid motion, I pulled the spear from the ground, turned toward Paul, and shoved the spear's point deep into his gut.

He gasped, pressing his hands over the wound as I pulled my weapon free. He stared at me, wide-eyed, for a moment, before tumbling to the ground.

"Moderate internal bleeding," I told him, taking a quick, detached glance at the wound. "Possible perforated lung. Trauma is severe, but unless you bleed out, not life threatening." I leaned a little closer to him. "For now," I hissed. "Stay down. Don't tempt me."

Jason and Flint were both still fighting. Chaos swirled around them. There had only been four mages, aside from Meri, and they were all down. But the nymphs were incredibly powerful, and had huge numbers. With each second they drained the Earthchild, the more likely it was the child would fall back into hibernation. And then all would be lost. I ran toward Rowan and the child, but had only gotten a few feet when I heard Meri's voice ring out behind me.

"Asa," she cried, and I could hear the threat in her voice. I froze. "Stop this at once!"

I looked over my shoulder. Meri's hand was stretched out toward me, silver lightning seething in her palm.

If I moved, Meri's magic would strike me before I could make it to Rowan's side, or to the child. I had no way to shield myself. And even if I could make it to the Earthchild's side, what good would it do? Even armed with the spear, there was no way that I could defeat all the nymphs that still clung to it.

"Put that weapon down," Meri commanded.

I hesitated, and then dropped the spear onto the ground. Holding my body carefully, so I was sure she could not see me, I pulled the clamshell from my pocket and, carefully, broke it into two, sharp pieces.

"Come over here, to me," she said. "Don't make me hurt you."

"Oh, Meri," I breathed. "You already have."

Then I took the broken fragment of shell, and sliced deeply into my palm.

It didn't hurt. The cold that poured out of me numbed my skin almost as soon as the surface broke. A small wave of fog rose up from my hand, like steam seething around a chunk of dry ice. I crouched and slammed my bloody palm against the earth.

I could *feel* the cold pouring out of me.

Frost formed on the ground around my hand, rolling out across the soil in a rapidly spreading sheet of sparkling white.

Not far from me, a nymph cried out. She wrenched her fingers away from the ground. As she brought her hand up to cradle it against her chest, I saw that her fingers were bloody.

Another nymph howled in pain, and then another. They began to pull away from the earth, tearing their hands out of the soil as though the dirt was biting at their fingers.

"What is wrong?" Desinda demanded. "Why are you stopping?"

"My quills!" one of the nymphs cried, gazing at her hands in shock. "The water froze, and they broke off!"

I gritted my teeth in a grim smile. The cold rolled out of me in waves, making my teeth chatter and my body shake. Ice built up on the ground around me, coating my knees and my other hand.

"You are out of your element," I shouted to Desinda, who was staring at her people in confused horror. "You were right about one thing. The cold here is brutal."

Silver light flashed by my face, so close I could feel the heat of it on my cheek.

"I won't miss again, Asa." Meri's words were hard, but her voice shook. Her fingers were closed in a tight fist, and silver light simmering between her clenched fingers. "Just stop fighting me, and come home. I don't want to harm you. All I ever wanted to do was to keep you safe. You're my daughter."

I gazed back at her, my hands full of ice and my heart full of venom. "Do what you want to me," I spat. "I'm not your daughter any longer."

Meri shook her head, tears spilling down her cheeks.

"I gave you every chance I could, child," she cried. "No mother could have done more. It breaks my heart that you will not let me save you." Then she opened her fist, and a silver orb drifted up from her hand, flashing and deadly, rippling in the air as it gathered itself to strike.

The ground moaned like a wounded creature. A deep cracking and tearing sound rumbled from all around. The ground beneath Meri's feet tilted, and she fell. The curse flew off course, missing me broadly.

I snapped my head around. Nymphs were still clustered around the Earthchild, but its eyes were wide open and staring at me. Then it looked past me, to where Rowan lay unconscious on the ground.

The child stretched out its hand. "Wake," it whispered.

I had never heard the child say a single word, hadn't thought it was even capable of human speech.

The force of its voice surged across the grass like a bomb imploding. The energy pounded into me, the Earthchild's word echoing over and over again in the air, shattering and thunderous. The intensity of it tore my hand from the earth and knocked me over onto my side. I could almost see the Earthchild's power flowing over the ground, reverberating over the surface of the soil.

Everything fell. The nymphs collapsed. Jason, Flint, and even Meri tumbled down.

Rowan was the only one left standing.

His skin was ashen gray. His wound had already started healing, but still bleed freely, dying his fur red. But he stood tall and straight. His body didn't shake. The Earthchild's command was something that called to the very core of his being. As long as his heart was beating, there was no pain so terrible, or injury so severe, that it could keep him from answering that call.

With a roar like thunder, Rowan threw himself at the nymphs. He ripped them away from the child, picking their bodies up in the air and tossing them aside, his face twisted with fury.

Desinda shrieked and darted toward him. She stretched out her hands. Venom dripped from her fingertips. Rowan rolled his body to the side, swung his arms up and around, and caught her deftly around the neck.

In one quick, smooth motion, he snapped her neck and tossed her lifeless body to the ground.

The nymphs wailed, the sound a shared cry of grief and confusion. Some of them rose and stumbled away, running with tears falling down their faces. Other nymphs ran to the side of their fallen queen. They picked her up in their arms and wept as they carried her body away. Rowan paid them no attention. He leaned down over the Earthchild, searching its face, making sure it was not harmed.

The child sat up. It reached out, and patted Rowan on the arm. I could see the wounds on Rowan's chest, still partially open, as though the Earthchild wasn't yet strong enough to heal him fully.

The child nodded to Rowan, and took his hand away from his shoulder.

Then Rowan rose, and came for Meri.

His chest rose and fell rapidly, and his lips pulled back from his teeth in a wide smile, his long stride closing the distance between them quickly.

Meri took a step back. Silver lightning pulsed in her palm and then flew, crashing into Rowan's chest. Rowan didn't pause, didn't even bother batting the curse away. He just came closer. Meri cried out in frustration and threw another burst of magic at Rowan, and then another.

Then she could not throw any more magic at him, because he had wrapped his hands around her neck.

"You made a fatal error," Rowan snarled. "If you had just attacked me, I might have spared you."

His fingers tightened. Meri's face began turning slightly purple. Tears ran down her cheeks.

"But you attacked the earth itself. You traded Jason's life away as if it meant nothing." Meri's fingers tore uselessly at Rowan's hands as his fingers squeezed tighter. "And you hurt Asa. I cannot forgive you for that."

My heart felt as numb and cold as the frost under my feet. This woman had raised me. But when I looked at her now, all I could feel was a deep, aching sorrow.

"Go ahead," Meri choked out, craning her head to the side to look at me. "You see?" she rasped. "You see what a monster this creature is?"

I stood right behind Rowan, though I didn't remember getting to my feet.

"It's okay," I told him, though I couldn't hide the tremor in my voice. "I know you have to."

Deep in her throat, Meri moaned.

Instantly, tears sprang to my eyes. Logically, I knew what she had done. But I hadn't learned to hate her yet. Love doesn't die just because it would make life simpler. I closed my eyes as a wave of bitter grief swept through me.

When I looked up, Rowan's eyes were fixed on my face.

There was a terrible moment of silence. Then Meri made a long, wheezing sound of relief.

I gasped. Rowan had loosened his hold around her neck.

"I will not do it," he said, staring at me as though his words shocked him as deeply as they did me. "I cannot hurt her, if it will cause you pain."

"I...I don't understand," I stammered. "She tried to kill you. She attacked the Earthchild."

"I know." Rowan's eyes glittered. "But you call her 'mother.' And I am *not* a beast."

Meri moved so fast that I couldn't quite track it, twisting and wrenching herself free of Rowan's hold. She raised a hand up toward the heavens. The sky darkened. Sudden lightning flashed. Wind sprang into existence out of nowhere and lifted Meri up off her feet.

For a second Meri hovered above us. "You and I are divided forever," she screamed at me. "I will never forgive you for this. Soon you will learn to fear me as much as I once loved you!"

The wind holding her up swirled thickly around her, and the sky turned a sickish tint of green. There was a flash of blinding light, and when I could see again, Meri and her mages were gone.

Jason and Flint came to stand beside me, and for a moment we all stared up, into the sky. Then Rowan's legs buckled. I ran to support him, but he gently pushed my hands away. The Earthchild had drawn closer and now stood a little off to the side, its eyes expectant.

Rowan's face was haggard as he took a few stumbling steps toward the child, and sank to his knees. Wordlessly, the child reached out, and lay a hand on Rowan's head. Rowan grunted, his back arching as the skin on his chest began to mend itself.

I stepped closer, standing right behind Rowan, looking on in wonder. As I watched, color seeped back into his checks. His skin brightened to its normal shade. Rowan heaved a deep, relieved sigh, and lay a hand against his healed skin. The child leaned over, and kissed Rowan gently on the forehead. It looked up over Rowan's shoulder, and smiled at me.

Then it was gone.

Rowan stumbled to his feet, and pulled me against his chest.

"I'm sorry," I told him through sudden tears.

"It is over now," he whispered into my ear. "We made it through."

"But she'll come back," I protested. "She won't ever let this go."

"She may come back, after a time," Rowan agreed. "And we will be ready when she does. Believe me, Asa." He put his hand under my chin and tilted my face up so he could stare into my eyes. "Whatever has happened, and whatever may come, even with all that you have lost...you are not alone. And we are going to be all right."

And somehow, pressed tight against him, I could almost believe that it was true.

TWENTY-FIVE

Two weeks later, standing next to Jason's battered red truck, I asked, "You're sure you don't want to wait and come with us tonight?"

Flint sat inside the cab, fiddling with the dials on the radio, a look of mixed wonder and amusement on his face. "You could leave first thing tomorrow instead. After the... ceremony." My voice hitched over the word, as my anxiety spiked.

Jason laughed and shook his head. "You're just nervous and want me to go with you," he said, adjusting the thick leather gloves he had taken to wearing all the time.

"You say that like it's a bad thing,"

"Rowan will be with you. You'll be fine," Jason promised. He glanced over his shoulder, to where Flint was waiting. "And I think my parents have waited long enough to meet their son."

"You're their son, too," I reminded him. "Nothing's changed that."

Jason shrugged, his lips pressed into a hard line. "I really hope they'll feel that way. But I'm not so sure."

"I am," I told him immediately. "I'm not saying that this will be easy. It'll be confusing, and they may need some time to think things through. But give them a chance."

"I'll try," Jason promised, though I could see his uncertainty.

"How long will you be gone?"

Jason shrugged. "Not sure. It doesn't really depend on me. We'll just have to see how things go. I'll be back before too long, though, either way." A smile crept back into his eyes. "I know you can't manage in the clinic without me for too long."

"I'll try not to burn it to the ground while you're gone," I told him. "What about Flint? What is he going to do?"

"I can honestly say that I have no idea what to expect from him. I don't think he knows what to expect from himself, either. To say that he has some issues would be putting it mildly."

"Well, that's only to be expected, considering all that he's gone through."

"I know. I know." Jason rubbed his face, as though suddenly deeply weary. "He's just got so much anger in him. It worries me."

"Worries you how?" I asked, concerned. "Does he scare you?"

"No. Nothing like that," Jason said, and then seemed to reconsider. "At least, no more than I scare myself. I just don't know what he needs. I'm kind of hoping my mom can help me to figure that out, to be honest. Maybe she'll have better luck than I have at getting him to talk."

"I'm sure she'll do everything she can," I agreed.

Jason hesitated, "How are you, Amy? Really. After everything that happened..."

"I can't talk about it." I cut him off, holding up a hand. I was sorry for the sharpness in my voice, but I couldn't help it. It was either nip this conversation in the bud or spend the next several hours crying uncontrollably. "Not yet. What happened with..." My voice faltered. I still couldn't say her name. "It's bad. It's going to be bad for a while. But I'll make it through."

"It's all right if you need to grieve," Jason told me, concern plain on his face, but I shook my head sharply.

"It would be, if I knew how to grieve for this. Tragedy is one thing. I've lived through that before. But betrayal is different. It poisons all your memories, makes you doubt everything that you thought you knew and felt..." A lump formed in my throat. I took a deep breath, waiting until I was sure my voice was steady before I spoke again. "Like I said. I can't talk about it."

"Okay." Jason held up his hands. "I get it. I really do. But when you're ready, Amy. I'll be here."

"Thanks," I told him, and meant it.

"All right, we're gonna hit the road. I'll be thinking of you tonight. I'm sorry to miss it, but I know you'll fill me in when I get back." He lifted his arms and, for a second, I thought he was going to hug me. But, even with his gloves, Jason was still wary of physical contact. Instead of a hug, he folded arms over his chest and gave a deep nod of farewell. I waved back, feeling an ache of disappointment. I could have used a hug. Then he climbed into his van, and waved before he pulled away.

When I turned around, I saw Rowan leaning against the wall of the barn, waiting for me.

"You didn't want to say goodbye?" I said, walking over to him. Rowan gave a quick shake of his head.

"I thought space would be more helpful to him," he said. I couldn't say I disagreed. Rowan smiled. "Are you ready? It is almost sunset." I took a deep breath, but it didn't make me feel any calmer.

"I don't like large crowds," I told Rowan, stepping forward so that he could take my hands in his. "And I don't like being the center of attention. I'm not so sure this is a good idea, after all."

"You will be surrounded by friends who wish you well." Rowan's thumb stroked the back of my hand. "And I will be beside you the whole time."

My heart swelled, and I leaned in to rest my head against his shoulder.

"Well, in that case," I said, "I guess I can do anything."

The centaur camp was decorated, in honor of the event. Fresh evergreen boughs and pine cones were strewn on the ground, and each centaur family had built its own small fire, so that the field was strewn with flickering light as the day darkened into night. I had been expecting solemn silence and the press of watching eyes; but instead when we arrived, the field was full of music and dancing. A low level of friendly chaos rolled over the grass like winter wind. Smoke swirled, filling the air with the smell of roasting meat. Laughter pealed. Parents called to their children to stop fighting with wooden swords and come to dinner, and various groups of musicians circulated, making no attempt to play together or find any sort of shared rhythm in their tunes. A circle of drummers pounded out a complex beat, a small band of centaurs playing pipes milled around, and small groups of singers with arms flung over each other's shoulders sang their own songs.

Somehow the disjointed melodies sounded exactly right.

The chief and Crinea were waiting. I saw them on the far side of the field, at the top of a small, flat-topped hill. Rowan squeezed my hand, and I took a deep breath as we began the long walk to the other side. I had been dreading stares and whispers. Instead, the first centaur who saw me cried out a happy greeting, and immediately grabbed my hands up in his own and began to spin me around in dance.

Rowan laughed and stood back to watch.

I never would have imagined that centaurs could dance, both because I would not have thought that four hoofed legs were amenable to dancing, and because they always gave the impression of being so warlike and fierce. But tonight, for the first time, I had been invited into their inner world, a place where they sang and danced with the same fierce wholeheartedness with which they fought their battles. Hooves flew and arms swung as the centaurs formed small, lopsided circles and twirled me round and round. They were much better at dancing than I was, but no one seemed to mind, and by the time that I had been swung around what seemed to be every campfire there, I finally found myself walking by Rowan's side up to meet the chief. My feet were sore, my calves were aching. I was out of breath and laughing, dripping with sweat, and far too happy to feel self-conscious.

There were murmured greetings, and then Rowan moved to stand a little distance away. Crinea stood on my left side, and the chief on my right. The throng quieted, and the chief turned to address me. He did not need to raise his booming voice to make it carry over the crowd.

"Healer," he said, "you have come to our aid more than once, and you have taken great risks on our behalf. More than one in this gathering stands here tonight only because of your skill and your fierce determination." He paused as cheers erupted into the night.

Several centaurs pawed at the ground as they clapped and whooped. Moments passed before they calmed enough for the chief to go on.

"You have endangered yourself for us, even when we did not ask it of you. Recently, you found a way to ensure the survival, not just of a few of us, but of our whole people. We sent the instructions for the medicine you invented far and wide, to every centaur tribe which we could contact. Already, no less than six tribes have responded, to inform us that your medicine succeeded in saving the life of a centaur child and its mother."

Exclamations of surprise and happiness rippled through the crowd. This time the chief paused to allow the silence to grow.

"This is a precious gift, beyond any price or reward that we could offer." He turned out to face his people. "In all of our legends, in all of the history which has been passed down to us, from parent to child and from chief to tribe, there is no story, no legend, of a non-centaur being inducted into a centaur tribe. But never before has there been one who so selflessly and profoundly came to our aid." He turned back to look at me, his eyes glowing with pure emotion. "We are forever grateful to you," he said. "In our hearts, you are one of us already. Tonight, will you join our tribe in custom and in name?"

I glanced over at Crinea, who beamed a beautiful smile at me, and at Rowan, who stood just out of the shadows, his arms folded over his chest, his expression both grave and approving.

"Yes," I told the chief, trying to speak loudly and to keep my voice from shaking. "I would be proud to join you."

The crowd clapped and sang out their approval.

The chief looked behind him and beckoned. Crinea's son, Archer, approached. Centaur children grow quickly, and he had grown almost a foot since the last time I had seen him for a checkup, just two months ago. His legs were long and thin, and his tail swished nervously behind him. His thick, curly brown hair had been carefully combed for the occasion, but still managed to fall into his face. His deep brown eyes were solemn with the importance of his role. He walked slowly, balancing a broad, sheathed sword on his hands.

When he reached the chief's side, the chief laid a hand on his shoulder before taking the sword.

"I bestow a weapon like this one on every member of our tribe, when they come of age, and have proven their worth in battle." He held the sword out to me. "Will you accept it, and with it, your place among us?"

I swallowed hard, but remembered the line Rowan had taught me. I felt a rush of gratitude that there hadn't been more to memorize.

I took the sword from the chief's open palm, and held it up so that the crowd could see. "With pride and with honor, I would stand as one of you," I declared.

The chief smiled broadly. "Then welcome to our ranks!" he cried, and the crowd burst back into dance and raucous music.

There was food then, and drink. Natia came and, laughing,

braided my hair in centaur fashion, decorating it with tiny, red, winter flowers. Crinea brought me a leather vest, such as the centaur women wear, and helped me slip it on over my shirt.

Rowan came and sat cross-legged beside me, so our knees never stopped touching. Every once in a while, he would rest his hand against the small of my back.

"You know," I told Crinea, motioning to the sword lying across my lap, "I haven't the faintest idea how to use this."

"Oh, don't worry," Crinea answered with a wicked smile. "You're part of the tribe now, and I'll soon fix that. Your training begins tomorrow."

"What?" I asked, blinking. "No one said anything about weapons training!"

Her son called out to her, and Crinea grinned at me and hurried away.

When I turned to look accusingly at Rowan, he was laughing.

"You knew about this, didn't you?" I asked, punching him lightly in the arm, and he held up his hands in mock surrender.

"It may have been mentioned to me," he said, and for a second, his face darkened. "I will admit that the idea of you learning to wield a weapon seemed wise."

The happiness in my heart quieted a little. "I know," I whispered back. "There are so many threats out still there. The invasives, the mages..." My words faltered. It still hurt too much to say Meri's name out loud.

Then I shook myself. I looked around. Firelight glowed, music swelled. I took a deep breath. "But whatever the future may hold, we are here now. We have tonight. And this is wonderful."

"There is much to be wary of," Rowan agreed. "But we have so many reasons to be glad. And tonight..." He kissed my neck. "Tonight is a night for rejoicing."

I leaned against him, and with his arms wrapped around me, I felt warm inside and out. I tilted my head back and looked up at the sky. Hundreds of stars blinked above us, seeming almost to dance to the music that the centaurs played.

Rowan followed my gaze up to the stars above.

"They are so beautiful," I breathed.

"Yes," Rowan agreed, and then chuckled. "You are an honorary centaur now," he reminded me. "Are you going to read the future in those stars?"

I looked over at him, locking my eyes with his. "I see struggle," I told him softly, "and worry. I see challenges that force us to find strength inside ourselves that we didn't even know we had. But I also see happiness. Laughter. And more than anything else, I see love."

"You aren't looking at the stars," Rowan told me softly. I smiled and nestled my head against his shoulder.

"I know," I whispered. "I don't need to. If I want to see my future, all I have to do is look at you."

THE END

Thank you for reading! Did you enjoy?
Please Add Your Review!

Find book one of the Outcast Mage novels, TRUTHSIGHT and discover more from author Miriam Greystone at www.miriamgreystone.com

---

Meet Amy. Mage. Healer. Outcast.

Amy has a gift for healing supernatural creatures. But the one person she can't save is herself.

Forced to abandon her magic and live in hiding, Amy spends her days working in the ER and her nights running a secret clinic for supernatural creatures. But everything changes on the night that she comes to the aid of a centaur infant and its mother. When Amy's medical skills alone aren't enough to save their lives, she is forced to use her magic, revealing her identity to the mages who want her dead.

Fleeing for her life, Amy's only hope for survival may lie with a mysterious being named Rowan, who has a hidden agenda of his own.

Now Amy must join forces with the creatures who were once her patients and fight to uncover the one secret that may be powerful enough to save them all.

For books in the world of romance and speculative fiction that embody Innovation, Creativity, and Affordability, check out City Owl Press at www.cityowlpress.com.

ACKNOWLEDGMENTS

So many people have been a vital part of bringing this book to life. I am very grateful to Heather McCorkle, who is an amazing editor and has been wonderful to work with from beginning to end. I am also thankful to Tina Moss, who is truly a publishing ninja, and the rest of the City Owl Team – I feel very lucky to work with you all!

My family means the world to me. My husband is a true friend and an amazing companion through all of life's ups and downs. My children are a constant source of joy, and the most important thing in the world to me. My sister is a friend who comes through for me and cheers me on, even when things are rough. My Dad's love and support is something that I treasure more than words can say, and he is an example and role model that I strive to emulate every day. Thank you so much, to all of you. I love you all so much.

I can't write these words without mentioning my mother, who read the draft of this manuscript, but isn't with us now to see the book come out. There are no words for loss like this, and I'm not really going to try to articulate it, other than to say that this book, and everything else I do, would never have happened without her. She is loved and remembered every day.

I have benefited immeasurably from the advice and guidance of my critique partners, Grace and Michelle. Their friendship, and their patience with me as I struggle through the writing process, has been a vital part of my growth as a writer. I honestly don't know where I would be as an author if I didn't have them in my life.

A huge thank you also goes to Leah Cypess, for reading and commenting on the manuscript, and for her advice and support.

And finally, thank you to all the people who read this book, who fall in love, as I have, with the characters on these pages. Thank you for caring, for reading, and for sharing your enthusiasm. You make all of this possible, and I am incredibly thankful to you.

Love,
Miriam

ABOUT THE AUTHOR

Miriam Greystone writes urban fantasy stories filled with magic, romance and the occasional centaur. She generally fuels her creativity with an insatiable appetite for reading and frequent episodes of Doctor Who. (And lots and lots of Diet Coke.) She lives just outside of Washington DC with her husband, her kids, and her badly behaved Australian Shepard. She loves to connect with fans, and you can join her FB group right below.

Reader Group: www.miriamgreystone.com/FBreadergroup

Facebook: www.facebook.com/miriam.greystone

Twitter: www.twitter.com/MiriamGreystone

Website: www.miriamgreystone.com

ABOUT THE PUBLISHER

City Owl Press is a cutting edge indie publishing company, bringing the world of romance and speculative fiction to discerning readers.

www.cityowlpress.com

www.ingramcontent.com/pod-product-compliance
Lightning Source LLC
Chambersburg PA
CBHW031308280626
47169CB00017B/915

* 9 7 8 1 9 4 4 7 2 8 7 3 1 *